ALL I EVER NEED

IS YOU

~ The Sullivans ~

Adam & Kerry

Bella Andre

ALL I EVER NEED IS YOU

Adam & Kerry ~ The Sullivans

© 2016 Bella Andre

Sign up for Bella's New Release Newsletter

http://eepurl.com/eXj22

bella@bellaandre.com

www.BellaAndre.com

Bella on Twitter: @bellaandre

Bella on Facebook: facebook.com/bellaandrefans

Seattle architect Adam Sullivan is well known for his brilliant historic building restorations—and for having absolutely no interest in love and marriage. He's happy for his siblings and cousins who have found true love, but though they're clearly hell-bent on seeing him settled, his family is just going to have to accept that Cupid's arrow will be skipping this Sullivan. That is, until he meets Kerry Dromoland…and suddenly Adam starts to question everything he once believed to be true about falling in love.

As one of the top wedding planners in Seattle, Kerry has been waiting her whole life to find her own true love. So even though Adam makes her heart race and her body heat up every time they're together, she knows better than to think he could be "the one." Still, knowing he's Seattle's biggest player doesn't make it any easier to resist his breathtaking kisses and wicked caresses…or the fact that he makes her smile more than any man ever has.

But when Kerry desperately needs Adam's help—and he comes through for her without the slightest hesitation—she begins to realize that there just might be more to the man she can't resist than she'd previously thought. Can the bad boy with no interest in being reformed—and the woman who has no interest in reforming a bad boy—find forever together?

A note from Bella

I know this will come as no surprise to those of you who have been reading my books for a while, but I have a thing for bad boys. Especially when the bad boy falls head over heels in love when he least expects it!

Which explains why I had the best time ever writing Adam Sullivan's story. As the resolutely single Seattle Sullivan—and the last of his siblings to find love—how could I pair him with anyone but a wedding planner who has been waiting for true love her whole life? What's more, the sparks between Adam and Kerry are so hot that I may have gotten scorched while writing *All I Ever Need Is You*.

I hope you love Adam and Kerry's book!

Happy reading,
Bella Andre

P.S. The New York Sullivans are coming soon! You will be meeting Drake, Alec, Suzanne, and Harrison in this book. Drake will be the next Sullivan to fall in love, this time in New York, and I'm really excited about his story. Please be sure to sign up for my New Release newsletter (www. BellaAndreFans.com/Newsletter) so that I can let you know as soon as new books are released!

CHAPTER ONE

How had it come to this?

Adam Sullivan couldn't believe he had a meeting with a wedding planner in a few minutes. Clearly, the universe was in the mood for a good practical joke.

His brother Rafe and his future sister-in-law Brooke were getting married on the beach at Lake Wenatchee in the Cascade Mountains in five weeks. When they'd initially told him their plans months ago, he'd been picturing hot dogs grilled over a campfire, hanging out in bathing suits on the beach, sailboat races, and a weekend of hiking through the surrounding mountains with his favorite people. But then, suddenly, they were working with some wedding planner, and Adam's visions of a relaxing weekend wedding had been shot to hell.

Wedding planners meant ties that were too tight, matching suits dyed ridiculous colors that no guy would ever willingly choose to wear, and endless toasts.

But when Adam walked into the foyer of Dromoland Weddings & Events, he was impressed despite himself. From the flowers on the reception desk to the painting on the facing wall of a glowing bride in a flowing white dress, laughing as she tossed her bouquet toward her bridesmaids—every detail of the office spoke elegantly of wedding dreams come true. There wasn't a single element he would have changed—something that rarely happened for an architect and builder who was always mentally tweaking the buildings and rooms he entered.

Both Rafe's and Brooke's work schedules had heated up just as they were in the crucial final planning stages for their wedding, and Rafe had been worried that Brooke might lose out on making her dream day come to life if they blew things with the wedding planner by bailing on another meeting with her. Adam hadn't thought twice before offering to step in on their behalf. Even though, as far as he was concerned, there had already been a heck of a lot of Sullivan weddings in the past couple of years. First Chase, Marcus, Gabe, Sophie, and Lori—his San Francisco cousins—had all tied the knot. And then Rafe, Mia, Dylan, and Ian, his three brothers and sister, were all either engaged or married now, too.

Love and marriage had taken over the West Coast Sullivans one by one, like an amusement park game where the goal was to fell the targets one after another. Only instead of winning huge stuffed animals, his cousins and siblings had ended up with rings on their fingers.

For all Adam's jokes, though, they all knew that he was happy for them. Truly happy that they'd each found someone they wanted to be with for the rest of their lives.

That didn't mean, however, that he was anywhere near that frame of mind himself. Women, he'd always believed, were to be enjoyed—for as long as the enjoyment lasted. Fortunately, the women he dated had always been of like mind, probably because he wasn't the kind of guy a girl looked at and thought, *Now, there's my forever.* And he was okay with that. More than okay. He had plenty of nieces and nephews to play with thanks to his cousins, and likely his siblings soon, too.

Sure, Adam knew what everyone was saying about him. He couldn't quite manage to block out the endlessly repeating refrains from the lovestruck. According to them, he just hadn't met the right woman yet. They said he didn't know what he was missing. And, evidently, he hadn't yet realized how love would change everything for him.

Adam's laughter rang out against the marble floors at the absurd thought of some woman walking into a room and changing his life forever. He'd never come close to feeling as if a lightning bolt had hit him, the way his brother Ian had with his fiancée, Tatiana. He couldn't imagine falling in love at first sight the way his brother Dylan had with his wife, Grace, and her son, Mason. There'd never been anyone he'd pined over for years the way his sister, Mia, had for her husband, Ford. And he couldn't think of anyone he'd known from childhood whom he would ever fall in love with the way Rafe had with Brooke.

Nope, his family was just going to have to accept that Cupid's arrow would be skipping this Sullivan.

On a recent business trip to the East Coast, where he'd met up with some of his Maine and New York cousins, he'd warned them that they were next, because he was officially passing the falling-in-love torch to them. He'd paid the bar tab that night out of pity for the poor suckers who had no idea just what was coming for them soon. All those gooey looks. The perpetually up-and-down emotions when the road to true love wasn't at all smooth. Not to mention the way they went a little crazy—more than a little crazy, actually—when they thought they'd lost the guy or girl of their dreams.

He'd seen all of that, and more, happen to his siblings and San Francisco cousins. But he was confident that it wasn't going to happen to him. That it *couldn't* possibly happen to him. In fact, he needed to get this meeting rolling soon or he'd be late for his date tonight with—

"Adam Sullivan?"

He turned at his name, and as he set eyes on the woman standing in front of him, he actually forgot how to speak for a moment. His brain turned into one big blank space, and his eyes went wide before he could stop it from happening.

Even when he gave his head a hard shake, he could still hardly believe his eyes. She was exactly what he'd imagined a high-gloss, high-class wedding planner would be. Perfect silk shirt and pencil skirt, heels that he knew his sister, Mia, would kill for, and not one strand of her long dark hair or makeup out of place. She was the polar opposite of the kind of woman he was normally attracted to.

And yet, only one thought would form in his whip-lashed brain: *Where the hell had she been all his life?*

* * *

By the time five o'clock rolled around, Kerry Dromoland had already had a long day, meeting with four current clients and a prospective client, as well. As a wedding planner, she was used to days like this—ones that started at five in the morning with no clear end in sight. But all day today, she'd been a little keyed up.

Rafe Sullivan and Brooke Jansen had asked her if one of Rafe's siblings could meet with her today due to business commitments that, unfortunately, couldn't be canceled. She'd assured them that it was perfectly fine. She often met with the sister of the bride or groom if they couldn't be present, and had been expecting them to send his sister, Mia, to meet with her. In the end, though, they'd let her know that Rafe's brother Adam would be meeting with her this afternoon.

Kerry hadn't needed to pull out the Sullivan family photo they'd given her to remember what Adam looked like. She'd been able to visualize, all too well, just how good-looking he was—the epitome of tall, dark, and handsome. His grin in the photo was super-sexy and so appealing she'd had to tear her gaze away before Rafe and Brooke caught her gaping like a fish at their brother.

All day long, whenever her heartbeat would kick up at the thought of him, she'd remind herself that she'd been around good-looking men like him zillions of times and had never had any trouble keeping her wits about her.

Only, now that he was standing in front of her, staring at her so intensely, she felt her knees actually go weak. Something that had never, ever happened before.

Something she'd been certain could *never* happen to

her.

Then again, thankfully, Kerry had enough presence of mind to realize that she'd never seen a more beautiful or more sexual man live and in the flesh. One glance was all it took for her to know that he was everything most women fantasized about. Wild. Rugged. Sex personified.

But Kerry had never fantasized about men like Adam Sullivan. She'd never believed the romantic myth that reformed players made the best husbands. Not when both her mother and her sister had shown her just what a terrible, painful myth that was.

"Promise me you'll wait for Mr. Perfect," was what her mother, Aileen, had made Kerry vow again and again in the years after their father had left them alone, a mother and two small girls with no money and no prospects. Nothing but unpaid bills and desperation. Kerry had been too young to remember much about her father, but according to her mother, he'd been Seattle's bad boy. One Aileen's own mother had warned her to stay away from, but had been foolishly unable to resist.

What Kerry did remember was how hard her mother had worked to give her and her sister, Colleen, a great childhood in one of the best neighborhoods in Seattle. Her mother had taken back her maiden name of Dromoland and started Dromoland Weddings &

Events twenty-five years ago with a laser-focused purpose: to build the best wedding-planning business in Seattle. But even back when she'd been scrambling for new clients, Kerry's mother had refused to work with any couples who she didn't believe were actually in love. She never wanted anyone to end up in a marriage like hers, where one had loved and the other had played. As a result, out of all the weddings her mother had planned during the twenty years she'd run the business, it was amazing just how few divorces there had been among her clients.

And yet, even though Kerry had never been the slightest bit tempted to break her vow to her mother, here she was fighting the urge to drool over the gorgeous player standing before her.

Especially when he smiled and said, "That's me. Are you Kerry Dromoland?"

He said her surname perfectly—Drum-*oh*-land—as if he'd spent some time in Ireland, and also managed to infuse it with searing heat. It was, she had to admit, an impressive feat. Even to a woman like her, who refused to be impressed or to fall for his sexy game.

"Yes, I'm Kerry." She forced herself to smile and move toward him with her hand outstretched. "It's lovely to meet you."

He quickly ate up the distance between them with his athletic stride. He clasped her hand in his at the same moment that he said, "Your eyes..." *Had anyone ever looked at her so closely?* "They're not emerald. Not jade, either." The longer he looked, holding on to her hand all the while, the drier her mouth became. "They're so much prettier than either stone could ever be."

More than one person had complimented her on her green eyes before, but never quite like that. She wouldn't have called his words poetry. How could she when there was such an unabashed sexual undertone to them? But at the same time, she couldn't dismiss the surprising eloquence of them. If only she could stop herself from blushing, her pale skin giving away the effect he was having on her.

Carefully drawing her hand back—she couldn't allow herself to be rude to her client's brother—she said, "Please join me in my office."

As she led the way, with every step she took she could feel his dark eyes on her. She'd been taught by her mother at an early age how to look elegant in every situation. But despite the fact that she hadn't intended her outfit to come across as sexy, she was suddenly extremely aware of the slightly translucent nature of her silk shirt, the way the waist dipped in to accentuate the flare of her hips, and the fact that the height of the heels she preferred wasn't at all modest.

Her office was a large, bright room with a plush

seating area, a glossy, round mahogany-topped table with three chairs, and her desk. It had never felt too small.

Until today.

When she was tempted to put a little space between them by sitting behind her desk rather than joining him on the couches, Kerry decided enough was enough and gave herself a silent talking-to. She was just in a weird mood, likely because she'd stayed up way too late watching bad reality TV the previous night and had started the day before the sun had even risen.

"Can I get you anything to drink? Coffee? Tea? A glass of wine? Or a beer?"

"You're prepared for everything, aren't you?"

For everything but you.

"That's my job," she said with a smile that she hoped masked her uncharacteristic nerves. "As is guessing that you'd probably go for the beer. I've got a locally brewed pale ale or a Guinness."

"It's five o'clock," he said with a grin, "so why not? And since I'm always up for celebrating my Irish roots—and yours, too—I'll have a Guinness. Have you visited Dromoland Castle in County Clare?"

"It's on my bucket list," she said with another smile before she got up to get him his drink. Again, she felt his gaze follow her across the room. She brought one for herself as well, even though she wasn't planning on having more than a sip.

He lifted his glass and once she'd raised hers, he said, "To Rafe and Brooke."

His simple, and very sweet, toast to his brother and his brother's fiancée made her smile. It also made her forget to keep her guard up as she clinked her glass to his, saying, "And to giving them a perfect wedding."

The drink was refreshingly cold in a room that had gone too hot from the moment he'd stepped inside and sent her every sense reeling in a way she'd never experienced before. The one small sip she'd planned to take wasn't nearly enough. Not when she could definitely use something to take the edge off.

Still, she put down her glass and picked up her tablet from the side table. "It's very nice of you to come to meet with me in Rafe and Brooke's place. I don't know how much they've told you about our wedding plans?"

"They've told me plenty."

His tone made it clear that he had clearly hit wedding-discussion fatigue. Working to keep from smiling at his obvious discomfort, she said, "I'd appreciate it if you could let them know that everything we've already discussed is well in place for their big day. However, there is one additional element that I would like to incorporate into the vows and then the reception."

She swiped her finger across her tablet and pulled

up a picture she'd drawn of a gazebo, with the blue lake and green mountains behind it and climbing vines up the sides. "I'm envisioning having this structure in the middle of the beach for their vows. And then for the reception, I would like to move it off to the side as a perfect place for their guests to have photos taken that will be ready for them to take home at the end of the night in their gift bags." When he didn't say anything, but just continued to stare at her drawing, she added, "If you're worried about the added expense, please don't be. I know a good, reasonably priced carpenter who can build the structure—"

"I'll build it."

She was surprised by his sudden offer. It wasn't that she didn't think he could build a great gazebo for the wedding. It was that he was one of the most sought-after architects on the West Coast. How could he possibly have time to do something like this?

"Your overall design is good," he continued, "but I'll want to change the roof line and the stairs a bit." Before she could even try to protest that he didn't need to build it, he said, "Did you draw this?"

"It's just a rough sketch so that you could visualize what I was thinking."

"It's a better drawing than most architects or graphic artists can do by hand. What's your training?"

"I'm not trained. I've just been drawing weddings

all my life." When he looked confused, she explained, "My mother started Dromoland Weddings & Events when I was a little girl, and I sometimes needed to stay with her during the weddings when she couldn't find a babysitter. She would give me crayons and paper to keep me from getting bored."

"You were never bored at those weddings, were you?"

"No." She smiled at the memory, a little girl watching all those beautiful brides and dashing grooms saying their vows, giving each other their first kiss, and dancing in each other's arms. "I loved it." Belatedly, she realized she'd lost her focus. Something else that never happened to her, especially during a meeting. "I'm sorry, I know you're a busy man. I didn't mean to veer us away from discussing the gazebo."

"I'm the one who veered," he said in that low voice that kept doing crazy things to her insides even though she knew better than to let it. "I was planning on heading up to the lake a few days before the wedding anyway, so I'll take care of building the gazebo while I'm there. For now, I'll do a drawing with my changes to run by you before I order the wood for it."

It was the perfect solution to her new plan for Rafe and Brooke's wedding, but all Kerry could feel was panic about having more meetings with Adam beyond this one. It didn't make sense, the kind of breathless impact he was having on her, especially when they'd only just met. But just because it didn't make sense, didn't mean her heart wasn't beating too fast or that her lips weren't tingling from nothing more than his gaze dropping and holding on them while she spoke.

Adam Sullivan was exactly the kind of man her mother had warned her about her entire life. Exactly the kind of man she needed to keep her distance from, no matter how much she might want to bring him closer instead.

"Rafe and Brooke have told me how busy you are with your work as an architect. It's wonderful that you want to help out with their wedding like this, and I know how much they would appreciate it, but I can't possibly—"

"He's my brother. She's one of my closest friends. Building this gazebo is the very least I can do for the two of them."

Yet again, it wasn't poetry, but his words were so heartfelt that Kerry couldn't help but lose a little piece of her heart to Adam right then and there.

"What else can I help with, Kerry?"

Yet another unexpected offer. One that somehow seemed sensual, even though that was *totally* crazy. Just as crazy as the fact that she could easily think of a dozen ways he could help her…and none of them had a thing to do with the wedding.

"Everything else is already arranged." She stood. "Thank you so much for coming to meet with me and for offering to help with the gazebo."

She held out her hand to shake his politely, but instead of pumping her hand once, he covered it with his and held on. "I want to see you again. And not just to go over my new drawings of the gazebo."

Inside, her heart was screaming, *Yes!* But she knew better, knew he was not only everything her mother had warned her about, but also every husband she'd ever seen stray, every groom she'd ever seen leave his bride at the altar so that he could continue to run wild.

"No, I can't."

"Are you seeing someone else?"

"I'm not, but I still can't go out with you." There were a dozen excuses she could have made—she was busy, he wasn't her type, she didn't date relatives of the couples she worked with—but she didn't want him to think dating her was up for negotiation. Gorgeous men with reputations as players were off-limits. Period.

And yet, despite the fact that she'd now said no to him twice in a row, he didn't seem at all daunted. "Do you always say no to something you want?"

It was on the tip of her tongue to say, *I don't want you,* but she was certain he'd know it for the utter lie that it would be. Thinking about the box of chocolates she was going to devour the second he left her office, she replied with utter honesty, "I never turn down Brooke's chocolate truffles."

But she was turning *him* down, beginning with pulling her hand from his and forcing herself to stop thinking about what kissing him would be like.

"I don't want to take up any more of your time," she said in her most polite tone. "I'll walk you out."

And though he didn't try to ask her out again, but simply walked beside her back to the front door of her building and then out into the downtown Seattle streets, Kerry couldn't shake the feeling that she wasn't anywhere close to being in the clear yet where he was concerned.

Not only did Adam Sullivan not play by any rules but his own, but something told her that he always won, too.

CHAPTER TWO

Adam closed his front door behind him at nine o'clock that evening and headed for his home office. He'd bought his home eight years ago. It had been a wreck—a teardown, according to everyone else who had seen it. But Adam had seen elegance beneath the rot and a foundation of strength in the beams behind the thick ivy covering the windows. The garden had looked beyond repair, too, but his mother hadn't been the least bit daunted, and over the years they'd spent plenty of weekends working to transform it into something pretty darned spectacular.

The house, however, had been entirely his project, and his passion. The restoration of the old Craftsman had grabbed him by the heart and had shown him what a difference it made when he was one hundred percent invested in a project. In the winter months, when he needed to draw plans or work up quotes, he'd light a fire in his den, sit down behind his antique Arts and Crafts desk, and get to work.

A great idea for the stairwell in one of the historic buildings he was reviving had come to him during dinner, and he wanted to get the sketch down right away. He was glad at least one good thing had come of his date tonight. He'd done his best to pay attention to the woman sitting across from him, an aspiring actress who had been all but throwing herself at him during their too-long meal. But Adam couldn't get the image of the shockingly sexy wedding planner out of his head. Heck, it was going to take some serious focus to sketch his idea tonight, given that Kerry was still front and center in his brain.

He grabbed his pencil and notepad and began to draw and make notes. Nearly an hour passed before he stopped to stretch out his back. After letting his initial sketch sit overnight, he knew he'd make more changes tomorrow.

Before leaving the den, he checked his watch and saw that it wasn't yet ten o'clock. Normally, he would still have been out with his date, usually back at her place by now. But since he'd dropped her off without so much as a good-night kiss—all while deftly ignoring her hints about getting together again—he'd gotten home pretty early.

Figuring Rafe and Brooke were probably still up, Adam dialed their number at the lake. Rafe picked up after two rings, sounding a little out of breath. "Good to hear from you. I'll put you on speaker."

Adam was grinning as he asked, "Are you two ready for your meeting report, or have I called at a bad time?" His brother and his fiancée couldn't keep their hands off each other, so he figured the odds were pretty darn high that he was interrupting something. And from what he could hear on their end, he was all but certain Brooke was currently throwing on some clothes.

"Hi, Adam." Yup, her voice sounded a little breathless, too. "How was your meeting with Kerry?"

"I was impressed with her. She's clearly good at what she does."

"I know, isn't she amazing? And even though she looks so perfect, she confessed that she has a terrible sweet tooth, so I've been sending her tons of chocolates. All of which she says are the best she's ever tasted," Brooke said happily. "She's even going to be using them in her weddings from now on!"

"That's great news, Brooke." Adam had known Brooke since she was a little girl and couldn't think of a woman who was a better fit for his brother. "You and your chocolates are going to take over the world."

"As long as people are happy eating them, that's all that matters to me," Brooke said in her typically modest way. "But, back to Kerry—considering how beautiful *and* intelligent she is, can you believe she's actually still single?"

Adam's eyebrows rose as he finally got confirmation that the meeting had been, at least partially, a setup. Clearly, Brooke had hopes that he and her wedding planner would make a connection.

He could have told them that he'd asked Kerry out. However, apart from the fact that she'd said no, he hated to set up his brother and Brooke for disappointment by getting their hopes up about his own happily-ever-after. Because even if Kerry *had* said yes, nothing would have changed for Adam. He still wasn't looking for forever—and he was absolutely certain that a wedding planner must be looking for just that.

Not that he'd given up on getting Kerry to say that yes, of course. Not by a long shot. He wouldn't be a Sullivan if he gave up that easily on an intelligent, sexy-as-hell woman who pushed every button he had—a woman he found himself wanting with a red-hot intensity that stunned him.

Still, even if he didn't want to get their hopes up, what fun would it be if he didn't play with the match-making couple a little bit?

"You should have told me what a looker she is."

"Did you really think so?" Brooke asked in a hopeful voice.

"Absolutely," he agreed. "My date tonight paled by comparison."

"Oh." He almost felt bad, Brooke sounded so disappointed. "You had a date tonight?"

"And he probably has one tomorrow with someone different," Rafe put in before getting down to business. "Kerry said there was a last-minute change she wanted to run by us. Did she present it to you?"

"She did, and you're going to have to add *artist* to your list of her great qualities, because the sketch she did of the gazebo she wants to build out on the beach was really good. The plan is that you two will say your vows in the gazebo, and then during the reception, it will be moved off to the edge of the property for your guests to have their pictures taken. Kerry is planning to have the photos developed on site and ready to go home with everyone at the end of the night."

"I *love* the idea of our guests taking home a personal keepsake from our wedding!" Brooke said enthusiastically.

"I agree about that part," Rafe said, "but I thought we had agreed to get married in front of a campfire?"

"Before you make a decision," Adam suggested, "let me send over the drawing so that you can see the way it will work with the setting. Honestly, I think it's better than the campfire plan. I need to make a few changes to the sketch first, so give me until midday tomorrow, okay?"

"Wait, why are *you* making changes to her sketch?"

Brooke asked.

"I'm going to be the one building it."

"She asked you to build it?"

"No. In fact, she tried to convince me that she could find a reasonably priced carpenter to do the work. But I wouldn't let her shake me off."

In more ways than one, he thought, as an idea came to him based on what Brooke had said earlier: Kerry had a sweet tooth. And Adam wasn't beyond taking advantage of that fact.

"That's amazing of you to offer—"

"Let me know what you think after I send over the drawing tomorrow, and if you do choose the gazebo, I'll be the one building it," he said, deliberately cutting off his future sister-in-law's protests. Sure, he was busy with work. But he was never too busy to pitch in for his family. "Now I'm going to hang up so that the two of you can get back to whatever you were doing that had you so out of breath when I interrupted you."

Adam could hear his brother laughing as he hung up. Hell, he'd be laughing too if he were heading to bed with a beautiful woman, rather than to an empty one.

All the more reason to get going on the plan he'd just hatched to get Kerry to reconsider that date with him.

★ ★ ★

A beautiful little silver box was delivered to Kerry the next day. Though she recognized the logo as belonging to a great local bakery, she still wasn't prepared for the absolutely gorgeous miniature cakes inside—one with a fondant bow-tie on top, the other with a lacy wedding veil made of icing. The thought of not promptly gobbling them down was laughable. Because, just as she'd said to Adam Sullivan at the end of their meeting, there were certain things she absolutely never said no to—cake being very high on the list—even if it meant she'd already ruined her lunch at nine in the morning.

Thought it had come as a total surprise, she was glad that the local bakery had sent her this out-of-the-blue reminder about how good they were. She hadn't used them for a wedding in far too long, and she decided to rectify that immediately. No question, sending her miniature cakes was a far better idea than a phone call or email from them would have been. Wedding cakes needed not only to taste delicious, but to look amazing, too. This perfect little sample had nailed it on all fronts.

She was in the middle of typing a thank-you email to the owner of the bakery when Joe, her regular delivery man, came rushing back into her office. "I can't believe I forgot to give you this." Though she assured him that no harm had been done, there was something about the handwriting on the note he handed her that had her wondering if that *no harm* sentiment was really going to be true.

Because, as she slid her finger beneath the flap of the envelope, she had the strangest feeling...

Kerry,

You know how many siblings and cousins I have, so I'm sure you can guess how many weddings I've been to in the past few years. I'm sure you already work with all the best bakers in Seattle, but I figured I'd send over something from one of my favorites.

I'll email you my changes to the gazebo drawing later today.

Enjoy the cake,
Adam

Her heart started to pitter-patter before she could stop it. Romance was her job. She often found herself giving gentle tutoring to her grooms on how to continue wooing their brides both before and after the wedding. She knew all the tricks, and yet this wooing was just subtle enough, and sweet enough, to get over even her walls.

Walls that were supposed to be particularly high and thick when it came to men like Adam.

Walls that suddenly looked like they might need some reinforcements to make sure they stayed strong.

He'd given her his email address during their meeting, so she quickly deleted the email to the bakery and sent him one instead.

Adam,

Silver's Bakery is one of my favorites, and the miniature cakes were delicious. Thank you for sending them to me.

I'm looking forward to receiving your new sketch of the gazebo.

Best,

Kerry

There. Done and dealt with in a professional but gracious manner. Surely the fact that she'd thanked him for his surprise without gushing like a teenager with a crush would show him that she'd meant it when she said she wasn't interested in dating him.

★ ★ ★

Alas, she'd known it wouldn't be that easy to shake off a man like Adam Sullivan, hadn't she, even though their email correspondence throughout the rest of that day about his changes to the gazebo—which she thought were great—had been perfectly professional.

Because when the next little box came the following morning, hadn't a part of her been waiting, and secretly hoping, for it?

Perhaps she should have refused to accept this second delivery from Joe, who remembered the card this time. At the very least, she should have told Joe to stop looking at her as if he knew there was romance in the air.

There most certainly was *not* any romance heading Kerry's way.

But when she didn't recognize the company logo on the pretty sea-green box, her curiosity got the best of her. She'd never be able to stand not taking at least a quick peek to see what he'd decided to send her today. Another delicious baked treat? Or...?

When she lifted the cover, she was more than a little surprised to see that Adam had mailed her candy this time. But not just any candy—gorgeous sugared, sparkly seashells and starfish and even one mini-meringue shaped like a wave about to crash onto the shore. Some looked to be sour, others sweet, but they were all beautiful.

And, as she soon found out when she popped one into her mouth, incredibly delicious, too.

She knew she was going to eat the entire box of candy by the end of the day. Unfortunately, the threat the candy posed to her hips wasn't her biggest problem. Not even close.

No, what had her truly worried was the fact that, as curious as she'd been about the contents of today's gift box, she was *much* more curious about what Adam had written in his second note to her. Especially when his gift was so perfectly spot-on for her tastes that it was almost as though meeting her only once had been enough for him to see through to all her secret delights.

> *Kerry,*
>
> *You know that big family of mine? One of my cousins out in Maine is a genius with sugar. It's just a hobby for now, but I've been trying to convince her to go pro.*
>
> *What do you think?*
> *Adam*

Seriously? He was not only sweet enough to volunteer to build the gazebo for Rafe and Brooke's wedding, but he was trying to encourage one of his cousins to turn her candy-making hobby into a career?

Kerry pushed back from her desk and walked out into the garden her mother had planted a little more than two decades ago. The roses were in full bloom, but today Kerry was so caught up in her spinning thoughts that she barely noticed them. Especially when she was still licking crystallized sugar from her fingers.

From the first moment she'd seen Adam standing across the room, she'd known he was a lady killer through and through. Now, however, she saw the error of her thinking—she'd assumed he used the same tired moves every other player did. Compliments, flowers and, of course, those ridiculously hot bedroom eyes.

But he was too smart for that. No, the game he was playing was on another level entirely.

He wasn't just trying to charm her with his gifts, he was also managing to help her source her business *and* showing her yet again that his family was important to him.

What was he going to send tomorrow?

The question jumped into her head before she could stop it, and that was when she knew that she needed to put a stop to his gifts. She'd call him up and say—

From the garden, the bell rang, announcing her first appointment of the day, and also snapping her out of her wild thoughts.

She was being silly. Adam Sullivan was one of the most successful architects in Seattle, with beautiful women constantly vying for his attention. He hadn't actually asked her out again. She was just jumping to conclusions because a secret little part of her wanted him to be pining for her.

But she knew that he had dozens of more important things to take care of than trying to woo her via a couple of cute little boxes full of sugar. Perhaps if he kept sending her surprises, then maybe that would mean that he was actually trying to romance her, but she couldn't imagine him continuing to take the time to come up with more surprises for a woman he'd only just met and who had turned down his offer to take her out on a date.

For the rest of the day, she deliberately pushed her thoughts of him to the background. But before she shut down her laptop for the night, she made sure to write him another polite email.

Adam,

Thank you for sending me the box of incredible candies. Your cousin truly is a genius and I would appreciate it if you could give me her contact information. Perhaps I could help with the first step in her going pro?

Best,

Kerry

★ ★ ★

The next morning, when the delivery man arrived with only one package—a sample of hand-painted dinnerware that she'd ordered from an artist in Oregon—

Kerry couldn't stop the sinking in her stomach. Though it was all for the best that Adam had stopped sending her surprises, what woman wouldn't want to know she was wanted by a man like him? Even if she wasn't interested...

But a few moments later, Joe walked back in, carrying another box. One that looked incredibly fragile. "I didn't want this to get crushed. Not when it's such a great-looking package."

Adam hadn't forgotten her.

Joe had been delivering packages to her for the past couple of years, and she knew he was happily married with two young children. Clearly, by the way he was smiling at her, he was hoping she'd find herself in the same place soon. "There's no card with this one."

She frowned. "There isn't?"

"I looked everywhere in my truck for it just in case it fell out, but I didn't find anything."

"Thanks, Joe. I'm pretty sure I know who it's from, even without the card."

His eyes twinkled, and though she could see he wanted to ask for more details, he was as professional as ever, simply wishing her a good day before heading out to make the rest of his morning deliveries.

She ran her finger over the lid, trying to guess what could possibly be inside, before finally opening it.

Oh my.

Kerry's breath went when she saw what was inside, and she suddenly wasn't so sure she'd be able to get it back any time soon. Not when she was staring down at an impeccably rendered model of Dromoland Castle, which her ancestors had begun building back in the late sixteenth century, made entirely out of candy, cookies, and frosting.

The castle smelled spicy and so yummy that she was tempted to lick the frosting to see if it would taste as good as it looked. Only, Kerry knew she had already given in to temptation one too many times where Adam was concerned. And clearly, another email wasn't going to cut it today. There was no telling herself, this time, that he was just trying to hook her up with new suppliers for her weddings.

No one had ever had something so amazing made for her before. She couldn't imagine why he wanted to date her so badly—maybe because she was the only female challenge he'd ever encountered? But despite all the lovely gifts, they hadn't changed her mind.

A few delicious sweets, no matter how breathtakingly original or perfect for her, didn't mean he would ever be a stick-to-one-woman kind of guy.

Quickly confirming that her first meeting wasn't for a couple of hours, she carefully closed the lid on the most amazing gift anyone had ever given her and picked up her purse. It was time to go see Adam in person to thank him for his latest gift.

And to tell him in no uncertain terms that she still wasn't going to date him.

CHAPTER THREE

Kerry had heard of Adam Sullivan long before he'd ever set foot inside her office for their meeting. For most of the past decade, he'd been considered the West Coast's top architect specializing in historic renovations. In fact, the building she lived in had been one of his first projects.

Still, she wasn't prepared for how lovely his office was. Not at all big or flashy, like that of an architect whose wedding she'd planned who had practically plated his office walls in gold, Adam's office was in an Arts and Crafts style building, and as far as she could tell, every piece was preserved. As she ran her hand over the gorgeous wood beam, she had to admit that the fact that he clearly loved history so much was yet another interesting facet to him.

Of course, that was right when he opened the front door and caught her fondling his building. She dropped her hand as if it were on fire.

Darn it, she was even being seduced by his building!

Unfortunately, looking at his gorgeous face didn't help her snap out of the seduction. What had she been thinking coming here today? A phone call would have worked just as well, and then she wouldn't have had to shove away this insta-lust that was shooting hot and fast through her veins every time she looked at him.

"Well, this is a nice surprise." His smile was so warm and sexy all at once that it sent the heartbeat she was working to slow jumping again. "Come inside."

Glad for the training her mother had instilled in her on how to be poised in any situation, no matter how nerve-racking, Kerry moved past him. The inside was even more stunning than the exterior. "Your office is beautiful."

"Thank you." He sounded pleased by her admiration. "I had my eye on it for years and made a dozen offers before the owner finally let me have it. Want a tour?"

She knew she should tell him no and get right to her point, but she'd always been drawn to beautiful things. Something that was going to be her downfall where Adam Sullivan was concerned, if she wasn't careful. But surely one little office tour wasn't going to send her swooning into his arms, was it?

"I'd love one."

He held out his hand to her, and she instinctively

reached out to take it. It wasn't until her skin touched his, and his searing warmth enveloped her, that she realized what she'd done.

Or how natural it felt.

Perhaps swooning in his arms wasn't so far in the distant future, after all.

He was a natural tour guide as he led her through each room and introduced her to his staff, all of whom seemed to worship him. And when he finally brought her through to his office and handed her a framed picture of what the building had looked like the day it became his—more than halfway to crumbling in on itself—Kerry almost started worshipping him, too.

"You saved it." She looked from the photo of the decrepit building to his dark eyes. "How did you do it?"

"Blood, sweat, and lots of help from my family. Keeping this picture on my desk reminds me that nothing is ever too far gone to be treated right."

She looked down at the picture again, and as she turned to take in his private domain, she was overwhelmed by his passion for what he did. Especially since she felt the same way about her career.

Giving herself a mental shake, she put the framed photo back on his desk. "I'm sure you're wondering why I'm here."

"Appreciating it, mostly."

She could feel her cheeks heating even as she said,

"First, I wanted to thank you in person for the lovely gifts and to ask where you found the person who made that incredible model of Dromoland Castle?"

"A friend I went to school with decided to stop working as an architect in order to make models out of candy. Pretty damned impressive, isn't it?"

"I've never seen anyone make something that complex or that whimsical all at the same time." Despite knowing she needed to stay on track with her real purpose for coming to see him, she had to tell him, "Driving over here, I couldn't stop thinking about how blown away my clients would be if we could hire your friend to make models for them. Maybe of the place where they had their first kiss or where he proposed and she said yes."

He wrote a number from memory on a yellow pad and handed it to her. "She's hoping to make a splash with the new business, so if you call, make sure to ask for pictures of her series inspired by her favorite buildings in the Pacific Northwest. Her Space Needle looked so great I nearly didn't eat it."

"You *ate* a model she made of the Space Needle?"

"Every last bite." He raised a questioning eyebrow. "Didn't you taste your castle?"

"I almost did, but I'm going to force myself to admire it for a little while before I gobble it down Cookie Monster-style."

His laughter rang out, filling her with even more warmth, even as she knew she was doing a *terrible* job of keeping her walls up around him. He was just so easy to be with, and she couldn't help but admire what he was doing with his life. Not to mention his heart-tugging devotion to his family.

"Have I mentioned how much I like you, Kerry?"

It was such a sweet thing to say—and so surprising—that she had to take a deep breath, and then another when the first one didn't do a darn thing to make her less lightheaded. Clearly, he was *brilliant* at this wooing stuff.

"Your gifts were all great. Your office building is amazing. And it's wonderful the way you're helping out with the gazebo at your brother's wedding. But I still can't go on a date with you."

"Why not?"

"I'm not in the wedding-planning business for money. I'm not even in it because my mother started this business twenty-five years ago. I do what I do because I believe in love. Love that's meant to be. Love that will last forever."

Again, he didn't look at all ruffled. "It's good that you believe in what you do. It must be why you enjoy it so much."

"I really do. Just as I can tell that you love what you do." Belatedly remembering that she hadn't come here to talk about the things they had in common, she said, "So now you must understand why we can't date."

"Sure. It makes perfect sense. You're looking for forever with someone and I'm not."

She'd already known he was direct, but even so, *wow*, she was surprised by his blunt statement. One that was perfectly accurate.

Kerry knew she should be relieved that he got it. That he could clearly see that the two of them could never work in a million years.

But the disappointment she was feeling was a heck of a long way from relief.

"Good," she made herself say. "I'm glad we both—"

"Want each other." He moved closer, and even though he wasn't touching her, her body came as alive as if he'd pulled her into his arms.

No one had ever spoken to her like this. Totally straightforward and honest. So honest that it made her head spin almost as much as breathing in his clean, masculine scent did.

"What are we going to do about how much we want each other, Kerry?"

A dozen naughty visions ran through her head of the two of them tangled up in each other, his hands in her hair, his mouth on hers.

Still, her reply was, "Nothing."

"Really?" He let his question hang between them,

right alongside all the sparks and heady desire that they were generating from nothing more than a conversation in his office. "Do you really think *nothing* is an option?"

There were few things Kerry appreciated in a person more than honesty. So maybe that was why his question made her stop and think instead of blurting out another automatic refusal. Really think for a few moments about everything he was suggesting.

If he had pushed her in any other way—if he had tried to pin her against his desk and kiss her into changing her mind—then she would have been able to reject him again outright. But the truth was that her body was humming just from being this close to him.

And, if she was being completely honest with herself, as much as she wished it were otherwise, he was right: Not going out on a date with him wasn't going to make this intense, if irrational, desire go away.

But could she do it? Could she take what she was fairly certain he was offering? Sex with no emotional strings. The option to scratch the itch with no expectations of anything more. No future. No forever.

Nothing more than pleasure.

Excitement fluttered within her belly at the shocking thought. Excitement that she could no longer deny had been building more and more within her since the moment their eyes had met in her office.

Kerry had never let herself entertain the idea of a sex-only relationship with anyone, not when she'd always been sure that someone would make the mistake of falling and that at least one heart would end up broken. Probably hers.

Any way she looked at things, though, she couldn't see herself ever falling in love with Adam.

Yes, he had a knack for sending the perfect gift. And he was also clearly devoted to his family. His brain was impressive, too. But she was looking for a life partner. For the one person she could trust no matter what. For the man who not only meant everything to her, but for whom she meant everything, too.

And Kerry couldn't imagine a world where Adam Sullivan would ever look at *any* woman like that.

Which meant, she was shocked to realize, that he was actually the safest possible man for her to enjoy a purely physical relationship with. Just long enough to scratch this itch that had been driving her a little crazy for the past three days. And then, when they both decided to go their separate ways, no harm would have been done to either of them.

All because love was absolutely out of the question.

In the span of several heartbeats, excitement shifted to heady anticipation. She'd come here to turn him down once and for all, and the truth was that she had done that. They weren't going out on a date. No romance. No expectations barring having a really good time getting naked with the sexiest man she'd ever met.

Adam continued to wait patiently for her response, even though she was certain he could hear her careening thoughts as loudly as if she were yelling them. And Kerry decided that if she was going to make this decision, she was going to do it with total confidence.

The knowledge that there would be no tears shed for Adam Sullivan at any point in the future made it easy to push back her shoulders and tilt up her chin so that she was nearly eye to eye with him in her heels.

"One night." She liked the sound of the two forbidden words more than she ever thought she could. "One night of just s—"

She halted on the word as her brain finally caught up with her mouth. But even though this conversation was unlike any she thought she'd ever have, she couldn't stop there. Not now. Not when the biggest, craziest leap of her life was suddenly—and desperately—calling to her.

"Just sex," she finally finished in a steady voice. "With no expectations of more."

"What if we both want more than one night?"

Her eyebrows went up. Was he actually negotiating with her?

Although the truth was that his endless nerve had

her body heating up just as much as everything else about him did. Her smile grew a little bigger as she said, "As long as we both always know it's just sex." She was pleased by the way the words *just sex* rolled from her lips so much more easily that time.

His own smile came slow and hot then, and she was as close to swooning as she had ever been as he said, "Not just a nice surprise. The best damned one I've ever had."

The things he could do to her with words had her wondering just what he was going to be capable of once mouth and hands and naked skin were involved. And oh, wasn't it lovely to know that she was actually going to find out?

Still, their negotiations weren't over yet. "Your brother and Brooke can't know. None of your family can know, either."

Now *his* eyebrows were going up. "You want me to be your secret?"

"Rafe and Brooke are very important clients. I won't jeopardize their wedding for any reason."

"Not even for hot sex with me?"

Honestly, by now she didn't want to walk away, not when her body was already humming and buzzing with desire. But if he couldn't even agree to this? "If you won't keep it a secret, then it looks like you and I won't—"

"How many siblings do you have?"

Frowning at the sudden change of subject, she said, "One. A sister."

"Then you've got to know just how good family is at getting up into your business and sniffing out anything even remotely secret. Fortunately, I have a few tricks of my own." He grinned, more than a little wickedly. "You want us to keep each other a secret, then that's what we'll do."

"Good." She was pleased, turned on...and out of her depth all at the same time. Which meant that she needed to turn back to what she knew better than anything else—putting together meetings and calendars. "Are you free Friday night?"

His nod was so easy that she had to wonder how many times he'd done this before. Then again, it didn't matter, did it? Because there was no place for jealousy in one night of sex.

Instinctively knowing they shouldn't bring anything personal into it, she said, "The Four Seasons is halfway between our offices." She'd been meaning to check out the recent renovations they'd made to the location for her clients. Her night with Adam could also double as research for her business. Perfect.

"I'll make the reservation," he said.

"Thank you." This was good, their being so businesslike and efficient. It was as far from setting up a date as she could imagine. "I should be able to get there by seven."

But *businesslike* and *efficient* went out of the window as he took another step closer to her, reaching out to brush away a lock of hair from her shoulder. Even through the layers of wool and silk, she could feel the heat of his touch, and barely fought back a shiver of need.

"Seven will work for me," he said, "although I hope you don't have anything you have to get to in the morning. Because I'm not planning on letting you get much sleep, Kerry."

Before she could respond—or even begin to untangle her overexcited synapses into thinking of a response that might make the slightest bit of sense—his secretary beeped him on the intercom.

"Jay Jones has arrived for your eleven o'clock meeting, Adam."

The sound of the buzzer yanked Kerry back to reality. One where she'd been about to ask—to *beg*—Adam to pretend that it was already Friday night.

"I have a meeting soon, too." She backed away from him so quickly that cool air rushed between them.

"I'll walk you out."

She nodded, calling on her poise as she said goodbye to his employees on her way out of the building.

After opening the front door for her, he stepped outside with her and closed it behind them.

She couldn't read his expression as he gazed at her, his eyes dark and intense. "Anything you need before Friday night, call me."

"The plans for the gazebo look great, so we shouldn't need to go over them again."

"I'm not talking about the gazebo or the wedding."

She'd known that, and knew he deserved her being just as direct as he was. "I'm not going to change my mind about meeting you on Friday." She wasn't going to wimp out, wasn't going to let nerves take away the only chance life had ever given her to focus solely on pleasure with no emotional repercussions. "But if *you* need anything before Friday—"

"Nothing is going to keep me from you, Kerry." His eyes darkened even further. "Nothing." With that, he leaned forward, and her heart nearly leapt out of her chest as he lightly pressed his lips to her cheek and whispered, "See you soon."

It was the kind of kiss friends gave one another. It should have been sweet. Perfectly innocent.

But, oh God, just the barest brush of his lips against her cheek was hands-down the hottest thing she'd ever experienced in her entire life.

Just minutes ago, when she'd made the decision to sleep with him, she'd been so confident, so rational, so certain that everything would be okay. But as she walked back to her car, her legs were a heck of a lot less steady than they'd ever been before.

If the brush of his lips on her cheek could turn her insides to mush, what would a real kiss do to her?

The question should have scared her. Should have made her spin around and tell him to forget the whole thing.

Instead, Kerry couldn't stop smiling.

CHAPTER FOUR

"Give me the sander." Adam's brother Dylan stood above him on the deck of the new boat he was building, holding out his hand. "Either your workmanship is slipping, or you've got something on your mind."

Adam looked down at the wood he'd been working on and knew his brother was right to take the tool away. He'd planned this Friday off weeks ago to help Dylan finish sanding the sloop, but work like this took a hell of a lot of concentration. And lately it seemed he could concentrate on only one thing. One woman.

Kerry Dromoland.

And the night they were going to spend together.

Dylan replaced the sander with a Coke for each of them, and they went out to the dock to drink it in the sun. Sitting on a couple of deck chairs, both of them kicked their feet up on the low table between them. Seattle was famous for rain, but when the sun came out, there were few places on earth that could rival its beauty. Particularly right here outside his brother's boathouse, golden rays glinting off the blue water as seagulls swooped down to catch fish.

"So, who is she?"

Adam shook his head. "You're getting to be worse than Mom. Marriage is obviously doing a number on you."

"The best damned number in the world," Dylan said with a grin. "You shouldn't knock a wife and kids until you try them."

"Kids?"

Dylan's grin became even wider. "We were going to try to keep it on the down-low for a few more weeks, but you dragged it out of me. Grace is pregnant."

"Congratulations." Adam raised his Coke to toast his brother, his grin just as big. "Adam Junior is a pretty good name, don't you think?"

Dylan laughed. "I'll make sure Grace puts it on the list."

"First tell her how happy I am for you guys. Then put my name at the top of your baby name list."

"What are we so happy about?" Rafe asked, surprising them both on the dock. He'd always been able to sneak up on them, even as a kid. No wonder he was such a great private investigator. No one ever saw him coming.

Dylan didn't even make a pretense of trying to

keep things on that down-low he'd mentioned. "Grace is pregnant."

"Incredible news." Rafe pulled Dylan into a hug. "Although I've got one piece of advice. You'd better tell Mia soon. Because if she ends up being the last to know, you're—" He slid a finger across his throat.

Dylan suddenly looked nervous. "I'd better call Grace to figure this whole spilling-the-beans thing out. Because if Mia or Mom hears the news from one of you first…"

As soon as Dylan got up to head back into the boathouse, Rafe took his seat. "I was just about to give you a call. You free tonight for dinner?"

Adam knew he had a hell of a poker face. Which was good, because he was about to use it. "Nope, I've got plans."

"Blonde or brunette?"

Adam gave his brother the laugh he was looking for. "Trying to live vicariously through me?"

"Hell, no." Rafe didn't look even remotely interested in being single again. "Brooke is the best thing that ever happened to me."

"You know I'm happy for you. For all of you. But every time you guys say stuff like that…" Adam mimed being sick.

"You'll understand one day," Rafe said, absolutely serious. "And too bad about dinner. I told Brooke it would be a long shot getting the four of us together tonight."

"Who's the fourth?"

"The wedding planner."

Though Adam felt his poker face slip, he needed to be absolutely sure. "Kerry's going to dinner with you tonight?"

"Hopefully. Brooke is probably on with her now to see if she can make it on such late notice, since we didn't know we'd be able to get into town until this morning." Rafe shot him a rather assessing look. "You sure you can't push back your plans a couple of hours so that the four of us could talk more about the gaze-bo?"

Adam made a show of thinking about it. "You know what? If it will make your blushing bride happy, I'm happy to change my plans. Why don't you let me make us a reservation for the Four Seasons restaurant? I'm pretty sure I can pull a few strings to get us in."

Both of their cell phones rang thirty seconds later. Rafe got up to take his call from Brooke just as Dromo-land Weddings & Events came up on Adam's screen.

Kerry didn't say hello, just barreled straight in. "I'm so sorry, but I can't meet you tonight after all. Not because I want to back out on our plans, but because Rafe and Brooke just asked me to have dinner with them. With the wedding coming up so soon, and they're so rarely in town, I couldn't say no."

"I'm glad you said yes. I'll be there, too."

"You will?"

"Rafe said they want to have dinner together so that the four of us can talk more about the gazebo plans."

"They do?"

"I'm pretty sure they're trying to set us up."

"They are?"

Kerry was always eloquent and poised. The fact that she was barely able to string words together right then meant that she was surprised and more than a little flustered.

"My entire family is hell-bent on marrying me off." Adam glanced over to his brother, on the phone with his fiancée, almost certain that Rafe and Brooke were working on taking their scheming up a level now that they knew both Kerry and Adam would be at dinner. "If I had to guess, I'd say they've decided you'd be a perfect addition to the family."

Her horrified silence said more than words ever could. Finally, she said, "You're joking, aren't you?"

"I'm sure Brooke will be calling you back any minute now to let you know that I'm coming, too. And if you listen real close, you'll hear the sound of gleeful matchmaking behind every word." Literally five seconds later, he heard the familiar click on the line that meant Kerry was getting another call.

"That's her now," Kerry confirmed.

"I'll see you tonight. Both during—and after—dinner."

"After?" Her earlier horror quickly turned to breathlessness. "You still want to meet after dinner?"

He could hear every one of the second thoughts she'd been having in her question. "I do, but that decision is still entirely up to you."

Because even though he'd never wanted a night more, he wouldn't let himself push her into anything she didn't want to do—he'd never forgive himself for taking something she wasn't ready to give.

He expected her to hang up to take Brooke's call, but she surprised him by saying instead, "I told you I wouldn't back out."

That should have been good enough for him. Any other fool would have taken her promise and run with it. But Adam wanted more from Kerry tonight than a promise to show up.

"I don't want you to meet me upstairs in the hotel suite after dinner because you gave your word. I want you to meet me because—"

"I want it." He could hear her breath catch slightly before she added, "And I want *you*."

CHAPTER FIVE

"Rafe, Brooke, it's lovely to see both of you!"

Kerry didn't hug all of her clients—her mother had been adamant that it wasn't professional behavior—but she'd always been so comfortable with Rafe and Brooke that moving beyond handshakes had happened quickly.

"You're always so gorgeous," Brooke said as she admired Kerry's wrap dress.

"So are you," Kerry said, wishing, not for the first time, that she had even a tenth of Brooke's curves.

"Thank you so much for meeting us on such short notice. I hope you like this restaurant. Adam chose it, and he's usually spot-on when it comes to good food."

Tonight they would be dining at the five-star restaurant in the hotel where Adam had reserved the penthouse suite for the night. Which meant that the whole time they were having dinner with his brother and future sister-in-law, Kerry wouldn't be able to forget that they'd be taking the elevator up a little while later.

Her brain came to an abrupt halt as her entire body suddenly came alive at the sight of Adam moving across the hotel lobby straight toward them. Her pale Irish skin meant she'd long ago had to learn how to keep her blushing to a minimum. But tonight, her self-control was just shaky enough that she felt the heat Adam always made her feel move across her cheeks.

"Kerry. It's good to see you again."

How did he manage to be better and better looking every time she saw him?

Instead of shaking her hand, he bent down to give her a soft kiss on the cheek, and she couldn't keep from breathing him in. He smelled like he'd just come out of a shower. It was all her brain needed to immediately run away with naughty visions of what he'd look like with warm water running down his naked muscles. That would have been enough to fluster her, but when she added the knowledge that, in a matter of hours, she was going to find out just how good he looked naked...

Oh God.

How was she ever going to make it through dinner in one piece? Especially when she needed to keep her nearly exploding lust for Adam a complete and total secret from his brother and his brother's fiancée?

Fortunately, she had a little time to compose her-self while he pulled Brooke into a bear hug and swung her around. Brooke's laughter rang through the otherwise hushed lobby, especially when Rafe growled, "Move your hands any lower and even being my brother won't save you."

"You know I love it when he gets all possessive like this," Brooke teased. "Say something totally inappropriate, Adam."

But before Adam could open his mouth, Rafe took his fiancée back into his arms and kissed her.

"Everyone in my family is like this," Adam told Kerry in a low voice. "Even my parents."

Though she knew her cheeks were hotter than ever at the way Brooke was clearly melting in Rafe's arms, Kerry resisted the urge to cover them with her hands. "It's very romantic."

When Adam made a sound that bordered on disgust, she was surprised to find herself smiling. Honestly, there was something incredibly refreshing about a man who didn't try to pretend about anything. Adam was quite obviously a man who wasn't trying to pull anything over on anyone. He believed what he believed and didn't care what anyone thought about those beliefs.

Even better, that knowledge that what she saw was what she'd get with Adam made her feel like she could breathe again.

At least, until they sat down and she realized he

hadn't been kidding about the matchmaking. Because after barely ten minutes of wedding talk, it seemed all Brooke and Rafe wanted to do was prove to Kerry just how compatible she and Adam were.

It didn't help, of course, when she and Adam ordered the exact same meal, down to the wine they preferred.

"Kerry, last time we met," Brooke said, "you were telling us about that hike you found just outside of the city. Adam loves to hike, and I'm sure he'd love to know about it, too."

"I sure would," he said, looking perfectly relaxed about the setup in progress. "Tell me all about it."

Clearly, he'd been down this matchmaking road many times before. And just as clearly, she could see that grinning and bearing it was the path of least resistance.

Deciding to take a page out of his book, she smiled at him and said, "It's straight uphill for four miles, but if you don't care about being able to breathe, the views are absolutely heavenly."

His eyebrows went up. "Are you talking about Mount Dickerman?"

"You know it?"

"It nearly killed me the last time I did it." He looked more than a little impressed. "One surprise after another, aren't you?"

For a moment, as he looked at her with a mixture of respect—and desire—she forgot there was anyone in the room but the two of them. Thank God the waiter came to remove their starters just then.

"Excuse me."

With as much poise as she could muster, Kerry left the table and headed for the ladies' room. She desperately needed a few moments alone to take a few deep breaths and settle down.

After locking the powder room door behind her, she closed her eyes and leaned back against the door, deliberately not looking at herself in the mirror. She didn't need to see how flushed her cheeks were, didn't need to confirm that her eyes were bright and sparkling.

The truth that she hadn't wanted to admit to herself—but now could no longer deny—was that she was filled to bursting with anticipation and need. Desire for Adam had grown from moment to moment, hour to hour, day to day, until she could hardly stand it. When she'd thought she was going to have to cancel on their night together, she'd practically wanted to scream with frustration. And now he was close. So close that *still* not being able to touch him was the most frustrating thing of all.

Combining all of that with nerves that just wouldn't quit—how could they when she'd never done anything even close to having a one-night stand before?—and she was a total mess. Top to bottom, inside and out.

Somehow, some way, she needed to tamp it all down until later tonight, when she could finally let herself go for a little while. Just long enough to find out if Adam Sullivan lived up to the late-night fantasies she'd been having about him all week.

Fortunately, she soon felt settled enough to return to the table. Unlocking the door, she was just stepping out of the hallway and into the restaurant when her phone buzzed in her bag.

After a lifetime in the wedding business, she was trained never to ignore a call. But it wasn't a panicked bride texting. It was Adam.

YOU LOOK BEAUTIFUL TONIGHT IN YOUR DRESS

Her heart jumped even faster as she stared at the compliment. He wasn't suddenly turning romantic on her, was he?

AND I CAN'T WAIT TO STRIP IT OFF YOU

She would never have thought it possible for her knees to go weak at the same time as laughter bubbled up and out of her. But Adam, it seemed, was turning everything she'd ever known, or expected, completely on its ear.

And when she looked up and straight into his intense yet laughing eyes, she realized what he was telling her—that it was okay to be nervous, but that she didn't have to be.

Because he would never lie to her or pretend to be someone he wasn't.

He would stick to every last part of their agreement to have fun in bed without ruining it with the threat of emotional entanglements that would never, ever work out for the two of them.

And most of all, he would make sure she had fun tonight, weak knees and all.

★ ★ ★

Adam loved Brooke like a sister, but little sisters could be seriously annoying sometimes. Especially when they got an idea in their heads that they refused to shake.

So while Kerry was in the bathroom clearly trying to regroup from the matchmaking onslaught, he turned to Brooke and Rafe and beat them to saying what were, no doubt, going to be the next words out of their mouths. "Kerry is beautiful. She's intelligent. She runs a successful business. And I like her a lot."

"I knew it!" Brooke exclaimed as she grabbed Rafe's arm in delight.

But Rafe was already shaking his head. "I don't think my brother is done just yet, sweetheart."

"One day," Adam continued, "she's going to find a guy who is perfect for her. And I really hope she does, because she deserves the kind of relationship that the two of you have found."

"That guy could be you!" Brooke insisted.

But they all knew better, knew that Adam wasn't anywhere close to looking for forever with anyone. All of his siblings had been ready when true love came. Brooke's childhood crush on Rafe had turned into a much more mature love when they'd found each other again as adults. Mia had fallen in love with Ford all those years ago, and when he'd come back into her life last year, the love that had never gone away had rekindled, brighter than ever. Their oldest brother, Ian, was clearly meant to be with Tatiana, even if he'd mistakenly thought he was no good at marriage because his first had been such a mistake. And Dylan had taken one look at Grace and her young son and known they were supposed to be his.

Adam was the odd man out. Which was perfectly okay with him.

Unfortunately, his family was having a hell of a time accepting that he liked flying solo. That he preferred it that way. And that even when a great woman like Kerry Dromoland came along, they would never be anything more than friends with benefits.

Having taken care of telling Brooke and Rafe to

back off in the nicest way possible, as the waiter brought their main courses over, Adam had sent Kerry a couple of texts. One meant to reassure her that she shouldn't let his family throw them off.

He hadn't been able to see her expression after she received the first text, but fortunately she was well within sight by the time he sent the second.

And her reaction was so freaking hot—from the way her cheeks flushed to the little stumble she made in her heels—that if they'd been having dinner with anyone else, he would have blown off the rest of the meal and taken her upstairs right then and there.

Adam stood and held out her chair for her. Her voice was a little husky as she murmured her thanks, and he was rewarded with the faintest trembling of her muscles against his fingertips when his hand accidentally brushed the middle of her back.

Jesus. He hadn't been lying when he said he couldn't wait to strip off her gorgeous dress. Every remaining minute at the dinner table with his brother and Brooke was going to be pure torture.

Kerry, however, remained the consummate dinner conversationalist. "You know how much I love your chocolates, Brooke, and all of my friends are getting hooked, too. Especially now that you have stores in the city. You must be thrilled by how much your business has grown in the past year."

"I am," Brooke said with a huge smile. "I honestly never thought my chocolates would be anything more than a small business by the lake."

"I always knew," Rafe said, giving his fiancée another one of his adoring looks. "Your chocolates are the best I've ever tasted." He was full of pride as he turned back to Kerry. "Brooke and her business partner are going to be opening several more chocolate truffle stores throughout Oregon and California soon."

"Oh, that's wonderful! You deserve every bit of your success."

"So do you. Your weddings are legendary."

Kerry laughed. "Promise me you'll say that to my mother if you ever meet her. She was so brilliant at planning weddings that sometimes it feels hard to live up to the legend."

Brooke smiled in a commiserating way. "As long as you promise to tell *my* mother how much you love my chocolates at the wedding."

"When we spoke on the phone last week I mentioned it at least a half-dozen times. And she agreed with me every single time."

"She did?" Brooke looked a little stunned by this news.

"She's clearly as addicted to your chocolates as the rest of us," Kerry said, instinctively knowing exactly what the bride needed to hear before spending time with her mother at her wedding.

When the waiter came to clear away their plates, then left them with the dessert menu, Kerry licked her lips in a completely natural—and extremely sexy— way. "Am I the only one here who wants one of everything?"

Adam caught the waiter's eye and waved him back over. "We'll try them all."

"You want to order every dessert on the menu, sir?"

"Yes."

When Adam turned back to Kerry, she was staring at him as if he were crazy. "I didn't actually mean it."

He could barely keep from reaching out to run his thumb over her gorgeous lower lip, still damp from her tongue. "Yes, you did. One bite of each, Kerry. Think how good that's going to taste."

"So good," she said back, her voice low and husky as she stared into his eyes as if she'd completely forgotten that Rafe and Brooke were still at the table with them. "Too good."

All night—hell, all week—Adam had been on edge waiting for this night with Kerry. But in that moment when she forgot to hide her desire for him, he nearly hit his breaking point.

He wanted her naked and in his arms as soon as possible, but he also wanted her to have what *she* wanted. Sugar, he already knew, made her happy.

And tonight was all about making Kerry happy.

Really, really happy.

Thirty minutes later, the four of them ended up doing a pretty good job on the desserts, even if Kerry barely had more than a taste of each one. Kerry and Rafe both tried to pay for dinner, but Adam beat them both to it, having told the maître d' to charge it to him when he'd made the reservation.

Finally, it was time to say their good-byes, and while Kerry and Brooke were hugging, Rafe asked him, "You heading home now?"

"Not quite yet."

"Still got that hot date?"

Guessing that Kerry had overheard Rafe's question because the restaurant happened to go quiet just in that moment, Adam made sure she could hear his response. "Crazy hot."

Her cheeks were flushed again as she turned to let him help her on with her coat. "It was nice to see you again, Kerry," he said.

And by the time she turned back to face him, her skin wasn't just flushed—her pupils had dilated, too, her breath coming just a little bit faster. "It was nice to see you, too. Thank you for dinner."

"It was my pleasure. I'm looking forward to seeing you again soon." He leaned close, pressed his lips to her cheek and whispered for her ears only, "Really soon."

With that, he waved good night to the three of them and headed toward the back of the hotel to the elevator that went up to the penthouse suites.

★ ★ ★

"I can't believe your brother is going on a date with someone else tonight!" Brooke was frowning as she and Rafe stood waiting outside the hotel for the valet to bring their car around. "The sparks jumping between the two of them were so hot I almost felt like a voyeur a few times during dinner. And he's already admitted that Kerry's perfect for him. So why won't he do anything about it?"

"Actually"—Rafe couldn't resist kissing her gorgeous mouth—"I wouldn't be so sure he's not doing something about it."

Brooke's eyebrows rose even as she moved closer to the man she loved and knew she'd never get enough of. "Wait, so even though he said all that stuff about hoping she finds some perfect guy one day, you think he's going after her anyway?"

"I think he believes every single word he said to us. Not just about how great she is, but about how he still isn't looking for anything serious." Rafe ran a hand over Brooke's hair. "But if you ask me, the way he looks at her says exactly the opposite."

"She was looking at him the same way, wasn't she?"

Rafe nodded. "She was."

"How long do you think they're going to fight the inevitable?"

"It didn't look like either of them was fighting too hard—at least when it came to the heat they were generating."

In fact, Rafe now had a pretty good idea about the identity of Adam's "crazy hot" date. He'd been able to read his brother's lips when he'd told Kerry he was looking forward to seeing her *really soon*. But just in case he was wrong, he didn't want to get Brooke's hopes all the way up quite yet.

"That's a good first step, I guess." Brooke bit her lip as she mulled over the situation some more. "But do you think there's anything else we can do to give them both a bigger push in the right direction?"

"I'm pretty sure we've done more than enough already by sending him in for that meeting with her this week and then getting them together for dinner tonight."

Looking a little guilty about their machinations, Brooke said, "I just want Adam to be happy."

"I know, sweetheart. We all do. But the truth is, there's only one thing that will do that for sure."

Brooke scrunched up her face. "No more match-making."

"No more matchmaking."

She sighed. "You're no fun."

"You sure about that? Because I have some pretty fun ideas about what we should do tonight when we get home." And when he leaned in even closer and began to whisper those wicked ideas to her, Brooke finally forgot about anyone but the man she couldn't wait to marry.

CHAPTER SIX

Kerry's heart pounded faster with every floor the elevator rose. Though she'd never done anything like this before, she'd still convinced herself that she could be cool. That she could walk into a hotel suite knowing she was going to have hot sex with a man she barely knew without blinking an eye.

Who had she been kidding?

Kerry could feel Adam's intense gaze on her the moment she stepped out of the elevator onto the penthouse level. They each already had their keys, but he hadn't waited for her in the room. She wondered if it was because he'd known how close she'd be to going back on her vow not to run. Not because she didn't want him. On the contrary, she'd never wanted anyone or anything this much. But simply because she was so far out of her comfort zone right now that she almost felt as if she were watching herself from a distance.

One step, and then one more, and then another— that was all it took to meet him in the middle of the hall, in front of the door to their suite. But when he didn't open the door with his key, she realized he was waiting for *her* to decide whether or not she truly wanted to do it.

Being a wedding planner meant Kerry dealt with people making big decisions all day long. She always told them that while it was great to take the time to consider all the options, they shouldn't worry about making the wrong choice. Because whichever way they went, she could absolutely promise them she would do whatever it took to make sure they were happy.

Happy. Kerry so badly wanted to be happy, too. If only just for one night with a beautiful man who set her every nerve alight.

Because the truth was that Adam Sullivan had made her smile more than any man ever had before. Remembering the way he'd ordered every dessert on the menu so that she could have a taste of each one made her smile through the nerves that were riding her. So, for tonight, she told herself as she lifted the key to the electronic pad, she wouldn't let herself worry about making the wrong choice.

She'd simply let herself be happy.

The door clicked open and she stepped inside first, with Adam locking the door behind him.

Unfortunately, the sound of the bolt clicking into

place—echoing loudly in her head as she realized they were now locked into the suite together—had her smile falling away as if it had never been there at all. She spun around and blurted, "Maybe this is a mistake."

Adam slid his hand through hers, and somehow, instead of it feeling as if he were trying to hold her down, it was more like he was trying to share his warmth.

"It isn't."

There were so many things she should already have done, all of them starting and ending with keeping her distance from him. But just as she hadn't been able to pull that off thus far, yet again she couldn't make herself pull her hand away from his. Still, she needed to ask, "How can you be so sure?"

"I was sure the first moment I set eyes on you that this is exactly where you and I are meant to be. Together." His eyes heated even further. "About to get naked."

She couldn't stop her next breath from catching in her throat. She wasn't used to playing this kind of sexy game. Wasn't used to any of this.

"I don't know what you're expecting from me."

Her words were almost a whisper, the opposite of the image of strength she'd hoped to give him. All her life Kerry had tried so hard to get everything right, but tonight, she just didn't know up from down. Right from wrong. All she knew was that some crazy longing, some fiery desire had sent her to this hotel to meet Adam tonight.

But what if that longing, that desire, fizzled into disappointment and regret?

"I'm only expecting one thing from you tonight, Kerry." Adam's words weren't much louder than hers had been. But they were completely steady. And utterly certain. "For you to let me give you pleasure." He used their connected hands to tug her just the slightest bit closer, close enough that she could feel the heat of his body. "More pleasure than you've ever had before." He took her other hand in his and rubbed each thumb in a circle over the palms of her hands. "More pleasure than you ever thought was possible."

Did he know that his words—and just the barest touch of his hands on hers—were already getting her more than halfway there?

And yet, the still barely rational part of her needed to know, "What about your pleasure?"

He smiled then, a smile with so much heat behind it that she lost what was left of her breath. "Making you feel good *is* what's going to give me pleasure."

Was he for real? None of the men she'd slept with before had considered her pleasure to be theirs, too. Was he just saying it to make sure she stayed long enough to take off her clothes?

He looked deep into her eyes. "Will you trust me, Kerry? I'm not asking for forever, just for tonight."

They were exactly the words that should have sent her running. After all, she'd been waiting her whole life for *forever*.

But, amazingly, it was the knowledge that one hot night didn't have to turn into a lifetime that had her shoulders finally relaxing.

Fun. She could just have fun tonight without it ruining the rest of her life. And pleasure, too. More pleasure than she'd ever had before. More pleasure than she'd ever thought was possible.

She didn't need to keep doubting, didn't need to keep worrying.

For one night she could just let go and *feel*.

"I will."

The words were barely out when he lowered his mouth only a breath from hers to seal the deal. And if somewhere in the back of her head her *I will* sounded a little too close to the marriage vows she'd heard countless brides say to their grooms, she forced the recognition away.

Adam Sullivan would never be her forever and she could never let herself forget it. No matter how good he might be able to make her feel.

Starting with a first kiss she wanted more than

she'd ever wanted anything in her entire life.

* * *

Adam swore he could taste Kerry's lips already, even though he hadn't kissed her yet. So sweet, but surprisingly spicy, too. And hot. So hot that he already knew their first kiss would blow every other one out of the water.

Lord, he wanted her. Wanted to strip off her clothes and have her naked beneath him. Right here in the suite's entry, and then again in the bathtub, and then in the enormous bed—all in a desperate attempt to try to sate his appetite for her. But at the same time, a part of him wanted to draw out the anticipation as long as possible. He'd always known anticipation was hot, but he hadn't had a clue it could be *this* hot.

And maybe he would have kept them just like that, their lips a breath away from touching, their bodies just as far apart, had it not been for the desperate little sound Kerry made. One that demanded his kiss as much as it begged for it.

As his lips finally touched hers, he found out that she truly did taste better than anything else ever had. The urge to devour nearly broke him, but he somehow managed to rein it in. Again and again he deliberately brushed his mouth so gently, so softly against hers that he knew she couldn't possibly be thinking about anything other than his next kiss. And with every brush of his lips against hers, she not only relaxed more and more, she also began to press her sweet curves closer and closer to him, her hands moving from his to come around his neck.

He cupped her hips with his hands at the same moment that he slicked his tongue over her lower lip. When she gasped with obvious pleasure, he couldn't resist taking the kiss deeper. Thankfully, she was right there with him, her tongue tangling with his as gentle-and-soft gave way to raw desire. He was a heartbeat from pressing her up against the door, tearing off her clothes, wrapping her legs around his waist, and driving into her when he forced himself to drag his mouth away from hers.

Her usually perfect lipstick was gone and her eyes were beautifully fuzzy as she looked up at him. "Adam?"

He now knew that her gorgeous mouth could strip his control away like nothing else ever had, but just hearing his name on her lips in that slightly breathless voice meant he had to tangle his hands in her hair and kiss her again.

There wasn't even a pretense of slow and soft this time as they jumped straight into the middle of the hottest kiss of his life. A kiss made even hotter by the way Kerry was rubbing against him as though she couldn't get close enough.

Just as he'd known it would be, it was even harder to pull away this time, and he groaned at the effort it took to hold himself in check, at least long enough to take off her clothes.

"The first time I looked at you, I wondered what you'd look like with your hair tangled from my hands, your mouth swollen from my kisses, your skin flushed from the heat between us." He took her hands in his and slowly moved them from his neck so that he could take a step back and look at her in her pretty dress with her hair falling over her shoulders. "I want to remember this, want both of us to remember the first time I stripped you bare."

Her breath caught again as he let her hands go and brushed her long hair back from her shoulders, then ran his hands down her back to her waist. Neither of them looked away from each other as he slowly untied the sash that held her dress closed. He could feel how hot her skin was beneath the thin silk and how sensitive she was to even the slightest touch as his fingertips brushed over the skin he was baring.

He slid open the fabric, pushed it all the way off so that it pooled around her feet, and stared, awestruck, at Kerry wearing nothing but sheer lace and heels.

"My God, you're beautiful." He'd known it all along, of course, but the contrast between the way she looked when she was almost nude and her previous buttoned-up elegance absolutely blew his mind.

Tracing the straps of her bra down from her shoulders to the soft flesh rising up out of the lace, he loved feeling her heartbeat skip as he cupped her fully in his hands. Her nipples beaded hard and needy against his palms, and there wasn't a man alive who would have had the self-control not to lower his mouth to them, lace and all.

Kerry reached for him and gripped his shoulders tightly as she arched into him. But he couldn't get enough of her like this, and without even the patience to unhook her bra, he yanked the sheer fabric down so that her breasts spilled out of the lace and into his hands and mouth.

Over and over again, she said his name as he loved first one breast and then the other and then both together when his greed for her overtook him. She was rocking her hips against his now, and it no longer mattered what he'd planned for tonight, how slowly he'd meant to strip her clothes away, how desperate he'd intended her to be before he finally put his hands, his mouth, on her.

He'd been a fool to think he could plan a damned thing where Kerry was concerned. Not when he wanted her this much.

And not when she clearly wanted him just as

much.

He lifted his mouth from her breasts at the same moment that he slid one hand down into the lace that covered the vee between her legs. And, sweet Lord, did he ever love the way her eyes widened at the sensation of his fingers slicking against her wet, hot skin.

"*Adam.*" She instinctively moved against him, and her lids lowered as he moved inside of her. "Good. It's so good." She bit her lower lip for a split second before she whispered, "Too good."

He wanted to watch her come apart for him. But even more, he wanted to *feel* her come apart against him—her mouth beneath his, her heart beating against his, her breasts pressed to his chest.

He slid deeper and swallowed her gasp with a kiss. With his free hand, he lifted one of her legs up around his hips, and she immediately rocked harder, faster, into his hand. The vibration of a moan rose up from her chest as her inner muscles began to pulse over his fingers.

Adam was still fully clothed, but even without taking anything off, this was the hottest sex he'd ever had in his life.

She rocked into him again and again, both of them taking her higher and higher until she stilled on a gasp, then shattered—utterly shattering him at the same time. And even when she finally started to settle against him, her breathing ragged, he continued to kiss her.

Adam couldn't get enough of any part of Kerry, especially her mouth. Their kisses had gone full circle already, from soft to desperate and back to sweet—but he knew it wouldn't be long before desperation caught them again. Especially when he swept her up into his arms, their lips still pressed together so that he drank in her sound of surprise and then her laughter at being carried through the suite.

Laughing while kissing wasn't something Adam had ever done before. But he suddenly found himself wanting to brush his fingertips over all the sensitive parts of Kerry's body and kiss her while she laughed and he laughed with her. He loved making her smile, loved knowing he'd pleased her. All he wanted tonight was to please her over and over and over again.

He lowered her onto the big bed, only moving his lips from hers because he needed to taste the rest of her. Needed to run kisses over every inch of her beautiful skin as he finally stripped her completely bare.

Thankfully, she wasn't nervous anymore, wasn't at all shy as he moved his hands and mouth down over her curves, from her shoulder, where he lightly sank in his teeth so that she shuddered, to the soft and sensitive undersides of her breasts. He moved lower then, dropping one kiss after another over her stomach and the upper curves of her hips. Lace still covered her, but not for long as he slowly tugged it down until she was finally completely bare. Totally perfect. And all his.

His.

Her beauty tugged at him, made him feel possessive.

Protective.

Ravenous.

In one quick move he had her thigh over his shoulder, his mouth on her core, and his tongue playing over the sweetest flesh imaginable. Her hips came off the bed, and he slid his hands beneath to help bring her even closer.

She was liquid heat against him, burning like fire from the inside out, and as she climaxed again against his lips and tongue, the sounds and sensations of her pleasure were nearly enough to send him over, too.

Making a woman who was always so controlled lose hold of it was the sexiest thing imaginable.

★ ★ ★

Kerry had never known such mind-bending pleasure. Had never actually thought anything so sweet, so sinful, could exist.

And if she had known it?

Well, she thought with a smile she couldn't possibly contain, she would never have waited so long to experience all of the shockingly good benefits of tangling with a bad boy. Especially when both of them clearly knew that what they shared beneath the sheets—or outside of the sheets, she thought with another smile—would never leave their hotel suite.

Knowing no one would come to harm from tonight, or any other night they decided to play these wicked and wonderful games together, made it easy for her to reach for him as he kissed his way back up her naked body. And to say, "It's my turn now."

Adam was much bigger than she, but desire—and desperation to get him out of his clothes—made her strong. Strong enough to turn them over in the bed so that he was beneath her and she was pressing a kiss over each inch of his chest that she bared as she undid his shirt.

"You taste so good." She licked out against the flexing muscles of his abdomen and they jumped beneath her tongue. "Amazingly good." She lifted her eyes to his as she put her hand on his belt buckle and said, "I want to taste more."

He groaned, and she felt him pulse against the palm she'd just laid flat over his erection. She could feel how big, how hard he was, had felt it as they'd kissed by the suite's front door. But it wasn't enough to feel him through fabric anymore—she needed him skin to skin.

Clearly wanting the same thing, he got the rest of his clothes off within seconds. Her brain scrambled as she looked at all those muscles, all that tanned skin, all that hunger for her. Jumbled enough that the only word she could think was *mine.*

For tonight at least, Adam Sullivan, with his dark, intense eyes, with a mouth made for kissing, and with those magical, knowing hands, was all hers.

Hers.

And then there was no room for thinking, no space for anything but instinct. And pleasure. She lowered her mouth to his chest first, running her lips south with soft and teasing kisses until she couldn't stand to tease either of them anymore as she ran her tongue over him. His hands tangled in her hair, her name falling from his lips again and again. Pleading and pleasured all at the same time. And then, finally, she took him inside on a hum of pleasure she couldn't contain.

His growl echoed in the room as she found herself suddenly lying back against the mattress, Adam kissing her with ferocious passion. He drew back from her lips just far enough to say, "Now, Kerry. I need you *now.*"

She knew it was his way of asking her, yet again, if she was ready for this. Ready for him. Even after what they'd already done—their hands and mouths all over each other—he obviously needed to know that she was still okay with taking the final step.

If any part of her had still been cold, his concern would have warmed her up completely. But she was already there—*beyond* ready to be with him. So instead of answering with words, she reached for one of the condoms he'd put on the bedside table and together they sheathed him. By the time his mouth found hers again, she was already wrapping her legs around his hips. In one perfect upthrust of her hips, she took him all the way inside.

In a heartbeat, he was unleashed. No more reserve, no more worry. Just wicked, sinful passion.

She met him thrust for thrust, stroke for stroke, gasp for gasp. And just as she'd never known there could be pleasure this sweet, she'd also never realized that she could become part of someone else. That Adam's heartbeat could mesh with her own. That his sweat could become hers. And that his pleasure would take her even higher than the very highest peak.

Together they climbed.

And together, wrapped in each other's arms, they fell.

CHAPTER SEVEN

Kissing.

And kissing.

Then kissing some more.

Kerry drank in every one of Adam's sweet kisses while his mouth never left hers. Her arms and legs were still wrapped all around him, his hands were tangled in her hair. And she had never felt so good in all her life.

Their post-sex make-out session kept her heart racing just as fast as it had when she was coming apart beneath him, her temperature just as high, her need just as desperate. There was no room, no space in their kisses for her to take a breath, but she didn't want that room. Didn't want that space. Not when everything felt so perfect, so right.

So *beautiful*.

He was heavy over her, but she loved his weight pressing her down into the mattress. Loved how secure it made her feel to know that he was as close to her as another person could possibly be. And that he didn't want to break their connection, either.

Finally, he lifted his mouth from hers, but only to rain kisses over her face. Again and again he'd press a half-dozen kisses over her cheek, or her eyelids, or the curve of her ear, or the tip of her chin, before returning to her mouth. And every time he came back, she was even hungrier for his lips against hers. For the slow stroke of his tongue over hers. For the nip of his teeth as sweet turned wild before turning breathlessly soft again. For the chance to drink in his groans of pleasure as she kissed him back just as passionately.

Forever. She could have kissed him like this forev—

Her phone rang, one of the two ring tones that she would never, ever ignore no matter what. Tonight, it was her sister's that was chiming barely a few feet from where she and Adam were wrapped around each other on the bed.

By the second ring, all the heat had drained out of her, replaced immediately by worry.

"Kerry?" Adam had clearly felt her tense up.

"I have to get that."

She could hear both the worry and the frustration in her own voice and knew that Adam wasn't at all the kind of clueless male who would miss it. Because even though she should be glad that Colleen had just saved her from letting her post-sex emotions, and all of Adam's amazingly passionate kisses, run away with her heart, she still couldn't help but be upset that the moment was now completely ruined.

Adam moved to let her slide out from beneath him. When he'd been lying over her and she'd been wrapped around him, she'd been so warm. But now, as the cool air in the room rushed over her skin, she couldn't repress a shiver.

He'd seen every inch of her tonight, but she still felt horribly exposed as she all but leapt off the bed to grab her phone before it went to voice mail. Because if her sister couldn't reach her, who knew what she'd decide to do next? Or how bad it would end up being.

"Colleen? It's Kerry—tell me what you need. Where are you?"

Her insides twisted as soon as she heard her sister's voice while Colleen gave her the name of a bar in a really bad part of Seattle. Slurred. High. Either on the verge of laughing or crying or both in that manic way Colleen often had when she went out on Friday nights to try to numb her emotions.

"I'm coming right now to get you," Kerry told her. "Don't go anywhere with anyone. Promise me you'll call me again if anyone tries anything."

But instead of giving her that promise, her sister hung up on her.

Kerry grabbed for her clothes and began to yank them on, not even the slightest bit concerned about her nakedness anymore. "I have to go," she told Adam, even though it had to have been obvious from him hearing her side of the conversation.

"I'll go with you."

He was already putting on his clothes as she told him, "Thanks, but I can handle this myself."

"Kerry." He was magnificent standing in front of her in only his pants, his chest bare. "The volume on your phone was up loud enough that I could hear the name of the bar you're headed for to pick up your friend."

"My sister."

"I get that your sister needs you, but I don't want you going to that part of town at all, let alone by yourself at this time of night."

"I've been there plenty of times to get her," she began, but even as she said it, she couldn't help remembering how scary most of those times had been. Or how last week her sister had been so wasted that Kerry could barely get her over to the car.

A car she didn't even have tonight, since she'd taken a taxi to the hotel.

She looked up into dark eyes that were comfortingly steady. "How fast can you drive?"

"As fast as you need me to go."

★ ★ ★

Kerry was glad that Adam didn't expect her to make conversation as they drove. He didn't waste any time trying to find a parking spot, either, just turned on his hazards and left his car right out front. Any other guy with an expensive car would have been freaking out about leaving it here. Heck, every time she left her car in this neighborhood to go into a bar and get her sister, she'd been relieved that it was still there by the time they got back outside. But Adam simply put his hand on Kerry's back as if to steady her while they walked through the crowd smoking cigarettes on the sidewalk.

"Colleen is taller and thinner than I am, with dark red hair to her shoulders."

Her sister was a beautiful woman. At least she had been until she'd started drinking and partying so hard. Colleen was too old, and too smart, for places like this. Kerry knew Colleen was hurt by what had happened between her and her ex-boyfriend, but how could her sister think that this was any way to fix it?

"I don't see her outside."

Kerry was more than a little frantic. *Please.* She prayed Colleen hadn't gotten into a car with some guy who would take advantage of her.

And as Kerry and Adam pushed through the crowd and into the bar, she was so thankful that he was there and that he'd insisted on coming with her. The sea of rough-looking men and women instinctively parted for him without him having to say or do anything threatening at all. Just from his sheer presence.

Thank God, it didn't take them long to find her sister dancing and drinking, although the guy she was with looked more than a little scary. Over the pounding music screaming from the speakers on the ceiling, Kerry yelled, "Colleen, I'm ready to take you home now."

Colleen's eyes were blurry and red as she turned to look at Kerry. There was barely recognition there, let alone any thanks that Kerry had rushed over to get her. "Go away," Colleen said as the song changed to one that allowed them all to hear. "I'm finally happy now with—"

"Zane."

Colleen gave him a big, messy smile and ran her hands down his arms. "Mmm, Zane. Make my little jailor go away."

Adam immediately stepped in and told the guy, "Colleen is going to have to take a rain check tonight."

Colleen's gaze shifted to Adam, at last. She tried to whistle, but she couldn't control her lips quite well enough, so only air came out. "Where did you come from, gorgeous?" Zane was instantly forgotten as Colleen reached for Adam.

Kerry had never felt so mortified in all her life. She'd assumed her previously perfect night with Adam couldn't get any worse.

She'd been wrong.

"Colleen, please," Kerry begged, "let's go home."

Her sister turned on her then. "Not all of us want a cold bed. Just because you're too uptight to know how to have a good time doesn't mean that the rest of us don't." She turned back to Adam. "Right, baby? That's why you're here, isn't it?"

Kerry knew her sister was too drunk to know what she was saying. But that didn't make it any easier to blink back the tears that were threatening to spill.

Fortunately, Adam still had his wits perfectly about him. "It's a nice night, Colleen. How about we go outside and get some fresh air?"

He didn't speak to her sister as if she were a loser. There was no pity in his voice. No revulsion, either. And Kerry had never appreciated anyone more.

Colleen shot her a triumphant look over her shoulder as Adam put his arm around her and began to lead her out of the bar. And thank God he was holding her up, because she could barely walk, and certainly not in a straight line. Kerry got on her other side, and together she and Adam all but dragged her sister toward the exit. They hadn't yet made it to the front door when Colleen let out a groan and went limp. Adam didn't miss a beat, catching her and lifting her into his arms to carry her outside.

"I'm sorry," Kerry said.

"Don't be."

And the crazy thing was that he really seemed to mean it. He didn't seem the least bit shocked by what had just happened. He simply laid her sister down in the backseat and was so kind as he took off his jacket and tucked it around her that Kerry found herself almost in tears.

"Where to?" he asked.

"I have to take her back to my place to make sure she's okay during the night."

Given that it was the absolutely worst possible ending to what had been the best night of her life, Kerry couldn't help but wonder if it was karmic punishment. Some sort of retribution for breaking her number-one rule: Don't hook up with a man who didn't have the potential to be *the one*.

Not that she would get the chance to make that mistake again, of course. Because she was absolutely certain that, apart from official wedding duties, she'd never see Adam again. Kerry had known their fling would end, of course, since that had always been the plan.

She just hadn't known that it would end on the same night it began.

CHAPTER EIGHT

Adam parked in the downstairs lot of Kerry's building, one of his favorite buildings in Seattle. He'd been honored to head up the historic restoration a decade ago, one of his first major projects.

The building fit Kerry well—classy and elegant, but not stuffy. Granted, he hadn't been willing to see that the first time he'd met her. No, he'd wanted to take her at face value. The glossy swing of her hair, the impeccably tailored and pressed clothes, the perfect face that seemed to be carved out of marble by a master.

But if he hadn't already learned just how wrong he was by now, tonight would have taken all of his assumptions and crushed them to bits. As soon as his hands had been tangled in her hair and her mouth had been beneath his, he'd realized that she was made up of more raw, elemental heat, more unfettered desire than any other woman he'd ever known. And after her sister had called, he'd realized just how hard Kerry had been working to project *perfect*. Only, it was clear her life wasn't even close to perfect. Because if she had a sister who needed to be saved from herself on a regular basis, what else was lurking in Kerry's shadows?

Before she could try to get her sister out of the backseat, he lifted Colleen into his arms.

"My place is just up on the second floor," Kerry said, leading the way over to the elevator. As they waited for it to make its way down to the garage, she gently brushed a hand over her sister's hair. Colleen didn't open her eyes, but he noticed the way she leaned into Kerry's touch.

Just the way he had tonight in their hotel suite.

Kerry's face was still too pale, her green eyes too full of concern as she looked at her sister. Adam's sister, Mia, had never been this much of a mess—not even close—but the handful of scrapes she had gotten into felt like they had taken years off his life. He couldn't imagine how difficult this was for Kerry. Because while she clearly wanted to help her sister, he wasn't sure just how interested Colleen was in being helped. Not if the disdain she'd heaped on Kerry in the bar was anything to go by.

"Not all of us want a cold bed. Just because you're too uptight to know how to have a good time, doesn't mean that the rest of us don't."

Kerry had looked like she'd been slapped, and even in the crappy bar lighting he'd caught the tears glistening in her eyes. He'd wanted to tell Kerry she wasn't at all cold. And that *uptight* was all wrong, too. But there hadn't been time to do that, not when getting her sister out of that hellhole was priority one.

As they stepped into the elevator, Adam wished he had the right words to make her feel better. His brother Dylan would have known just what to say right now. Rafe probably would have, too. But Adam had always been one to comfort by action rather than words, just as he was doing right now. Still, he wanted to do more, wished there was some way he could take care of Colleen's problems for Kerry.

No woman had ever made him feel so protective. And not because she was weak. Beneath the veneer of gloss and elegance, Adam believed Kerry Dromoland just might be the toughest woman he'd ever met. Not only did she run her business with perfect precision, but she also wasn't the slightest bit afraid to head into the worst parts of town to help her sister.

They got off the elevator, and her front door was only a few steps away. At first glance, as she let them inside, the space wasn't too different from her office— perfectly decorated, from the furniture to the artwork and even the patterns on the rugs. But unlike her office, there were little things throughout that gave away hints as to the real woman beneath the gorgeous veneer. The jar of candy on the counter. The sweatshirt thrown over the back of a dining room chair. And especially the pile of romance novels by the side of the couch.

"If you could bring my sister into my guest room, that would be great."

Following Kerry down the hall, he'd only just stepped over the guest room's threshold when Colleen suddenly groaned. He knew that sound, and it was never a good one.

"Where's the bathroom?"

Kerry pointed, and he moved as fast as he could without jostling Colleen too much.

But just as he put Colleen down on her feet on the tiled bathroom floor, Kerry moved in to put her arms around her sister. "You've been amazing, but I can't let you do any more for her tonight. You shouldn't have to deal with this."

She'd barely finished her sentence when Colleen's eyes fluttered open and she said, "I'm going to be sick."

"Please, Adam," Kerry said. "She'll hate knowing you saw her like this."

He shut the door behind him a beat before Colleen's retching and crying started. Adam knew exactly how this was going to play out. Kerry would take care of her sister, then stay up all night watching over her.

But who would take care of Kerry?

By the time Adam made it out to her kitchen, he'd

decided that *he* would.

No doubt Kerry would need coffee when she emerged from the bathroom. He sure as hell would in her position. Adam's mother had made sure he and his brothers weren't useless in the kitchen or around the house, so he easily knew his way around a pot of coffee.

As he found everything he needed to make it, he thought about family and all that came with it. He'd always been thankful for his, for the way they all stood by each other no matter what, and he liked knowing Kerry clearly felt the same about her family.

But from what he could see, there was a big differ- ence between his family and hers—no one in his family had ever pretended to be perfect. His parents had never expected it from Adam and his siblings. They'd simply expected them to be kind, and hoped that any mistakes they made would be something to learn from. Adam hadn't met Kerry's mother, but from what she'd said at dinner about her mother doing spot checks on her "empire" all the time, he had a sense of just how much weight her mother expected Kerry to carry on her shoulders. And to do it effortlessly, as well.

An hour later, Kerry's hair was damp and curling softly around her shoulders as she walked into her kitchen. She'd not only showered, but had also changed into leggings and an oversized University of

Washington sweatshirt. She looked utterly unlike the perfectly polished woman he'd first met a week ago—and totally adorable. Even more beautiful, in fact, than he'd already thought she was.

She stopped in her tracks halfway into the room. "What are you still doing here?"

"I was thinking you could probably use a cup of coffee."

He poured it for her and brought it over before she could tell him that she didn't need it. He'd seen how hard she worked to take care of everything herself, but sometimes you needed support, whether you wanted to admit it or not.

"How did you know coffee was *exactly* what I needed right now?"

She took the cup from him and drank. Not dainty sips, but big, thirsty gulps.

Staying to make her coffee hadn't been about sex—yes, they'd had an amazing night together, but after seeing what she was going through in helping her sister, he'd simply wanted to take care of her. Still, he wasn't going to blame himself for enjoying the sight of her *perfect* walls falling away or for thinking she was even sexier behind those crumbling walls.

After Kerry had finished the cup and gone to pour herself a refill from the pot, she said, "You're good at silence. At letting a person process their thoughts."

"You can thank my father for that. He's the best listener there is."

She gave a faint little smile. "From everything Rafe and Brooke and you have told me, your parents sound really amazing. I can't wait to meet them at the wedding." But too soon, her smile fell away and she sighed as she picked up the coffee cup and took another sip.

He'd given her a little silence and coffee. Now he'd give her the chance to get some of tonight off her chest if that's what she needed. "Do you want to talk about it?"

She sighed again. "I just feel really embarrassed about everything tonight and how it all turned out."

"There's nothing at all embarrassing about being there for your family and helping them when times are rough. Trust me, we've all been there." He moved closer and put his hand on her cheek. "On both sides."

For a moment, she closed her eyes and leaned into his touch. He loved the feel of her soft skin against his palm, her eyelashes brushing over him. He also loved knowing that she felt she could rely on him for a little while.

When she finally drew back, she leaned against the kitchen counter, her expression bleak. "My sister thought the world revolved around her boyfriend. There wasn't anything she wouldn't do or give to him.

But then it turned out he was lying and cheating and stealing from her. Pretty much everything you can imagine. And she just fell apart after that. I keep hoping she'll stop treating herself like dirt over it, but..." She sighed again. "Maybe tonight will be the wake-up call she needs."

Adam hoped it would be, too, although the way Colleen had behaved tonight didn't have him holding his breath. Something told him her sister was still a ways from actually hitting bottom, no matter how bad tonight had been.

"How long has this been going on?" he asked.

Kerry scrunched up her nose, so cute and uninhibited that he found himself not only wanting her more, but liking her more, too.

"About three months."

"You've been heading into dangerous neighborhoods to bring her home for three months?" He couldn't mask the alarm in his voice, and he could see her shoulders stiffen as she reacted to it.

"I've been careful."

He forced himself to bite his tongue, a very difficult task when he was worried as all hell for her. "I'm sure you have, but the next time she calls you for a late-night bar pickup, I'd really appreciate it if you'd call me to come with you."

Kerry raised an eyebrow at that. "Thanks for the

offer, but I don't think you'd appreciate me calling in the middle of one of your dates to ask you to drop everything for Colleen."

Not for Colleen, for *Kerry*. And not only was no one other woman on his horizon right now, but at this point he couldn't honestly imagine being interested in anyone but Kerry.

"No," he clarified, "what I wouldn't appreciate is finding out you went back into one of those dangerous hellholes without me."

He couldn't quite read her expression as she said, "You're stubborn."

"So are you. But there's a big difference between stubborn and foolish. And we both know you and Colleen have been lucky so far to get out of those places unscathed. I'd like to keep things that way." He'd heard her ask her sister for a promise to be safe earlier that night. Now he decided to ask Kerry for the same thing. "Promise me you'll call me if you ever feel that you need to."

He watched her battle silently with herself, clearly caught between her belief that she needed to be self-sufficient at all times and the knowledge that she really *had* been lucky to get out of those neighborhoods in one piece so many times over the past three months.

"Okay," she finally said. "I promise to call. But hopefully I won't have to, because Colleen will decide it's time to turn over a new leaf." Kerry looked more than a little uncomfortable as she added, "Please don't say anything about this to Rafe and Brooke. I'd hate for them to think I'm not one hundred percent there for them and their wedding, when I am."

"They know you are," he said softly. "And I can't imagine anything would ever make them think differently. But what happened tonight is just between you and me."

"All of it?" she confirmed.

"That's what we agreed on, isn't it?"

When Kerry nodded, though it should have been a relief to know that they were on the same page about having secret hot hookups with absolutely no relationship pressure, strangely, it wasn't. Instead, he found that the idea of keeping the night they'd spent together a secret grated on him. Big time.

"Thank you again, Adam. Not just for helping me with Colleen, but for—"

He stopped her by threading his hands through her hair and pulling her close for a kiss. She didn't need to thank him for anything, and he figured the best way to make her stop trying was to do what he'd been wanting to do ever since she'd walked into the kitchen sweet and fresh from the shower.

Kerry didn't resist his kiss, but slicked her tongue out across his instead, as if she was still just as hungry for him as he still was for her. They'd been kissing when her sister called—kissing in a way that he'd never kissed another woman, a way that was so good it seemed to have no beginning and no end. Now, it was so tempting to continue where they'd left off. He could so easily lift her into his arms, carry her into her bedroom, strip her bare again, and drown in her sweet scent, her moans of pleasure, run his hands over every inch of her soft skin before finally giving them the release they both craved.

But moving things to her house hadn't been in their original plan. And even more than he wanted to be with her again, he needed to know that she'd come through tonight's ordeal in one piece.

Forcing himself to drag his mouth away from hers, he asked, "Do you need me to stay?"

She shook her head without so much as a pause. "No. You've already done too much."

But even though that was his cue, he didn't let go of her. Not yet. Not when her skin was so soft, so warm, so touchable. And not when all he could think about was kissing her again.

"Do you want me to stay?"

The words were out of his mouth before he could stop them. Before he'd even realized the slight shift from *need* to *want* was coming. But even though a part of him wanted to take back the too-revealing question, he found that he wanted to know her answer more.

A flash of longing winged across her face—deep and intense—but it was gone so fast that if he hadn't been watching her so intently, he might have missed it. It hadn't been a fair question, he knew. Not when they had an agreement. An arrangement. One that was based on hot sex with no emotional strings.

Only, how could either of them deny that tonight had definitely tied some strings? And though he could have told himself that it was simply needing to band together to help her sister that made him feel this close to Kerry now, he couldn't forget how close to her he'd felt while they'd been making love. Closer than he'd ever been to anyone else. Even hours later, the pleasure still lingered. Enough that he knew better than to ruin it by pushing for something in these too-early morning hours that they'd agreed neither of them wanted.

Kerry had no interest in reforming a bad boy—and Adam had no interest in being reformed. Their arrangement was perfect as it was, and he wouldn't make the mistake of ruining it.

"Adam…"

He stopped her from having to say anything more with another kiss. A softer one this time.

"Try to get some rest, okay?"

"I will." She gave him a small smile. "Good night,

Adam."

He finally forced himself to drop his hands and take a step away from her. "Good night, Kerry."

CHAPTER NINE

It was only noon on Saturday, but Kerry was already drinking her third espresso of the day. Colleen had been sick again in the middle of the night, and Kerry hadn't had the heart to ask her sister to clean it up herself. And when Colleen had begged her not to tell their mother what had happened at the bar, Kerry had agreed, just as she had a dozen times before, not to say a word.

Colleen's horrible Friday nights were their little secret. So very different from the secrets they'd shared when they were little girls—secrets over stealing a cookie or wearing lipstick at school. Kerry had never been so thankful to have to go meet with potential new clients on a Saturday, nor so guilty about not being able to spend any more time nursing her sister.

The only problem was that there was something off about this new couple. Something Kerry couldn't quite put her finger on. From the moment they'd walked in the door, she'd felt the tension between them. Kerry didn't expect the men and women she worked with to agree on everything. But not being able to find common ground on any of the dozen preliminary questions she'd asked them? Honestly, there were times when it had been almost painful to be in the same room with them.

She often saw brides and grooms disagree with their mothers or future mothers-in-law, but usually the bride and groom were on the same team. How, she'd found herself wondering, had these two even reached the point of becoming engaged? And even if they did end up agreeing on enough to make it to the wedding, did they stand a chance of making it past that?

Kerry knew what her mother would have done. Aileen Dromoland would have politely but firmly informed the couple that she was not the right wedding planner for them. And her mother would have been perfectly sure that she'd made the right decision.

But what if there was something Kerry was missing? What if the couple had simply had a rotten morning just like hers, and were normally loving with each other? Or what if she was simply projecting her own frustration onto them?

Because the truth was that she was still more than a little upset about the way her one incredible night with Adam had been cut short so abruptly.

As if he could read her mind, his name popped up

on her cell phone as it began ringing on her desk.

She'd been wrecked by the time he'd left last night and had expected to fall asleep the second she hit the bed. Instead, as soon as she'd closed her eyes, her brain had taken her back to the hotel bed she'd shared with him just hours before for a slow-motion replay of every sexy moment.

Even thinking about it now had her barely stifling a little moan. Adam had been so amazing, so far beyond any sexual experience she'd ever had before.

It would have been so easy to believe that there'd been more than just sex between them, even before he'd pitched in to help her with her sister. She could have told herself that the way he'd kissed her, the way he'd caressed her, had seemed to transcend "just sex." Fortunately, however, she knew all those orgasms could easily mess with a girl's head and heart, even a heart like hers that was so carefully guarded from anyone but the man who would eventually be her one true love. Just as soon as she met that guy, of course.

Still, for all her rationalizations and reminders, her belly still fluttered as she picked up his call. "Adam, hi."

"Kerry." She liked the way he said her name, a little low and rumbly. Liked it more than she should. "How's your sister feeling today?"

Yet again, he surprised her with how sweet he could be. Probably, she figured again, it came down to his mother raising him right. Claudia Sullivan was surely a very interesting woman, and Kerry greatly looked forward to finally meeting her at Rafe and Brooke's wedding, even if it would likely take a heck of a lot of work to hide her affair with Adam from his mother.

"Just as you'd expect," Kerry told him. "She has a splitting headache and pretty much feels like dirt." Colleen hadn't seemed to remember the things she'd said about how cold Kerry was. But all of that was better forgotten, even if there were never going to be any apologies coming. "Hopefully by the time she heads in to her emergency-dispatch job tonight, she'll be back to her usual self." And hopefully she wouldn't hit the repeat button again next Friday night.

"And how are you?"

Kerry barely kept the words *Better now that you've called* from falling out. "A little tired, but I was actually just about to call to thank you again for everything you did to help last night."

"How many times do I have to tell you to stop thanking me?"

She'd particularly liked the way he'd stopped her last night, with a kiss that had melted down her brain one cell at a time.

"Now," he said before she could even try to answer his question, "for the other reason I'm calling."

Ugh, this is it. The part where he said, *Thanks for a few hot hours in the sack, but your situation is way too complicated, so let's call it done now.* She'd agree with him, of course, and wouldn't ever let on that she felt otherwise. In fact, now that she thought about it, wouldn't it be better if she were the one to end things first?

But before she could, he was saying, "Do you have a wedding next Friday night?"

Surprise had her answering before thinking better of it. "No, not next Friday."

"Good." His voice had lowered even more, the one word so warm and sexy she felt as if he'd reached out through the phone to touch her. "How about keeping it free for me and another fun hotel visit?"

Her heart skipped, leapt, *sang!* And her smile was so big that she was glad he couldn't see it. Not when it gave away far too clearly just how thrilled she was to know that he *didn't* want to stop their sexy no-strings fling just yet.

Soon, she knew it would end. But any woman who had experienced the kind of pleasure he'd given her would have wanted more. She wasn't weak for wanting him again, she was simply human. Human enough, evidently, that she continually had to remind herself that it was just sex. Really phenomenal sex, of course, but just sex nonetheless.

She was about to agree, when she remembered. "Colleen and I were talking about staying in, watching a movie, and eating pizza together next Friday. That's the night that's always the hardest for her."

"You're a good sister. Tell me, how does she do on Thursday nights?"

"Pretty good, usually."

"Then how about you and I aim to make it *really* good?"

Her breath caught in her chest. "Yes, let's."

★ ★ ★

The skies were clear and blue on Thursday afternoon as Adam stood with his father, Max, in front of a big old Queen Anne that had seen better days. In fact, at this point, it actually felt like knocking it down would be putting it out of its misery. But something about the place kept pulling at Adam, so he'd decided to get a second opinion from the man he most respected. It didn't hurt, of course, that Max Sullivan knew wood carvings better than pretty much anyone.

After his father had lost his job a couple of decades ago, when he'd come home from another crappy interview, he'd disappear into his workshop in the backyard and would carve wood until he was able to smile again. Adam and his siblings all joined his father in there over the years—even Mia, who ended up with some mad carving skills—and Adam was glad for what he'd learned from his father. But a job like this, with turned porch columns and hand-cut trim around the eaves and windows, needed a specialist's opinion.

In his typical way, his father hadn't said much as Adam took him through and around the outside of the house. They'd both worn hard hats, and although that hadn't helped when his father's foot went through a stair riser, it had made Adam feel a little safer walking through the place.

The neighborhood had been quiet when they'd arrived a couple of hours ago. Now, as kids got out of school, it wasn't quiet anymore. But it was a good kind of loud—kids having fun, moms and dads chatting as they wheeled strollers past each other, dogs barking excitedly as their little owners finally came back home to play with them. It reminded Adam of his childhood neighborhood, where his parents still lived on the other side of town.

And yet, at the very end of the street where the pavement turned to forest, this house had been left neglected. He hadn't dug too far into its history yet, but from what he could tell, it looked like a fairly standard story. The couple who owned it hadn't had any children and the nieces and nephews they'd left it to hadn't lived close enough to want the house, nor had their heirs been able to agree on what to do with it.

Over the years, it had been left forgotten until some-one in the family had finally realized they were sitting on valuable Seattle property in a great family neigh-borhood. The house was being sold as a teardown, but when Mia had emailed the listing to him from her realty office, she'd told him to take a look before he made up his mind.

Even as an adult, Adam relied on his family for so much. Not only their professional support, but support on every other level, too. Friendship. Respect. Love.

All of which brought him back to Kerry, the way so many things had since he'd met her a little over a week ago. She'd taken care of her sister without even a moment's hesitation, just as he would have any of his siblings.

But that was where the similarities ended. Because his siblings had never been as cruel to him as her sister had been to her. If they had, he wouldn't have stood there and taken it. Of course he would have helped them get back home and into bed—but he also would have told them where they could shove their crappy attitude.

His chest hurt every time he thought about the way Kerry had withstood Colleen's harsh words, and his jaw clenched every time he thought about the fact that she hadn't seemed at all surprised by them. He'd wanted to find out what else her sister had said to her so that he could tell her none of those bad things were true, and that she should never believe what someone so messed up had to say about her.

Only good things. *All* good things. That was what he wanted for Kerry—all the good and beautiful things that she gave to everyone she planned weddings for.

Actually, more sizzling-hot sex was right at the top of the list, too. Especially when five days had turned out to be *way* too long to go between their hotel meet-ups. Hell, given how good they'd been together, they could have spent the last five days naked together in the penthouse suite without needing more than a little food and water every now and again.

His father cleared his throat, drawing Adam back to the sidewalk they were standing on and the house in front of them.

"If you take this on, Adam, it's going to be a hell of a lot of work." His father turned away from the house to look at him. "You're looking for a challenge, aren't you?"

Again, Adam found himself thinking of Kerry. He hadn't thought he was looking for a challenge with her, but from the first moment he'd set eyes on her and realized she wasn't like any other woman he'd ever known, he'd immediately wanted to find out more. The more he found out, the more he wanted to know. Not just because the sex had been mind-blowing, either. But because she continued to fascinate him in every way.

"I've got more than enough on my plate right now," he told his father. "Too much to even be considering taking on a house like this, where something tells me I'd have to give it one hundred percent focus."

Adam always worked on multiple projects at once. When he started to get a little bored with one, he could jump to another. He'd never actually focused on only one building, figuring that split-focus was just who he was. But could he change for this house? Or, rather, could this house change him?

Despite its current wrecked state, there was something about it that told him once upon a time it had been someone's special place, and he couldn't quiet the voice inside that wanted to make it special again.

"No one would blame you if you decided to let this one go. She's going to be damned prickly," his father said. "Parts of her will probably fall down around you right when you're trying to put her back together."

It hadn't escaped his notice that, though Adam's working with the house was still in a very hypothetical—and unlikely—stage, his father wasn't speaking in *maybe* and *might*. No, Max Sullivan had already moved on to *will* and *are*.

And Adam couldn't miss that tug in his own gut

that told him this place might be the ultimate diamond in the rough. Not for an investor or even a Realtor like his sister, but for Adam himself.

"Still," his father added in his deep, steady voice, "it's always hard to walk away from something beautiful, isn't it? Especially when you can sense that giving her your full attention will make both of you happy."

"We still talking about the house now, Dad?" Or had Rafe or Brooke said something to his parents about Kerry—and the sparks that had very clearly been jumping between them at dinner on Friday night at the hotel?

"I don't know. Are we?" His father grinned. "Or is there something you brought me here to talk about other than this house?"

Adam had never been one to kiss and tell. And he'd never wanted, or needed, to pull his parents aside to talk about love and broken hearts, either. But, strangely, instead of outright brushing off his father's question, he realized he actually did have another question for him.

"There's someone I want to help with something personal, but she's pretty tough. Pretty stubborn, too. She doesn't think she needs anyone to help her, but—" Constant frustration and worry had ridden Adam since Saturday morning. Because if anything happened to Kerry while she was helping her sister...

"Tough and stubborn, huh?" His father looked more than a little taken aback at hearing that. "Doesn't sound like the kind of woman you usually date."

Adam wasn't surprised that his father was fishing for details—it was just the way of things. Not because his father wanted to control his kids' lives in any way. Max and Claudia Sullivan only wanted them to be happy. And his parents believed, with one hundred percent certainty, that true love was their children's surefire path to happiness.

"We're not dating," Adam clarified. "I'm not even sure she wants me to be her friend, actually. But I need to be there for her anyway." Because if Kerry kept letting her sister wound her the way she had at the bar... Adam had to deliberately unclench his jaw.

"Of all the kids," his father said after a moment, "you were always the one who immediately reached for the hammer and nails. Or the glue and staples. You hated to watch things fall apart, not if you thought you could save them before that happened. Even if that meant trying to hold things together with your bare hands, like that bird's nest that you wouldn't let go of when you were eight because every time you put it down it fell apart. But sometimes, all you can do is trust that people are going to figure out how to rebuild things for themselves, and let them know that you're always there as a true friend if they ever do want to reach out for you."

"I wish I could use glue and staples to fix this situation." Even though Adam knew his father was right, that didn't make it any easier to stand by while Kerry got hurt.

A few minutes later, after his father had gotten into his car and was about to drive away, he rolled down his window. "I'm not sure I was as much help as you'd hoped I'd be, but if you need anything else—"

Adam could easily finish his father's sentence. "You're always there."

CHAPTER TEN

That evening at the hotel, Adam checked his phone half a dozen times for a message from Kerry. But at forty minutes past seven there was nothing—no email, no text, not even in response to his. He hoped she hadn't bailed on him, even as he worried that something might have happened to hold her up. Something worse than just a meeting that had gone on too long. An accident or—

Thank God, she came in from the sidewalk just then, her long dark hair blowing back as she moved quickly toward him. "I'm sorry I'm so late. The traffic was horrible. I could have gotten out and walked here faster if not for my heels. And my stupid phone was dead."

His only response was to grab her hand, taking her overnight bag in the other.

"Adam?"

Despite the question in her voice, she let him pull her past the reception desk and the bar and into the elevator that was conveniently open for them. He jammed in the room key that would take them straight to the penthouse suite.

The doors were closing as she asked, "Is everything okay?"

"No. But it will be soon."

His hands were already in her hair, and he caught the flash of surprised pleasure in her eyes just before he slammed his mouth against hers.

There was no sweet ramp-up tonight, no gentle whispers. Only the rawest, hottest need.

In both of them.

She wrapped her arms around his neck and met his kiss with such fierce passion that he groaned into her mouth. *"More."* He could barely wrap his brain around anything other than that right now. "I need more of you."

"Yes." She tore at the buttons on his shirt, and a few popped off and landed on the marble floor of the elevator. *"God, yes."*

Permission granted, he put his hands on her hips and lifted her so that she could wrap her legs around him. She was wearing something pretty and likely expensive that he knew he shouldn't tear off her. But when her skirt caught on her thighs, there were just way too many layers of fabric between them.

And he wanted her naked.

Now.

The back seam of her skirt tore open with one hard tug of his hands, and she immediately took advantage of the freedom, wrapping her long legs around his hips. The heat of her—and the soft press of her curves against every inch of him—made everything flash to white in his brain for a few seconds. And when one of her hands moved from around his neck to his belt buckle, he nearly lost it completely, right then and there in the elevator.

The soft bell that rang as they made it to the top of the building almost wasn't enough to pierce through. Lust had never held him so tightly in its grip before, but he'd worked on enough of these buildings to know that there had to be a video camera in the elevator. The last thing he was going to do tonight was share Kerry in all her gorgeous, naked beauty with the guys in the security room. Especially when he knew she would be the most beautiful thing they'd ever seen.

She was his, damn it.

Only his.

Fortunately, like last week's hotel, theirs was the only penthouse suite, so all they needed to do was make it out of the elevator and in the door. And then he would tear off her clothes and devour every inch of her.

But he couldn't make himself move away from her.

Not yet. Not when she was rocking her hips into him and he knew how close she was. So ready for him that all it would take was the barest brush of his hand inside silk to take her over the edge.

From the moment he'd left her house on Saturday morning, he'd wanted this. Wanted to have her in his arms. Wanted to lick across her skin. Wanted to hear the sweet sounds she made when she came apart. Wanted to be inside of her more than he needed to take his next breath.

Tearing his mouth from hers on a rough curse, he yanked the key card out of the elevator, then covered the open seam at the back of her hips with his hands so that the security guys couldn't ogle even that. "Hang on tight." He carried her out of the elevator and to their door, nearly kicking it open when the card wouldn't read at first.

Finally, the damn thing opened up, and in a matter of seconds he had it closed again and locked behind them with Kerry pressed against it. The words, "I'll buy you a new outfit," were barely out of his mouth when he tore again, this time from her neck down. The belt at her waist was the only thing holding the fabric up anymore, but even though a part of him was frustrated that she *still* wasn't naked, another part of him needed to stop and drink her in.

The first time he'd set eyes on her, though she'd

been glossy and elegant and perfect, he'd seen her like this in his mind's eye. Her hair tangled from his hands. Her mouth swollen from his kisses. Her skin flushed with desire as she begged him to touch her. To take her.

But with her hands deftly yanking open his belt, he knew now wasn't the time to stand back and stare. *Later*, he promised himself. Later tonight, he'd look his fill as she lay naked and soft in his arms.

Look...and run his hands over every inch of her.

By the time she'd undone his zipper, her bra was off and he was gorging himself on the sweetest tasting skin in the world, first one breast and then the other, over and over again.

Her hands faltered on the band of his boxers as she moaned and arched into his mouth. Without the elevator's cameras on them anymore, he was finally able to hook one of her legs over his hip and slide one hand into her panties.

He loved hearing his name fall from her lips in the exact moment that he found her slick and hot. Again and again, she gasped out his name as she rocked into him. And when she shattered with his fingers in her and his mouth on her breasts, he not only knew without a doubt what heaven felt like—he also knew that even though he'd never done one thing good enough to deserve to be here, he wasn't ever going to willingly walk away from the most beautiful, most responsive, sweetest lover he'd ever known.

His hands shook as he grabbed a condom, tore open the wrapper and shoved it on just seconds before she jumped up into his arms again, wrapped her legs around him, and took him all the way inside.

"Nothing has ever felt this good." He thrust up into her at the same time as she came down onto him, taking him so deep that he nearly saw stars. *"Nothing but you."*

He needed her mouth beneath his again, always needed to be kissing her, even when he would normally have simply been gunning for the finish line. And just as their kisses had taken him even higher last weekend, tonight he felt his chest clench even tighter as she kissed him back. Their tongues tangled, their teeth caught on each other's lips, her hands gripped his shoulders for dear life as he brought her down over him again and again and again.

Until all they could both do was just hold on tight to each other, kissing and kissing and kissing as blazing pleasure shook through both of them.

★ ★ ★

Like the first time they'd made love, they didn't stop kissing for a long time. Only when her arms and legs started to tremble where she was wrapped around him did Adam finally let her go—only to sweep her off her feet to carry her into the enormous bathroom and run a bath.

Sinking into a tub of hot water had never been so good, especially with the most gorgeous man in all creation lying behind her, cradling her body with his.

She leaned her head back against his shoulder and closed her eyes, sighing. How wonderful it was to finally have a chance to relax for a few minutes. Especially since she was still a little off from a second meeting with that difficult couple today, and trying to decide whether or not she should cut them loose.

"Too tired for more?" Adam murmured against her neck.

"I might be persuaded to wake up in a little while," she said as he gently ran his fingertips over her bare shoulder. She wasn't even close to having her fill of him, that was for sure, but as a huge yawn escaped her, the truth was that for a few precious moments, all she wanted was to give in to doing absolutely nothing.

Thankfully, Adam seemed to understand exactly what she was feeling, even though he could easily have turned his gentle caresses into far more sensual ones. Soon, that was exactly what she'd want. But for now, though she knew their meet-ups were supposed to be just about sex, ever since she'd been to his office, she'd been even more curious about what he did. And it would be lovely to think about someone else's job for a while.

"Tell me about some fabulous building you worked on today."

"You want to talk about work right now?"

"I've always been interested in architecture. And not that your ego needs any boost—"

"Anytime you want to stroke my ego—or any part of me—you should feel free."

She couldn't help but laugh. Adam might have the world's best self-esteem, but he was also fun and cute. It was quite a package, especially when he had his strong arms wrapped around her in a big bathtub.

"As I was saying," she continued, "I think what you do—and how well you do it—is really fascinating."

The kiss he pressed to her shoulder told her how much he liked her compliment. "Thanks, but I don't know how fascinated you'd be with the place I was looking at today."

"Why? What's wrong with it?"

"Everything."

"I thought you said there was no project too big?"

"Funny, you sound just like my father." She could tell Adam was thinking about the house again because his hands were moving over her skin absently now, rather than with the devastating sensual purpose he usually had. "You saw the picture of what my office looked like before I got my hands on it. Well, this place is in even worse shape."

"But?" She could hear the interest in his voice even as he tried to convince her that it was a lost cause.

"But at the same time it's in a great neighborhood, right at the end of a curving lane, with an incredible oak tree in the front yard."

His words stirred up a picture in her head of her favorite house as a child, so clearly that she had to tell him, "I know this might sound crazy, but I think I might know the house you're talking about."

"It's on Seaview Lane."

Her exhaustion suddenly fled as she squirmed around in the tub so that she was straddling him. "Oh, Adam, the most amazing old couple lived there. They built the house together, and it was just so beautiful, all of the hand-carved wood, the inlaid floors, the stained glass in the windows upstairs. They made all of that themselves as a team. They were so sweet together, always holding hands, always giving each other little smooches, rocking together on the front porch. They didn't have any kids of their own, so they'd invite the local kids and our parents to have picnics under the huge old oak tree. And you wouldn't believe the way they'd decorate the whole place for Christmas. It was more than just the light shows you see now—everything was handmade with such love and passion."

It wasn't until she came to a stop that she realized Adam was staring up at her with such intensity that her breath caught in her throat.

"Do you have any idea how gorgeous you are when you're naked in the bath with me, talking about houses?" He reached up to tangle his hands in her wet hair and pull her mouth down to his for a kiss that seared through every cell in her body. "Do you have any idea how damned gorgeous you are every single second?"

Every kiss he gave her took her deeper and made her more and more desperate to get even closer to him than they already were, wrapped around each other in the tub. And, oh, how she loved the way his large hands slipped and slid over her wet curves, moving over her breasts and then to her waist and hips and back up again. They'd only just taken each other against the door, but she needed him again.

"Adam."

"I know, sweetheart. I need you again, too."

The endearment shouldn't have sounded right for two people who were just having fun hotel sex once a week, but *everything* was right just then. Especially when she realized he'd thought to put protection on the edge of the tub.

Moments later, he was ready for her and was she ever ready for him. His hands on her waist helped to guide her down over him slowly, so slowly that she gasped at how good it felt to have him inside of her. Every last one of her nerve endings was already on fire when his tongue slicked over her nipples...and then going slow wasn't an option anymore. Because she needed more, needed to sink all the way down onto his rock-hard muscles, needed him to keep raking the edge of his teeth over her breasts one after the other.

Fireworks had already gone off inside her once tonight, so brilliantly that she'd nearly been blinded. But as this second climax started to take her over, from the tips of her toes all the way to the top of her head, she was amazed to realize that when she was in Adam's arms, there were always brighter and brighter colors to see and even bigger and bigger explosions to experience.

And then, his hands were back in her hair and his mouth was on hers again, kissing her through not only her orgasm but also his own, and then beyond...just the way they had each time before.

Finally, with one more swipe of his tongue over her lower lip, he let her up for air. "We weren't done talking about the house yet, were we?"

Every part of her felt warm and sated as she smiled and shook her head. "No, not yet."

"How about we continue our conversation in bed?"

If the water hadn't begun to cool so rapidly, she

might have voted for staying in the tub with him forever. "Throw in a couple of steaks, a bottle of wine, and some fresh-baked bread, and you've got a deal."

A few minutes later they were both wrapped in plush bathrobes, he'd called for room service, and they were sitting on top of the soft duvet drinking from a couple of mini bottles of wine from the minibar.

"I've thought about the couple who lived in that house more than once since we moved away fifteen years ago," Kerry said, "but I always assumed their house must have sold to some lucky family. If it's in as bad a state as you're saying, I'm guessing that's not what happened."

"Unfortunately, it went to some distant family members who forgot all about it."

"You have to save it, Adam."

"Because you loved it as a child?"

"Yes, partly because I loved it as a kid. But also because that house, more than any I've ever known, represents true love. A love so pure," she teased, "that even you couldn't have missed it."

He shook his head, feigning disgust, but she felt as though she was starting to see through him just a little bit.

"You're planning to go by to see it, aren't you?" he asked her.

Clearly, she thought, he was starting to see through

her a little bit, too. "Sitting beneath that oak tree was always one of my favorite places to be."

He frowned. "I'd hate for your good memories to be changed."

"Don't worry." His concern was so sweet that she had to reach up to stroke his bristly cheek. "They won't be, no matter how bad you think it looks."

"How about we go together? That way I can show you why it's not a completely lost cause."

"I knew it," she said, leaning in even closer so that she could kiss him. "You were already thinking of taking the house on."

He kissed her back before saying, "Maybe."

"No," she said softly, "you're not a maybe kind of guy."

The sudden tension in the room had her realizing that she must have overstepped somehow. Did he think she was talking about them? Or that she was wishing for more than the agreement they'd made?

Kerry wished she could read his expression, wished she could figure out how to take things back to the playful, sexy place. Fortunately, the ringing of the suite's doorbell broke the slightly tense moment.

"Hang tight, I'll go get our food."

Adam was effortlessly gorgeous as he took off the robe and pulled on a pair of jeans to head out of the bedroom and into the connected sitting room. She could still hardly believe that she'd slept with him—or that she'd ever considered *not* sleeping with him for one second. Because even with that one weird moment they'd just had, having sex with Adam Sullivan was the best thing she'd ever done in her entire life.

The *very best* thing.

CHAPTER ELEVEN

"Your turn now," Adam said between bites. "Tell me how things are going with the wedding biz."

Kerry laughed as she took a bite of bread, swallowing it down with some red wine before saying, "You can't possibly want to hear about the minute details of planning happily-ever-afters."

"I like listening to you be passionate, whatever the subject. Especially," he added with a wicked grin, "when you're being passionate about something on my lap in the bathtub."

She threw the rest of her roll at him as she laughed again. He liked seeing her loose like this, her hair down and tangled around her shoulders, her mouth curving up again and again into easy smiles.

"Well, if you insist," she said with her own little wicked glint in her eyes, "I'd be happy to tell you *all* about the couple I met with for the second time today."

Surprisingly, he found he really was interested.

Still, he had to tease her by saying, "Let me guess. They were disgustingly, droolingly in love and they called each other Poopsie and Button."

He was expecting her to laugh again, but she frowned instead. "Actually, they weren't like that at all."

She looked so sad about it that he pushed the tray of food aside so that he could pull her onto his lap and put his arms around her. "Then what were they doing in your office?"

She sighed, leaning closer to him. "That's what I keep asking myself." He pressed a kiss to her neck, and she shivered a little at the sensation before saying, "They couldn't agree on anything. Not location. Not size. Not style. Not even the month to have the wedding."

"Maybe," he suggested, "he feels like a fish out of water talking to a wedding planner."

"I'd have known if that were the problem," she said with a shake of her head. "This was different. Like they were both determined to push at each other."

"But they've gotten this far, right? To the point where she's wearing a ring that he gave her and they're talking with the best wedding planner in the business."

That got him a small smile, which he was glad to see. "True."

"Some of the buildings I've loved working with

most are the ones where, when I've pushed, she's pushed back just as hard."

"Your buildings are feminine?"

"Most of them."

She rolled her eyes. "Figures."

He gave her shoulder a little nip. "Can I get back to my point now?"

She lowered her mouth to his shoulder and nipped him back. "Go ahead."

Of course, instead of finishing his thought, he needed to slide his hands into her already tangled hair to kiss her breathless. They were both breathing hard by the time he finally let her up for air.

"I think I get your point now." She looked back down at his mouth, then up to his eyes. "They probably have such great sex that nothing else matters."

He should have jumped to agree with her. But for the first time in his life, he found he couldn't play the part of the player who only had sex on the brain.

"I'm the last guy to say sex isn't important. But there's got to be more than that if things are going to work long term." When she didn't respond, simply stared at him as if seeing him for the first time, he tried to explain. "My siblings, my cousins—I've seen the way they are with their spouses. Sure, they can't keep their hands off each other, but that's just a part of what binds them together."

"What else do they have?"

"Respect. Trust. Dedication."

"Wow, I'm impressed. You didn't even need to think about that list."

"Like I said, I've seen an awful lot of couples in love, with my parents right at the top of the list."

"Maybe you should have been a wedding planner instead of an architect."

He put his mouth to hers, found her tongue with his, and then gently bit it.

She was laughing even before he let it go. "Did you just bite my tongue?" she asked through her laughter.

"Someone had to for saying that."

He loved the feel of her shaking with laughter on his lap. So much that he really didn't want to let her go any time soon.

"Look, all I'm saying is that maybe they like the pushing. Maybe they both like the challenge. Maybe they'd be bored with someone exactly like them, someone who thinks the exact same way. Maybe they like the excitement of knowing their partner will always surprise them."

"I've never looked at things that way." She looked pensive. "I always thought friction was a bad thing in relationships."

How, he wondered, had they progressed to talking so seriously about relationships? What they did on their nights together was supposed to be just sex. Instead, somehow, he was having to work to stop himself from thinking about how a real relationship with Kerry wouldn't be boring, because they didn't think the same way at all. Because she always surprised him.

Sex. He needed to turn the focus of their night back to sex, and quickly, before things went any deeper and they both had regrets in the morning when they came to their senses.

"All this talk of friction"—her skin was soft beneath his lips as he laid her back on the bed, peeled open her robe, lifted her arms up over her head, and began to kiss his way down her gorgeously naked body—"has given me an idea. Want to hear it?"

"Maybe," she said as she licked her lips, "you should just show me instead."

"It would be my pleasure." He grinned as he pulled the satin sash from her robe. "And yours, too, I hope. Have you ever been tied up before?"

"What?" She sat up with a start. "No." She shook her head. "God, no."

She looked so adorable when she was shocked that he had to kiss her. "Good."

"Good?" She looked confused and maybe even a little irritated, too. "Why is that good?"

"Because," he said as he gave her another kiss, "I like knowing I'm going to be your first."

"You're *not* going to be my first. I can't let you tie me up."

"Why not?"

She made a little growly sound at the same question he'd asked her when she'd first told him she couldn't date him, and he was hard-pressed not to grin like a fool. There really was something to this oil-and-water stuff, it seemed.

She was just so much fun, both to wind up, and then to watch come unfurled in his arms.

"Because."

He couldn't hold in his laughter anymore. Fortunately, by now her lips were twitching at the corners, too. "One good reason, Kerry. Give me one good reason why I shouldn't use this strip of satin to tie your wrists to the headboard."

"Here's one *great* reason: I'm not like the other women you've been with."

"I've never for one single second thought that you were." He dropped the sash so that he could put his hands on either side of her face. "And if I ever do anything to you that makes you feel like you are—if I ever do anything that you don't like—promise you'll tell me so that I can do everything in my power to make it up to you."

★ ★ ★

All her adult life, Kerry had stuck to her list of what was and wasn't acceptable. Obviously, letting a man tie her up in bed was on the *not acceptable* list. Then again, since she was already having a sexy night in a hotel with a totally inappropriate man...

"I've liked everything you've done to me." But that wasn't good enough, wasn't anywhere near close to the full truth, so she made herself tell him, "I've *loved* it."

The way he kissed her told her how much he liked hearing it. And then she surprised them both by shrugging off the robe, lying back against the pillows, and lifting her arms over her head.

"Tie me up." Heat flared in his eyes, but when he didn't move to do it right away, she knew he was concerned that she might not really mean it. So she added, "Show me how much I'm going to love this, too."

Finally, he smiled, and reached for her wrists with the sash. "You'll never look at a headboard the same way again, that's for sure."

Despite her sudden nerves at trying another new thing with Adam, she had to smile back. His grins were infectious.

Heck, everything about him drew her in. His smart mouth. His wicked smiles. His passionate kisses. His brilliant hands, always knowing just how—and where—to touch her.

When he'd finished tying her up, he shifted back to look at her, his heated gaze slowly roving head to toe and then back up again. "You've got to be the most beautiful woman I've ever set eyes on."

She could feel her skin flush, both at the way he was taking in her nakedness and at his compliment. "Thank you."

"Jesus, hearing you say that prim little *thank you* while I've got you tied to the bed... You just might be the end of me, Kerry." His eyes looked a little wild and a muscle in his jaw was jumping as he directed her. "Tug on the sash."

She tried to move her arms, but though she wasn't in any pain, they didn't have much give. She was well and truly at his mercy now. But though she supposed she should have been nervous about giving herself over to him this way, the only thing pumping through her veins right then was a desperate anticipation.

"Looks like you're all mine to play with now, aren't you?"

Did he know how his question—just on the edge of wicked—made her heart feel as though it were going to pump out of her chest? Or how badly she wanted him to kiss her?

And then, just like magic, his mouth was on hers. Warm and heady, reassuring and wild, all at the same time. She got so lost in his kiss that she almost forgot her hands were tied up until she tried to reach for him. That was when he finally drew away from her mouth.

"Every inch of you," he promised. "I'm not going to miss a spot."

And, oh my, did he ever make good on his promise as he took advantage of having her at his mercy. He ran his fingers and lips and tongue over her curves, her hollows, lingering at the most sensitive spots. Higher and higher he took her with every caress, with every sensual stroke of his fingers over her until she was simultaneously shattering and begging for more of him.

Thankfully, he didn't keep teasing. Maybe because he could see that she was at the breaking point. Or maybe because that was right where he was himself. Barely able to survive staying apart, when all either of them wanted anymore—all either of them *needed* anymore—was to be connected in the most elemental way possible.

Her name was on his lips, and his was on hers, as he cupped her face in his hands. The moment hung between them like a gift you couldn't wait to open, but wanted to savor for just one more moment before you tore off the wrapping paper. And then, a heartbeat after he'd sheathed himself, his mouth was on hers again as he thrust into her.

Unable to get her arms around him to hold him close, she wrapped her legs around his hips and rode him, taking everything he was giving her and giving it back to him tenfold. Her climax crashed over her, and Adam's did, too, as her release sent him over the edge.

Kerry had never felt so blissfully wild. So wonderfully savage.

Or so perfectly free.

★ ★ ★

When Kerry could finally get her breath back, she said, "Do you think the designer knew people were going to use this headboard like that?"

Adam's laughter warmed her up all over again. "I sure hope so."

She shouldn't be shocked, not anymore. Not when he'd just blown her mind in a thousand new ways. But she needed to know. "Do you ever design things for…"

"For kinky clients?"

She nodded.

"Well…" He had her right there on the edge, waiting for his answer. "I never design and tell."

"I need you to untie me so that I can smack you."

"Sounds to me like that's exactly why I should keep you tied up a little longer." He ran the tip of one finger down over her curves. "Oh, look, here's another reason."

She should be sated, should be done by now after having made love with him three times already tonight. But, of course, her body instinctively arched into his touch.

"God, you tempt me." He kissed her. "Do you have any important meetings tomorrow?"

She couldn't hold back her groan as reality came crashing back in, even with her hands still tied to the headboard. "Seven a.m. A breakfast meeting."

"And I thought my nine o'clock was early." He didn't look any happier about it than she felt as he untied the sash and gently began to massage her arms, from her wrists up to her shoulders. "Next time, we both need to clear the decks the morning after."

Next time. It shouldn't thrill her so much to know they'd be doing this again. But, boy oh boy, did it ever.

He looked over at her overnight bag. "You brought clothes for tomorrow?"

Not wanting it to seem as though she expected them to spend the night together, she explained, "I like to be prepared, just in case the outfit I wore tonight got ruined before I left." Which it definitely had, given that it was currently lying in shreds by the door.

"Let's stay here tonight, then," he suggested. "Just crawl under the covers right now to get as much sleep as we can."

The rational part of Kerry—a part that seemed to

shrink further and further every second she was with Adam—told her she shouldn't stay, because actually sleeping together had to be a bad idea. But between the busy week she'd already had and all the magnificent things he'd done to her tonight, she could barely keep her eyes open.

Besides, what could one night in the same bed hurt?

"Okay." Her voice sounded a little slurred even to her own ears. "I should go brush my teeth." Because of course she'd packed her toothbrush, too. *Be prepared for everything, both in life and during a wedding.* She'd learned that from her mother.

But Adam was already pulling the covers over both of them and curling his big, strong body around hers. "You can do that tomorrow morning." He pressed a kiss to the top of her head. "I had a great night with you, Kerry."

Her usual walls were down far enough as she hurtled toward sleep that she didn't question the urge to tell him, "I had the *best* night with you, Adam. The very best."

And when he responded by pulling her even tighter against him, feeling more content and safer than she ever had, she fell into a dreamless sleep.

CHAPTER TWELVE

The following day, Kerry ran from one meeting to the next, putting out potential fires left and right. By that night, she was nearly convinced that the previous one at the hotel with Adam must have been a dream. She'd been too busy all day to get in touch, and she knew from what he'd told her at the hotel that he'd had just as packed a schedule. That was one of the nice things about not actually dating each other, she told herself. Neither of them had to feel guilty if they couldn't fit each other in apart from a handful of hours having hot sex every now and then.

By the time she left the office and made it home, she couldn't wait to change out of her suit and heels, throw on her most comfortable jeans and a sweatshirt, and collapse on the couch. She'd left her sister several messages—voice mails, emails, and texts—about getting together as they'd planned the previous weekend, but it wasn't until nine o'clock that Colleen finally answered one of them.

"Hey, Kerr, I won't be able to make it over to-night."

Kerry's stomach immediately sank. She'd known this would happen, hadn't she? Just like every time her sister told her they were going to have a girls' Friday night in—and ended up bailing to go party instead. The last thing Kerry wanted to do was put real clothes and makeup back on, but if she could keep her sister out of trouble, she'd do it.

"Why don't I meet you wherever you are? We could still have our girls' night out."

"There's not exactly room for one more right now." She could hear Colleen laughing with whatever loser she was with as he said he'd be happy to have her sister join them.

"Call me later, okay?" Kerry pleaded. "I can come join you any time if you change your mind."

"Drinks are here, got to go."

Kerry was about to press the call-back button on her phone, but stopped herself. If she pestered Colleen too much, then she might not call later if she needed help getting home. It was such a fine line trying to support and help her sister while not upsetting her so much that she pulled away entirely.

Kerry wasn't at all sure that she was walking the right side of that line. If only there was someone she could talk to about this.

As if on cue, her phone buzzed again. But it wasn't Colleen. It was a text from Adam.

HOW'S THE MOVIE AND PIZZA WITH YOUR SISTER?

Kerry's heart melted. He was so sweet to even remember her plans for tonight, let alone check in to make sure it was all going according to plan.

As she typed in her response, however, she knew he wasn't going to like her answer. She made herself send it anyway. The best thing about Adam—apart from all the super, crazy-hot sex they were having—was that they were always honest with each other.

COLLEEN CHANGED HER MIND ABOUT TONIGHT

Her phone rang a second later.

"Where is she?" Adam asked.

Kerry didn't even try to hold in her worried sigh. "I don't know. I offered to go with her, but she didn't think that was a very good idea because she was already with someone. He, however, seemed to think it was a super idea to spend the night with two sisters."

Though Adam wasn't there, she could see his expression, knew his jaw would be clenching. The curse he uttered confirmed it.

"Did you get to the movie or pizza before she

bailed on you?"

"No."

"A friend of mine makes the best pie in Seattle. I'll have him send one over to your place. See you in fifteen."

* * *

Exactly fifteen minutes later, Kerry went to answer the knock at the door.

A quarter of an hour had been exactly long enough to tie herself up in knots about how things were supposed to play out between the two of them tonight. If they'd been meeting to have sex, kissing him hello would make sense. But since he was clearly just coming over to keep her company because he was worried about her—and also so that he'd be there to accompany her into the bad part of town just in case her sister called later—what exactly did that mean tonight was all about?

Kerry hadn't wanted to examine anything beyond their incredible sexual escapades on Thursday, but the truth was that they'd done nearly as much talking as having hot sex. And she'd liked doing both. A lot.

Adam was fun and smart. Surprisingly insightful, too, particularly when it came to relationships. For someone who had no interest in a lasting relationship of his own, he wasn't at all blind to the way things played out for the people he loved. Whereas while Kerry's job revolved around love, she far too often felt as though she didn't have the first clue about what truly made a relationship work.

Her thoughts in a hopeless tangle, she opened the door and found Adam grinning at her, so perfectly, shockingly gorgeous that everything fell out of her head. Everything except being glad he was there.

"Hi."

He responded in exactly the way she now realized she'd been secretly wishing for—with a kiss that left her breathless. And the truth was that if the pizza delivery guy hadn't showed up just then, she might have stood in her open front door and kissed Adam Sullivan all night long.

A short while later, they were sitting on her couch devouring pizza that truly was the best she'd ever had, while debating what movie to watch.

"No sappy chick flicks," he said.

"No movies with pointless violence," she retorted.

"Nothing foreign with subtitles." He actually shuddered as he said it.

"Nothing where people get naked for absolutely no reason," she said with a shake of her head.

He looked at her in surprise. "There needs to be a reason for people to get naked?"

Kerry threw a piece of pepperoni at him, but he

somehow managed to catch it in his mouth.

"Remind me never to feed you anything heavy," he said with a smile that made her heart dance around in her chest. "You love to toss your food at me every time we eat together, don't you?"

"Only when you irritate me."

"Like I said—every time we eat together."

Kerry wanted to tell him how nice it was that he'd come over to help keep her from worrying incessantly about her sister all night long. But something told her he already knew it, and saying it aloud would probably only make things awkward between them. They were having too much fun to let any awkwardness in.

"Nothing sappy, no pointless violence, no subtitles or naked people." He ticked through their list. "So if *Sorority House Massacre* in French is out, then it looks like all we're left with is *Star Wars*. The ultimate good-versus-evil story. Plus it has the best line ever put into a movie."

"Use the Force, Luke," she said before he could. Yet again, he'd surprised her—this time by coming up with the perfect movie. "I haven't seen *Star Wars* in years."

"Years?" He looked pained. He grabbed her remote. "How do you work this thing?"

"My house, my remote." She quickly found the movie on her smart TV and soon they were caught up in the epic story.

Her couch wasn't huge, but even if it had been, she suspected she would still have ended up snuggled in Adam's arms. Partly because he wasn't at all shy about pulling her into them. But also because his arms were right where she wanted to be on yet another Friday night where she was waiting for her sister to call for pickup.

Throughout the movie, he kept lightly stroking her hand, or her leg, or her shoulder. She didn't get the sense that he was deliberately trying to seduce her, but with every minute that passed, each light caress managed to drive her higher. And then higher still. Until she was practically holding her breath waiting for the next one to come, wondering where he'd brush up against her this time.

She should tell him to stop. After all, this was just a friends' night at home, rather than a night for one of their wild hotel sexcapades. But she couldn't get the words past her throat. Didn't want him to stop touching her. Not when she'd never known it was possible for her body to feel this alive with all her clothes on in her living room, while Princess Leia was telling Luke Skywalker it wasn't over yet.

By the time the movie ended, Kerry was so wound up that she simply couldn't think straight. Couldn't remember why she shouldn't flip around on the couch and devour his mouth in the way she'd been dreaming of for the past two hours.

Seconds later she was straddling him, her hands tangled in his dark hair, giving silent thanks that his gorgeous mouth was almost beneath hers. "I know we're not in a hotel, but—"

His lips stole away the rest of what she'd been about to say at the exact moment that her phone rang.

She tore her mouth away from his with a curse. Too late, she remembered exactly why she should have done more—heck, done anything at all—to keep a friendly distance from Adam tonight.

Not only because what she'd just done had been about to blur the very clear lines they'd set up for their arrangement, but also because the whole reason he was over in the first place was to wait with her for her sister's call.

"Colleen, where are you?"

"The Salty Dawg, but you don't need to get me. I've got a ride."

Kerry cursed again as the line went dead. "It sounds like she's planning to leave with someone."

"One of my cousins is a race-car driver," Adam told her. "He's taught me a few things over the years."

She grabbed her bag and hurried out to his car, which he gunned up and out of her neighborhood in true race-car fashion. "What if we're too late?"

"Then I'll have Rafe trace her cell phone ASAP."

"He can do that?"

"You know he's a P.I. He can do pretty much anything, even if not all of it is completely legal." Despite the speed at which Adam was driving, he reached out for her hand and squeezed it. "Either way, we're going to find your sister tonight and bring her home safe and sound."

The first time they'd done this, Kerry hadn't wanted to let herself believe having this kind of support was more than a one-time anomaly. But here he was again, sitting beside her, helping in every way he could, promising her that she didn't need to worry because he was just going to keep helping.

Kerry had tried not to be angry with her sister these past months. She'd tried to understand how hard it had been for Colleen to get over the hurt of her relationship crumbling.

But now Kerry couldn't stop herself from wishing she could have one Friday night where she wasn't on babysitting duty for her fully grown sister. Just one Friday night where she didn't have to keep pretending that she had any control whatsoever over the situation.

The flash of anger was short-lived, though, when she thought about how much worse things could be if her sister *didn't* call some night for pickup, and instead went home with one of the losers.

The thought of anything happening to Colleen

made Kerry's blood run cold. Cold enough to put out the fire Adam had so deftly stoked while they'd watched *Star Wars*. And by the time they made it to the bar, it felt like having pizza on the couch together had happened in a different lifetime.

She shot out of Adam's car, and he was only a couple of steps behind her when she nearly plowed into Colleen and her guy-of-the-night weaving their way out of the bar.

"Thank God," Kerry breathed. She believed Rafe could have traced Colleen's whereabouts, but it would have taken time. Time in which any number of horrible things could have happened to her sister.

Colleen's eyes were blurred with drink, but they still went wide when she saw Adam step up beside Kerry.

"Wait, I remember you. The hot guy from last weekend who wouldn't let me stay and have more fun." Colleen turned to Kerry. "You're fucking him, aren't you?" She made a move to high-five her, but stumbled and Kerry had to catch her instead. "Not such a little goody-two-shoes, are you, out having sexytimes with Mr. Hunk. What other dirty secrets are you hiding from me?"

"Enough." Adam's tone was hard. Hard enough to have her sister's mouth turn down into a pout. "We're leaving. Now."

"Why do you always have to come to ruin my fun?"

But Kerry could see that Adam wasn't feeling particularly charitable tonight. Was it because he was upset that their *sexytimes* had been interrupted? Or was it something else? Something that made Kerry's chest ache because she could only think of one reason he'd stick up for her.

Because he cared.

★ ★ ★

Just like the previous week, despite the fight she put up getting into Adam's car, Colleen was fast asleep by the time they got back to Kerry's house. And after she finished cleaning her sister up and putting her to bed, this time Kerry wasn't surprised to find Adam waiting in her kitchen.

"You can't keep doing this," he said the second she walked into the room.

She'd been hoping for comfort. But she'd known that he was going to confront her, hadn't she? If only because she'd finally come to the point herself where even *she* had to admit that she couldn't keep on like this forever.

Still, since she didn't have any other answers yet,

she couldn't just let Colleen down. "How can I just turn my back on my sister? What if I don't go pick her up next Friday night and she gets hurt?"

"You can't stop your sister from getting hurt if that's what she wants."

"Why can't I?"

Even though she knew she shouldn't be taking it out on him, Kerry didn't know what else to do with all of the anger that kept bubbling up inside her tonight. She felt as if it had been bottled up forever. Not just in the past three months, but long before that.

And not just anger bottled up, either. Her sensuality. Her passion.

Herself.

"You know why, Kerry."

"But if I'm not there for her, she'll think she's all alone."

Kerry knew she was being stubborn, knew he was making a good point, but she honestly couldn't see any other path right now.

"I can't stand listening to her talk to you—*about you*—the way she does." He took her hand and drew her closer. "You're perfect just the way you are, Kerry. Beyond perfect." He tipped her chin up with his free hand so that she had to look him in the eyes. "Tell me you know that."

When she opened her mouth, all that came out was a choked sob. He wrapped his arms around her and pulled her close, for the second time that night.

Somewhere in the back of her mind, she knew any other man would have kept arguing with her to try to force her to see things his way. But Adam was simply letting her rest her head on his shoulder for a little while and stroking her back while she let all of the stress, all of the strain of the evening drain slowly out of her.

Tired. She was so tired. But even though asking Adam to stay the night would be the easiest thing—and the most comforting by miles—she had just enough sense left to know that the lines between them had already been pushed *way* too far.

The last thing she wanted was for things to get blurry between them. Not when it was so lovely to have a man like him in her life. One with whom she could laugh and have hot sex, and not have to worry for one single second about anything more. About *perfect*. Or *forever*.

Or, most of all, about setting herself up to be hurt or let down by him like all the other women in her family had with the men they'd thought were their forevers.

"Thanks for tonight," she said when she could finally force herself to move out of his arms. Arms that had given her more comfort—and pleasure—than she'd ever known before. "I know it's probably pretty different from how you normally spend your Friday nights."

"I wouldn't have wanted to be anywhere else."

She knew he never lied to her, but still, it was difficult to take his words at face value. "*Star Wars* is a pretty great movie," she joked.

But he didn't laugh. Just said, "Are we still on to see the house in your old neighborhood tomorrow?"

The cautious voice inside was telling her she should postpone their visit to the house. That the two of them needed space. That *she* needed some space, at the very least, to get her head back on straight about what she and Adam were. And more important, were *not*.

But just as she hadn't been able to resist letting him hold her on the couch while they'd watched the movie, she couldn't resist the thought of seeing him again tomorrow. Especially when it would be the perfect thing to look forward to while dealing with her sister's Saturday morning hangover.

"I'll text you after my midday wedding."

She wasn't surprised when he kissed her good-bye. At least, not by the kiss itself. But she was surprised by how gentle his kiss was.

And by how much she missed him after she shut the door behind him and he drove away.

CHAPTER THIRTEEN

Three nights in a row.

Adam couldn't think of the last time he'd seen a woman he wasn't related to that many consecutive nights. Sure, he'd dated plenty of women. And had enjoyed being with most of them in one way or another. But there'd never been anyone serious for him, no one he'd wanted to see more than once a week. It had always been easy to come up with excuses as to why he couldn't be available more often, why they both should keep their personal space wide and open. And any woman who had pushed for more than that had been cut loose.

Only, Kerry wasn't the one pushing for more. It was all him, over and over again.

He was the one who had texted her last night to check on how things were going with her sister. And he was the one who had made sure they were still going to meet here at the crumbling house in her old neighborhood.

The craziest thing of all? It wasn't suffocating. It wasn't boring. And he wasn't regretting it. Probably, he figured, because none of their meet-ups had been dates. It was amazing how that took all the pressure off and made it so that he could actually be friends with a woman while having great sex, too.

And Lord knew he *really* wasn't regretting getting a nice eyeful of Kerry stepping out of a taxi and walking toward him in another one of those super-sexy wrap dresses. Especially when the sun behind her was making it just see-through enough that he could drink in her gorgeous curves without even taking off her clothes.

His mouth watered and his hands fairly itched to grab her and pin her to the trunk of the oak tree she loved so much so that he could ravage her mouth, just so that he could finally feel at least the slightest bit sated. Because *sated* sure as hell hadn't happened yet. On the contrary, the more he had of her, the more he wanted.

"Sorry I'm late again."

He didn't pin her against the tree, but he did tangle up her perfect hairstyle with his hands when he threaded his fingers into the silky strands and kissed her. "I forgive you," he said when he finally let her up for air. "After all, everyone has to have a fault."

"It's not a fault," she protested. "It's the traffic in

this town. They should really do something about it, like put in better public transportation or make the freeways wider." But when he simply raised an eyebrow in response, she sighed. "Okay, maybe it's one of my faults."

"Wait, you have more than one?"

He loved the sound of her laughter. "You're the last person I should be saying this to, but yes, I *definitely* have more than one. Count yourself lucky if the only one you ever have to deal with is my tiny little problem getting to anything outside of work obligations on time. If you saw more of me, I'm sure you'd be overwhelmed by the need to point out all the things I should be working on."

Normally he would have counted himself lucky that he wouldn't have to learn too much about the woman he was sleeping with. He'd never been interested in drama. Never looked for someone to fix. And he still wasn't looking for drama or to change anyone.

But though he'd helped Kerry out a couple of times with her sister and knew that her family situation wasn't going to get any simpler anytime soon, he still wasn't itching to ditch. If anything, he'd been racking his brain trying to figure out how to help her. Hell, he'd nearly called his mother to ask for advice.

Fortunately, he'd had a good enough hold on his rational brain to put down the phone before he got

Claudia Sullivan all in a tizzy over her hold-out-on-love son calling with a question about how to help a woman with a family problem. His mom was an insightful woman, but Adam knew she was far too focused on getting her last kid happily married to be able to see that Kerry was just a friend. One who rocked his world in the sack, but who was still not ever going to be more than just a friend.

A good enough friend, already, that he knew he needed to force himself to stop mentally undressing her and turn his focus back to the house that she had loved so much once upon a time.

She was still holding his hand as she stared at the house, and he used their connection to take her closer to the oak tree that he hoped could help anchor her in happy memories rather than sadness over what had happened to the property.

Especially because he couldn't read her expression.

"Oh, Adam." He couldn't read her tone, either, and he was just about to jump in to say something soothing when she continued, "I still love it just as much as I always did."

She'd surprised him a dozen times before now, but never as much as she did just then, when she managed to see beauty amidst the dirt and rubble, neglect and overgrowth.

He was speechless as she drew him closer to the

house and ran her hand over the curved porch columns, just as his father had earlier that week. "I want to live here. In this house. On this property." Her eyes were bright with excitement as she turned to him. "Will you help me restore it to its former glory?"

He could have said a half-dozen things right then. Could have warned her about all the problems she was bound to encounter. Could have rattled off dollar figures that would have made her head spin. Could have explained how difficult the county was likely to be about the property if they did, in fact, deem it to be historic.

He'd come here today planning to tell her not to get her hopes up too high, because renovating this place was going to be a positively enormous project that would test even the steadiest nerves.

But now that she was all rose-colored glasses and memories of love, he didn't want to do one damned thing to dim her light, her pleasure, or her excitement.

"Yes, I'll help you."

She threw her arms around his neck, and he twirled her around, not caring if they looked like they were straight out of a sappy rom-com.

"Every step of the way, Kerry, I'll be here."

This time she was the one kissing him, dragging him under, fast and hot, with her passion.

Her joy.

"I want you." He'd never tasted anything so sweet. Never wanted anyone as much as he wanted her. "Now."

She echoed the *now* against his lips, and the only way he could stop himself from taking her right there and then on the front porch was to forcefully remind himself that they were standing outside in a neighborhood filled with families and kids who could walk past at any second. The inside of the house was out, too, because it would start falling down around them if they got too crazy.

"My house." He could barely fit the words in between kisses. "Come to my house. It's close. Closer than a hotel."

It should have been lust that drove him to make the suggestion, but the truth was that it was more than that. He wanted to test her will to resist him, test her belief that walking away from him one day would be so easy. Maybe it wasn't fair, maybe it wasn't even entirely rational, but the way he needed her right now—he needed to know that she needed him that badly, too. Badly enough to throw away their rules for one night and come to his house instead of a hotel.

But she didn't even blink, didn't pause before asking, "How fast can you get us there?"

Every time she'd asked him that before, it was to go save her sister. Tonight, though, her need for speed was for them and them alone.

"Depends on whether you're distracting me or not."

Lightning fast, she was taking his hand and pulling him down the street to his car. He was careful driving out of the neighborhood—and she made sure to keep her hands to herself—but once they hit the freeway, he gunned it. And so did she, already starting to unbutton his shirt.

"Three minutes. We just need three more minutes."

He knew she had to be able to feel his heart pounding like crazy beneath her fingertips. And his heart wasn't the only thing pounding, so when she reached for his belt, he put his hand over hers and held it still.

"If we crash, I don't get to have you. Give me two minutes to get home."

Two of the longest minutes of his life, especially when she leaned over and lightly bit his earlobe.

"Sixty seconds." Which was one minute that he might not live through, not if she kept doing that thing with her tongue.

Finally, they were inside his garage. And then all bets—and any rules that had ever been there between them—were off.

Her dress was up and over her head before she could blink. Her bra and panties torn off and tossed to the floor of his car.

"Come here."

He shoved his seat back and together they got her onto his lap as fast as possible. Her breasts were perfection in his hands, and then his mouth, and her hips were already grinding onto the jeans he hadn't let her take off him while he was driving. She was already making those gorgeous sounds that told him how close she was to the edge, and he'd never needed anything so much in his life as he needed to hear her come just then.

"I need to watch you come for me." He tugged at her hair with one hand so that he could look into her eyes. With the other, he gripped her hip to bring her even closer. "I need to feel it." He lowered his mouth to her neck to nip at her skin and whispered into her ear, "I need to taste it, too."

Her mouth parted on a gasp, and when he looked back at her, her eyes were fluttering half-closed as the tremors shook her. They rode her climax together, and though he loved being able to see her face as she came, he needed her mouth too badly not to take it with his.

He'd meant what he said about needing to taste her. Not just her lips, but all of her. And as tempting as it was to take her there in his car, he needed to lay her out on a bed so that he could have better access to all of her incredibly tempting curves and hollows and beautifully sensitive spots.

He lifted her out of his car and got them to his bedroom as quickly as he could. It was the first time he'd ever wished for a smaller house. Hell, a one-room studio would have been perfect so that he could have walked in the door and just tossed her down onto the bed. It didn't help that she kept distracting him with kisses and roving hands while he tried to get through the living room and up the stairs.

Finally, he kicked open his bedroom door and dropped her onto his bed. Her breath whooshed out of her as she landed, but she was laughing as he leapt over her and pinned her hands above her head, her lovely thighs open on either side of his knees.

Beyond rational thought or action now, he bit at her lower lip, hard enough that she gasped again, but then immediately did the same to him. No woman had ever made him feel this wild. No other woman had ever made him completely lose control. And no other woman could have goaded him into even more wildness the way she did.

He rained kiss-bites all over her skin, her breasts, her rib cage, her waist, the curve of her hips…and then he was momentarily lost. Lost in the taste of her silky sweet flesh as he ate up her arousal, sending her straight toward a second climax as quickly as he had the first one.

He loved hearing his name on her lips, how desperate she sounded as she shattered again. Only now, he didn't have to wait to get her from the car to his bedroom. This time he was already there, having yanked off his own pants while he was eating up every inch of her perfect skin. A heartbeat later he had a condom on, and before she could begin to come down from her climax, he was inside of her, and she was wrapping her arms and legs around him and giving him even more of herself.

More of her sweetness. More of her passion. More of everything that he couldn't get enough of.

More.

More.

More.

Until they both went hurtling over the brilliant edge of pleasure, her mouth and body beneath his the most perfect fit in the world.

CHAPTER FOURTEEN

When Kerry woke the next morning, she couldn't believe last night could possibly have been real.

Because how could any two people need each other that badly? So much that they'd gone from his bed to his shower. And then the rug in front of the fireplace in his bedroom. And then again to his bed.

They hadn't stopped for food. Hadn't needed to drink anything, either, not when they'd been utterly drunk on each other. Again and again, he'd sent her reeling with pleasure—and she'd done the same with him. Only pure exhaustion had been able to douse their fire.

Now, Adam Sullivan lay sound asleep beside her in his huge bed, which had already been unmade when he'd first devoured her on it and was now little more than a tangle of sheets and limbs. The first rays of the sun were just beginning to illuminate the room, but mostly him, as if it were specifically seeking him out so that it could shine over him.

For the first time since she'd met him, Kerry was able to stare. To admire the strong lines of his cheekbones and jaw, the mouth that she found herself daydreaming about during meetings, his long dark lashes. She'd never imagined waking up in bed with a man like him, who could have walked straight out of a magazine or off the movie screen. More than that, she'd never dreamed that a man like him would want her the way he wanted her.

The passion between them was…

Honestly, she didn't know how to begin processing it. And it was tempting, so very tempting, to not overthink what was happening between them. Just to keep letting it happen. Over and over and over and over again until every cell in her body was celebrating being alive and in Adam's arms.

But she knew better.

She'd known all along that she needed to keep her guard up around him. Stupidly, she'd thought it would be easy. Easier, anyway, to keep one foot on the brake at all times and her eyes firmly on pleasure and nothing else.

Yes, last night had been pure pleasure, start to finish. There was no question at all about that. But it had been more than just pleasure. And she thought she knew why: Their other nights together had been planned meet-ups at hotels, but last night had not only been totally spontaneous, it had also been born of more than lust, more than desire.

Joy—pure, unfettered joy—had propelled her into Adam's arms. All because he'd rediscovered her dream house and had promised to bring it back to its former glory with her.

It was that joy that scared her. Because while the sex was great, it was the happiness she felt with Adam that she knew she'd never be able to replace when their arrangement came to its inevitable end.

She was a fun change for him right now, utterly unlike the other women he'd been with—just as he was a total change for her. That was why it was so exciting. Such a rush that they'd both thrown caution to the wind for a night and ended up in his big, warm bedroom instead of staying in neutral hotel territory.

Adam's imprint wasn't only on the walls and ceilings and floors of the home he'd restored, it was also on every piece of furniture and book and framed painting. She couldn't take a breath without breathing him in, too.

Where pleasure had swamped her all night long, morning now brought panic rushing in to replace it. She needed to get out of his bed, and fast—before she got to the point where she never wanted to get out of it at all.

Kerry had shifted less than an inch away from Adam when his arm came around her waist, and he tugged her so that she was lying across his chest. Chest to chest, she could feel his heart beating against hers. But it wasn't his nakedness, or hers, that made hers beat faster.

It was the smile on his lips, and in his eyes, that stole her breath. And sent an even deeper terror racing through her. Because she liked his smile—*loved* his smile—so much that she realized she wanted it to be the first thing she saw when she woke up every morning for the rest of her life.

"Morning."

"Good morning."

She put everything she had into hiding her panic from him, but a frown had already begun to steal away his smile. "What's wrong?"

"Nothing." She made herself smile, hoping it reached her eyes the way his had. "I just need to get going to make it to my office on time."

He continued to frown, but instead of pushing her, he simply said, "I'll make you breakfast first."

The words *I'll make you breakfast* shouldn't have her heart twisting up in her chest. She was being ridiculous. Melodramatic. Clearly, the endless hours of mind-blowing sex actually *had* blown out a whole host of her brain cells, and now she was functioning on less than a full set.

She'd let the house—and Adam's amazing kisses—sweep her away yesterday. But in the clear light of a new day, his easy offer to make her breakfast told her without a shadow of a doubt that she hadn't been nearly careful enough about not blurring the lines.

Not to mention the fact that it had felt *way* too much like they were making love last night when it should have been nothing more than naughty, wicked sex.

The last thing she wanted to do was move off his deliciously hard—and aroused—body. But she couldn't stay here and keep having sex with him. Not when every kiss, every touch, would only drag her deeper into the danger zone.

She could feel him fighting with himself about letting go of her, but finally her feet were on the floor again, and she was holding a blanket in front of her, even though there was nothing he hadn't seen by now.

Kerry meant to say, *Thanks for offering to make breakfast, but I really do need to go,* only somehow the words that actually came out were, "We can't do this again."

"What the hell?" He was out of bed and standing in front of her so fast she nearly stumbled, and he had to reach out to steady her. "You're calling our arrangement quits?"

"No." She couldn't do that. Wasn't strong enough to actually end what had become the most magical, wonderful thing that had ever happened to her. "Just this. Being here. At your house. Or at mine."

He ran a hand over his face, through his hair. "I didn't get enough sleep to understand what you're talking about."

"Hotels. We agreed to meet in hotels. Neutral ground without all of our things, without personal stuff around."

"Fine." He bit the word out, hard and fast. "We'll make sure we stay in hotels from now on."

"Good."

"Great," he said, even though he didn't look like he thought it was great at all.

God, having this conversation shouldn't make her chest clench. And she shouldn't dread getting out the rest of it. But they couldn't move forward until they got one other big thing cleared up.

"Yesterday, at the house, I didn't exactly give you a chance to say no to helping me with it."

"There was no gun to my head. I want to restore it. You want to live in it. So what's the problem?"

She'd seen Adam flirt. She'd seen him tease. She'd seen him care. She'd even seen him angry at her sister. But she'd never seen him—or felt him—be angry at *her* before. And because it stung, she stung back.

"The *problem* is that you and I will have to work together on the house."

"You've changed your mind about working with me?"

"No. You're the best. Of course I want to work with you." She was as frustrated as he was, couldn't he see that? She sighed, knowing she was doing this, saying things all wrong. "But if working on the house together ends up extending past all of this"—she gestured to the bed where they'd had such wild, fabulous sex—"it might get messy."

"You like having sex with me, right?"

She nodded. "Of course I do. You *know* I do."

"Good, because I like having sex with you. And I can't see that changing anytime soon."

"But what if you—" She stopped herself, hoping he hadn't noticed her slip. "But what if some reason pops up where we both decide we're done having sex, and then we have to keep seeing each other because of the house?"

"You're worrying about nothing, Kerry. We're both adults. It's not going to get messy."

"So you're saying that you think we can keep things totally compartmentalized, and that the sex we're currently meeting up for in hotels will in no way impact the work we'll do together on the house?"

His dark eyes held hers for a long moment before he finally said, through what sounded like gritted teeth, "Sure."

"Great," she forced herself to say past the lump in her throat. "I'm glad we've talked through any potential issues." Through sheer force of will, she finally managed to move away. "I should get my dress from the car so that I can head out."

"I'll get it." His words were more clipped than usual. "Go take a shower. Your clothes will be here when you're done."

He had on a pair of jeans and was walking out the door before she could figure out how to say she'd had a great time with him the night before and was sorry that she'd made such a mess of the morning. Which, she figured as she headed into the bathroom, was probably all for the best, given that she couldn't get anything right this morning anyway.

* * *

Adam needed to get a grip.

But, damn it, the conversation he and Kerry had just had in his bedroom had thoroughly pissed him off.

He yanked open the door to his garage, hard enough that it nearly came off its hinges, then did the same to his car door.

Why did Kerry always have to look for problems?

He grabbed her dress, her shoes and bag, but left her bra and panties because those were unsalvageable.

Why couldn't she just go with the flow?

He slammed his car door shut.

Why couldn't she just let her hair down and have fun for once in her life?

He slammed the door to the garage shut, too.

Why did she keep assuming he was going to be a jerk about everything?

He headed back through the entryway and kitchen, still fuming as he headed up the stairs.

Couldn't she see that she was his friend and he didn't screw over his friends?

Adam stopped halfway up the stairs, cursing again as he finally realized that, while she might have played things wrong this morning, he sure as hell hadn't done much better by snapping at her as soon as she brought up her worries.

Kerry had been clear from the start about meeting at hotels and keeping sex separate from everything else. First it was his family and the wedding that she hadn't wanted to be affected by their hooking up. Now, they'd added in a house.

She was right. Things could get complicated if they let them.

So they wouldn't let them.

He put her bag on the seat of the leather chair by the fireplace, laid out her dress along the back, and put her shoes down beside it, then headed into the kitchen to make some coffee and wait for her. When she came out fifteen minutes later, looking and smelling fresh and beautiful, he didn't waste any time in handing her a cup of coffee—or getting straight to the point.

"I'm sorry."

She had the cup halfway to her mouth when she froze. "You're sorry?"

"Very." His parents had taught him loads of important things over the years, but one of the most important was knowing how to apologize sincerely, and not to feel like less of a man for it. "I like you, Kerry. I like you a lot."

She still seemed unsure about where he was going, but she said, "I like you, too."

"I know we started off all of this"—he gestured up to his bedroom the way she had earlier—"as strangers, but we're friends now. Aren't we?"

She nodded. "Yes." She seemed almost surprised to realize that it was true. "We're friends."

"I don't hurt my friends." He took the cup and put it on the kitchen counter so that he could take her hands in his. "However long you and I decide to keep having sex, once it's over, I'm not going to hurt you, and I can't see you wanting to hurt me, either."

"I don't want that. I would never want to hurt you, Adam."

He had to smile at the way she said it so sweetly, so earnestly. "Good."

Finally, he did what he'd been wanting to do since the moment he'd awakened and seen her staring at him—he kissed her. Long and deep and sweet, so that she couldn't help but press close and wrap herself around him in that way he absolutely loved.

"I've heard the suites at the Fairmont Olympic are top-notch. How does next week look for you?"

For a moment she seemed surprised by the question, but she was quickly back to her usual practical self as she reached for her phone in her bag to check her calendar.

"It's pretty packed. What about you?"

After checking his own calendar, he said, "Mine is jammed, too. Everything but Thursday night."

She looked at her schedule again. "You know," she said slowly, "I could probably shift my Thursday night meeting without much trouble. Do you want me to try to do that?"

"Does it rain in Seattle?"

She laughed, and the sweet sound of it helped relax the muscles in his chest that had been clenched from the moment she'd jumped out of his bed.

"I'll text you as soon as I know for sure if Thursday will work." She moved back against him and kissed him again. "I have a big wedding this afternoon so I really do have to get going now, but thank you for an amazing Saturday night."

The offer to give her just as amazing a Sunday morning was on the tip of his tongue, but now that things seemed back on an even keel again, he didn't want to ruin it by begging her to stay, especially now that he knew she had to work today.

"Let me just grab a shirt, and I'll take you home."

"Thanks, but I've already called a cab, which I believe is waiting for me outside." She gave him one more quick kiss, then said, "See you Thursday," and walked out his front door without a backward glance.

Adam had never been with a woman this self-sufficient or independent.

It almost stung a guy's pride.

CHAPTER FIFTEEN

Kerry had been to hundreds of weddings, but she was enthralled by them every single time. No two weddings were the same. Some were sweet. Some were fun. Some were out-and-out parties. Some were formal affairs. Some mixed together a dash of everything. But at the core of them all was love.

When people found out she'd taken over the family wedding-planning business from her mother, they often asked her if she'd rather be doing something else. But weddings were where Kerry's heart was—in that moment when the groom lifted his bride's veil and tears of joy slid down people's cheeks as everyone gave in to a moment so radiant, so pure that it didn't matter how cynical, how steeped in "reality" they normally were.

But today's wedding was already on her favorites list, and the guests were only just beginning to arrive at the beautiful grounds of the private arboretum on the shores of Lake Washington. The reason was simple:

The bride and groom were clearly each other's best friend. Every time she'd met with them, she'd been struck by how wonderful they were together. Over the months that she'd worked with them on the large wedding, she'd seen them laugh and kiss and dance like lovers—and she'd seen how well they worked together to deal with difficult things, too.

Over the years, Kerry's vision of the love she wanted for herself had taken clearer and clearer shape as she'd not only watched so many couples come together, but also paid close attention to which ones *stayed* together.

Of course, she wanted heat and can't-keep-their-hands-off-each-other passion. But more than anything, she wanted her husband to be her best friend, and she wanted to be his. She wanted him to be the person she whispered all her secrets to in the middle of the night. She wanted her shoulder to be the one he cried on behind closed doors.

The thing was, Kerry had never really been friends with a man before, might never have thought it was even possible until this morning, when Adam had said he was her friend and she realized she was his, too.

She'd been full of angst and worries over everything when she'd awakened in his bed. She'd been so afraid that they had made a huge mistake. But after they talked things through—with Adam ending up being the surprisingly rational, calm one when she hadn't been able to find one single rational, calm bone in her body—she was able to smile again as she thought about him.

How unexpected their relationship was. Adam Sullivan was the last person she would ever have thought she could become friends with. And yet, their relationship was one of the most wonderful she'd ever had.

He not only knew just how to make her laugh, but also precisely when she needed that laughter.

He was easy to talk to about the things that mattered to her, and she loved listening to him talk about what got him juiced up, too.

Seeing him smile always made her smile.

And few things in her life had been as comforting as simply holding his hand.

At first, she'd wanted to keep things straight and clear between them because she'd been afraid of getting her heart broken. But now, there was even more at stake. Because she didn't want to do anything to lose his friendship. Not when he'd come to mean so much to her, so quickly.

Before Adam, her life hadn't been bad by any stretch of the imagination, but in the past two weeks, it had been bright and colorful in a way that she hadn't known it could be. Part of it was the hot sex—of course she knew that had to be a factor. But if she'd been having sex with someone she didn't like, they wouldn't be hanging out and talking afterward. They wouldn't be laughing together.

And they definitely wouldn't be looking out for each other.

As the caterer gave her an update through her headset on their preparations for the post-wedding reception, Kerry knew now wasn't the time to be thinking about her night or her morning with Adam. She had a job to do, and do well.

The groom's mother had been one of her mother's clients, a widow who had found love for a second time twenty-five years ago, and Aileen Dromoland had hinted on the phone that she might drop by. If ever there was a wedding to get right, it was this one.

Kerry always wanted her mother to feel that her daughter had done right by the company she'd worked so hard to build. So since it wouldn't do to let either the bride and groom or her mother down, she corralled her focus and got back to work on making sure all of today's moving pieces worked in perfect concert with each other.

The crush of guests arriving to take their seats began in earnest now that the ceremony was scheduled to start in less than fifteen minutes. Kerry had already checked in with the bride, her bridesmaids, and her parents, and all of them were relaxed and happy in the final minutes before the wedding began. The groom and his crew were also equally at ease, and she gave silent thanks that everything was so well on track.

Ushering an older couple to their seats came as second nature to her, and she enjoyed her chat with them about the gorgeous Seattle weather and how lucky they were to be there today. More than three hundred people would be attending. The groom was a prominent financier, and the bride owned one of the best beauty salons in the city. It stood to reason that their guests were an uncommonly good-looking and successful bunch.

Still, she couldn't help but think that none of them were quite as good-looking as Adam. Perhaps she was biased, she thought with a little flush of pleasure she couldn't quite contain, given that she had firsthand knowledge of just how gorgeous he was head to toe, clothes on *and* off.

A message from the florist popped up on her iPad, and she realized she'd lost focus again. It was so unlike her to daydream while on the job.

Then again, it was also *extremely* unlike her to meet up with a gorgeous, totally unsuitable man for wild sex.

Giving her head a shake, she turned to greet another guest. But her greeting stuck in her throat when she realized she was looking at her favorite face, the one she couldn't seem to get out of her head no matter how hard she tried.

"Adam?" Her tongue felt all tied up, probably due to the way her heart and stomach immediately started jumping around whenever he stood this close to her. "What are you doing here?"

He held up his invitation. "My friends Jodi and Paul cordially requested the honor of my presence at their wedding and reception this afternoon."

"You're one of their wedding guests?" She usually knew the guest list like the back of her hand, but the bride and groom had made theirs months ago and, amazingly, had stuck to it with so few changes that she hadn't thought she needed to review it.

He grinned as he said, "You're their wedding planner?"

She couldn't help but smile back. And why shouldn't she? After all, it wasn't a crime to be friends with Adam Sullivan. It was only the sex part that she didn't want anyone to know about.

"When I mentioned I had a wedding this afternoon, why didn't you say anything?"

He looked a little chastened as he admitted, "I might not have exactly remembered the wedding was *this* weekend. But if I'd known I would get to see you here this afternoon, I definitely wouldn't have forgotten."

"Figures you'd almost forget about your friends' wedding." The only reason she held back her eye roll was because they weren't alone. But she planned on letting it loose on him in a big way once it was just the two of them again on Thursday night. "Although I don't know how much you'll see m—"

The caterer said something to her through her earpiece, and she cut herself off to quickly answer another question. At the same time, the iPad she was holding was buzzing with one message after another, all of them potential fires that needed to be put out, so she quickly typed a half-dozen messages back to keep everything on track.

When she looked up again, she was surprised to realize Adam was still standing in front of her. "I forgot you were still here."

He put his hand over his chest. "Ouch."

For a moment she couldn't tell if he was teasing or not, but then she realized he was working to fight back another grin. "Honestly, it's a really nice surprise that you're here," she told him, and she meant it. Maybe she should have been worried that he would do his best to distract her in his far-too-charming way, but the truth was that she was too happy about seeing him again to care. "And I also want to apologize in advance for the next zillion times I can't give you anywhere near my full attention today."

"Don't apologize for doing your job." But he gave her a look she knew too well, one that promised he wasn't even close to done having fun with her yet. "And I won't apologize when I steal you away from it all for a dance later."

She opened her mouth to remind him that she was there to work and not party, but before she could get a word out, he pointed to her iPad. "Looks like a dozen new messages have come in for you in the last thirty seconds, so I'll go take my seat."

With a soft kiss on her cheek, he was heading off into the crowd and being heartily greeted by pretty much everyone, male and female.

Kerry knew she'd already been thinking about Adam Sullivan far too much. Far too happily, too, despite the fact that they could never be more than friends with really great benefits. And yet, as she took care of a dozen last-second details before the ceremony began, she didn't do anything to squash the extra spring in her step or the extra-fast beat of her heart.

★ ★ ★

Adam made sure to take a seat where he could see his friends standing in front of the officiant *and* observe Kerry at the same time. She looked so professional, and utterly in control of every detail, as she stood just to the side of the last row of guests.

After the huge number of family weddings Adam had been to during the past couple of years, he knew a thing or two about them. Enough to know that putting on one this big was a massive undertaking. Odds were she was being given a dozen different updates from her staff and contractors through her headset, but she didn't look the least bit stressed out.

And then, as the officiant began to lead the bride and groom into their vows, he watched her reach up to her ear and take out her earpiece.

He grinned, easily guessing that she didn't want to miss even one word of the mushy stuff.

Adam was happy for his friends, but even though they were making major vows to each other today, they took a backseat to the chance to be with Kerry for a little while outside of one of their hotel suites. Considering she'd made it perfectly clear just hours ago that their relationship needed to stop growing outside of those hotels and work on the house she wanted him to revive, today's wedding had gone from a waste of a perfectly good sunny weekend day to a total bonus.

And yet, over the next few minutes, the vows his friends had written for each other hit him harder than any wedding vows had in recent memory. Not only because the couple clearly dug each other and planned to do whatever it took to make their love last, but also because of the look on Kerry's face as they pledged themselves to each other.

How many times had she heard people make similar vows to each other? Hundreds, at the very least, he figured.

And yet, as he watched her eyes tear up and her beautiful mouth wobble slightly at the corners when the couple sealed their vows with a kiss, the marriage vows clearly meant as much to her today as they must have the first time she'd heard them.

What, he suddenly wondered, would it be like for Kerry to hear those vows on her own wedding day? To say them herself to the man she was vowing to love, to cherish, to remain with forever? How much more would it mean to her to know that *she* had finally found the love she'd been waiting for?

Adam's chest tightened.

It was hard to picture Kerry with another guy. Impossible, actually. Even harder than it was for him to picture himself as a groom in a tux in front of friends and family saying things about sickness and health.

Strange that he could see himself getting hitched more easily than he could see Kerry letting some other guy slip a ring on her finger.

Everyone around him jumped out of their seats to applaud the newly married couple as they walked down the aisle, and he lost sight of Kerry. By the time the crowd cleared out, she was gone. She had a show to run, and he planned to let her do her job. But though he normally avoided the dance floor at weddings—it was where the desperate single women always pounced—today it was the part he was most looking forward to.

Because it meant he'd get to hold Kerry in his arms for a few minutes.

The next couple of hours were perfectly orchestrated, and though he knew they must be flying by for his newly married friends, for Adam they dragged on and on, until the band *finally* started up and the happy couple took the floor for their first dance.

Adam didn't waste one single second after it ended to take Kerry's hand in his. "Our turn now."

She looked momentarily surprised—and pleased—to find her hand in his. But though he sensed she wanted the dance as much as he did, she said, "Any other time, I'd love to. But I'm here to work today, not to party with the guests."

"Looks like everything's going great," he said with a gesture to the very happy people all around them who were full of food and cake and champagne. "Besides, you want all of the bride and groom's guests to be happy, don't you?"

Figuring he'd already given her more than fair warning, with one deft move, he put her iPad on a nearby table, then sent her into a graceful spin. One that had her forgetting the rules for a moment as she laughed and came back, breathless, into his arms.

His friends looked over at them with big smiles, and when Kerry saw that they weren't at all upset to see their wedding planner dancing with one of their guests, she finally relaxed.

He already knew she was the perfect fit in his arms, but this was a different dance than any they'd ever done before, and he wanted to savor every second of it. Her head on his shoulder, her delicious scent, the beautiful sound of her voice as she softly sang along with the classic crooner song, the softness of the skin at her wrist where he was gently rubbing his thumb along her pulse point.

For hours, time had dragged on endlessly. But now that he wanted it to slow, it raced forward faster than ever before. The song was ending too soon, leaving him only a handful of seconds with Kerry in his arms before he lost her until Thursday.

"Kerry?"

In a split second, her body went from loose and languid to taut as a bow. She stepped out of his arms before he could try to keep her close.

"Mother." Kerry's voice had a sharpness in it that hadn't been there just minutes before. "I'm so glad you were able to come to the wedding."

Adam could see where Kerry's beauty had come

from. Her mother was a stunning woman. A little too thin, perhaps, but otherwise she looked barely two decades older than her daughter.

Her mother gave her a kiss on both cheeks in the British style. "I would have been here earlier, but I'm afraid the event I was chairing ran long."

Adam extended his hand and smiled as he said, "It's a pleasure to finally meet you, Ms. Dromoland. I'm—"

"Adam Sullivan, the architect." Kerry's mother shook his hand. "I recognize you from the story I recently read about your work on the historic women's club. I'm very impressed with the way you revived the building."

"Thank you, I enjoyed working on it."

Despite her compliment on his professional skills, Adam had a sense that Kerry's mother wasn't necessarily impressed with much else about him. Clearly, she knew of his reputation as a ladies' man. Just as clearly, she wasn't thrilled to find one of her precious daughters in his arms. If he had a daughter and found her dancing with a guy like him, he'd feel precisely the same way.

The thought didn't sit quite right with him.

"How did you two meet?" Kerry's mother asked them, clearly assuming they hadn't just met at today's wedding.

"Adam's brother Rafe is working with us for his

wedding. Adam helped design a marvelous gazebo for the event. He's also volunteered to build it, which is very sweet of him."

Adam had to work to fight back a grin at the way Kerry was trying so hard to come up with a list of unarguably good points in his favor. At the same time, he wondered at her use of the word *us* as she'd spoken about working on Rafe and Brooke's wedding. Was Kerry's mother still involved in the business? That wasn't the impression he'd gotten so far, but maybe he'd missed something along the way.

"I'm also a good friend of Jodi and Paul," he added, "which is why I'm here today."

"What do you think of today's wedding?"

"Pretty much every Sullivan on the West Coast has gotten married in the past couple of years, so I've been to plenty of weddings, but the truth is that today's wedding is by far the best one I've attended."

Kerry's mother was silent for a long moment as she studied his face to assess how genuine his statement was. Finally, she said, "Kerry is the best wedding planner on any coast."

Kerry looked more than a little surprised—and very pleased—by her mother's praise. "I learned from the very best."

Her mother smiled at her, and he liked seeing the deep warmth in the other woman's eyes toward her daughter. Kerry deserved to be loved by absolutely everyone.

"Everything except dancing with the guests rather than making sure everything is running smoothly," her mother added, with a small upturn of her lips.

When he felt Kerry stiffen beside him again, knowing she was still mortified to be caught goofing off for a few minutes while on the job, he took her hand and held it as he said, "I didn't give her much choice, I'm afraid."

"Nonsense." Her mother was still smiling, but the slight edge was back in her tone as she looked down at their linked hands. "One always has a choice."

With that, she kissed Kerry's cheeks again, said how lovely it was to meet him, and went to mingle.

"Thanks for the dance," Kerry said, but she sounded distracted, her eyes following her mother's movement across the lawn beneath the fairy lights.

Kerry's hand was far too cold, and he covered it with both of his to try to warm her up. "Your mom is one seriously elegant lady. I'm glad I finally got to meet her. I see where you get your strength from. And your beauty."

Finally, Kerry's eyes met his again. "She's amazing. And," she said with an upturn of her lips that didn't quite reach her eyes, "probably worried that I'm dropping the ball big-time by goofing off with one of the guests. I really should get back to work now to make sure everything's beyond perfect."

She tried to slide her hands from his, but he wasn't ready to let go just yet. "I want to dance with you again. Not tonight," he said before she protested that she couldn't goof off with him twice in one night, "but soon." He lifted her hand to his lips and pressed a kiss to the back of it before handing her back her iPad. "Time to let you go back to showing everyone why you're the best wedding planner on any coast."

And though she smiled as she took the device from him, he didn't like the worry that was barely a layer down. Nor did he care for the way she ran herself off her feet the rest of the night to make up for a dance that she clearly thought had been a terrible transgression.

He finally understood why she'd been utterly adamant that no one learn of their nights together. Not only because she didn't want Rafe and Brooke to question her professionalism, but also because she was terrified of disappointing her mother.

The thing was, Ms. Dromoland clearly adored Kerry, and despite the fact that she obviously had high expectations, he wasn't convinced that her mother was quite as full of demands and expectations as she thought.

There must be something more to the way Kerry

bent over backward for her mother and sister, another reason why she felt she always had to look and behave so perfectly. Something that ran deeper than he had a handle on yet.

Then again, the truth was that there was plenty about Kerry he couldn't get a handle on. The way he couldn't stop thinking about her, for one. Or wanting her.

Or just plain smiling every time he thought about her.

CHAPTER SIXTEEN

The following Thursday night, as Kerry walked from her office toward the hotel, she was glad for the fresh air and a few minutes alone to clear her head before she met up with Adam.

Again and again over the week she'd replayed her dance with him—and the subsequent conversation with her mother—in her head.

The dance had been unlike any other Kerry had ever experienced. Throughout her teens, both Kerry and her sister had taken ballroom-dancing classes, and that knowledge had helped Kerry a great deal as she worked with brides and grooms who were nervous about their wedding dance. But though Adam was incredibly skilled on his feet, it wasn't skill that'd had her heart leaping around in her chest or her soul feeling as though it was taking flight in his arms. She'd wished the dance could have gone on forever, that she'd never have to let him go.

Regret washed over her again at the way she'd all

but jumped out of his arms when her mother had said her name. Of course, he'd been sweet about it, and nothing but gracious with her mother. After that, Kerry had been swept back into the myriad details of her job, being pulled in so many directions by her wedding staff and the guests that when Adam came to say good-bye, she'd barely had a chance to say good-bye herself.

By the time she'd finally left the wedding site, she was stunned to realize how lonely the thought of going home alone was. Especially now that she knew how warm and wonderful it was to share Adam's bed.

But that wasn't their deal. Wasn't what they'd agreed on. Wasn't the plan that *she'd* reminded them they needed to stick to.

Not allowing herself to be a coward, Kerry had called her mother Monday morning to see if she enjoyed the wedding and had any suggestions. Where Kerry was good with details and organization, her mother's gift had been in the tiny things that ended up making all the difference. Kerry had been touched to hear her mother tell Adam that she was the best wedding planner on any coast, but she also wanted Aileen to be honest about where she still had room for improvement.

"The wedding was perfect, darling, although I'm sure it wasn't easy to keep your focus on work when

Adam Sullivan couldn't keep his eyes off you."

Kerry had been glad her mother couldn't see her mouth drop open, or the flush of pleasure that she couldn't stop from moving over her from knowing how much Adam wanted her.

Trying not to betray either reaction, she'd replied, "If you do think of anything at the wedding that needed improvement, please don't hesitate to tell me. And as for Adam..." She hadn't wanted to lie to her mother—she'd never get away with it anyway. "We became friends while working together on his brother's wedding. He's a very nice man."

Her mother had let the silence ride just long enough that Kerry knew they weren't yet done discussing him. "Yes, I've heard he's a very nice man. Especially when he's around beautiful women."

Kerry hadn't been able to keep from defending him—and, she supposed, herself at the same time. "He's been nothing but kind and generous. A true friend." Surely, her mother had to know that Kerry wasn't foolish enough to fall in love with an utterly unsuitable man, not after having done such a good job of steering clear of bad love her entire life.

"I'm not sure friends look at each other the way you both were during your dance, darling—or that men and women are ever very good at being friends without complications ensuing. But I've never had any reason to doubt you before, so I won't begin now."

Her mother's warning to stay away from romantic entanglement with Adam hadn't needed to be explicitly said to be perfectly clear. Of course, Kerry couldn't possibly have told her mother that both she and Adam knew the rules and had a strict arrangement where the nights they spent together couldn't possibly become more than hot sex between friends. If her mother ever found out about Kerry and Adam's hotel hookups, she would be beside herself with worry.

And yet, even knowing how deeply her mother disapproved of even the idea of Kerry spending time with Adam wasn't enough to convince Kerry to cancel her night with him. Not when she was really looking forward to seeing him tonight at the hotel.

Not just for sex—although she was definitely looking forward to that—but because she wanted to hear about everything in his life. Things like the projects he was working on and whether he'd spent time with his family this week. She wanted to hear about the good parts, and the frustrating ones, too. And then she wanted to tell him all the little things she knew he'd appreciate, like the incredible historic house of one of her new clients and the little boy who had given the funniest wedding toast she'd ever heard.

Kerry was halfway to the hotel when her phone dinged from inside her purse. Though ignoring a ringing phone was strictly against the rules of all wedding planners—even higher than dancing with one of the wedding guests—she was tempted to turn it off. The last thing she wanted was for work to derail her night with Adam. They'd both been so busy this week that the only contact they'd had with each other since Sunday's wedding were a few emails and text messages about the house she was in the process of trying to buy.

He'd sent over the original plans from the county for her to study so that she could discuss what she'd like to change inside the house. But she loved it just as it was. She didn't want to change anything about it. She simply wanted to see it come back to life—and know that she could spend hers there, as well.

Fortunately, the number on the screen was the only one she wanted to pick up tonight. "Adam, hi."

She knew he could probably hear the smile on her lips, but she didn't need to hide her pleasure at hearing from a friend. One of the best she'd ever had, actually, despite whatever her mother believed about a woman and a man not being able to be friends.

"Kerry, I kept trying to get away to call, but there are so many problems with this renovation project I just took on in mid-rebuild that if I so much as left the room it was likely to collapse on everyone's heads and take out all ten of the guys I brought in."

"What can I do to help?" Adam had been there for her again and again. Tonight, she'd be there for him. And she'd also stuff down her selfish disappointment about not getting to be with him in the hotel.

"You could hire a sniper to take out the guy who was running this project before me."

"How did you know that all wedding planners have a sniper on speed dial?"

He laughed. "Damn it, I didn't want to be late tonight. Any night but this."

Hearing how much he regretted having to bail on their night together had her chest squeezing tight. But it was a good kind of squeezing, almost as if he'd put his arms around her and was holding her close.

"Where's the building?"

The address he gave her wasn't far from where she was standing. "I'll bring everyone dinner."

"Dinner?" She could hear a half-dozen male voices chiming in behind Adam. "You can't even imagine how big a hero you'd be if you brought us dinner, especially since we skipped lunch, we've run out of snacks and drinks, and we've got hours left here tonight."

Kerry made a quick call to her favorite caterer, who also ran a great deli close to the building they were working on. Judy didn't ask questions when Kerry said she needed munchies and drinks for twenty ASAP.

Adam had said he'd brought ten men with him, but she figured they'd each eat for two if they'd missed lunch. With Judy on the snack delivery, Kerry headed into the Mexican burrito place on the next corner, one she'd heard great things about.

Twenty minutes later, she was getting into a taxi with four huge bags of food. No one would go hungry tonight, that was for sure. And even if she didn't get to spend an entire night with Adam, at least she'd be with him for a few wonderful minutes.

★ ★ ★

"Kerry, you're a goddess."

Adam's smile lit her up from the inside out as he popped a hard hat on her head, then took the bags from her and handed them to his guys. His men all agreed that she was indeed the best as he quickly introduced her. Each of them was polite and charming as they took turns shaking her hand. It was an awful lot of testosterone in one place, and she'd be lying if she said she wasn't just the tiniest bit overwhelmed by them.

But Adam didn't dig into the food with everyone else. Instead, he told her, "I've made a few notes about the blueprints for the house we looked at last week. I know you love it as is, but there are a few things we should discuss. The blueprints are in the next room."

He took her hand and led her through to another construction zone. Kerry thought it was fairly easy to make beauty out of things when they were already in order, but she'd always been amazed by anyone who could find order in a mess like this.

Adam Sullivan was clearly a magician, one who wasn't scared off by a ton of work and a boatload of cleanup. Nor was he put off by digging through the rubble to find the beauty waiting many layers down.

He shoved a heavy door halfway closed, which was as far as it could go, and then they both moved into each other's arms at the same time. His hunger, her need—they were both so strong that the building could have started to fall down around them and neither would have noticed or cared. Not when they simply couldn't get enough of each other's mouths. Not when their hands couldn't touch enough skin. Not when she could have listened to him say her name over and over again for the rest of her life and never tire of hearing it.

And not when her week without him finally ended in the most perfect way—with his arms around her and her arms around him.

"I'd rip off all your clothes right now if I didn't know that my guys would enjoy it *way* too much knowing what we're up to in here."

"Maybe I'm supposed to care, but right now I don't. I just want you, Adam. That's all I want. Just you."

Heat flared in his eyes at her words, and his mouth came down on hers so hard it should have hurt, but all she could feel was pleasure. The pleasure of being with the only person she'd ever truly been free with—the man who had shown her how much beauty there was in that freedom.

Unfortunately, he dragged his mouth from hers a few moments later. "Forget my guys outside. Swear to God, if I didn't think this room would actually cave in around us, I'd already be inside of you."

Her breath caught in her throat at his wickedly hot words.

"That sound is going to fuel my fantasies for a hell of a long time. Especially," he said as he bent his head to her neck, "if I can get you to make it again right now."

The delicious feel of his stubble along the sensitive underside of her chin as he nipped and kissed her easily had her gasping with pleasure. But instead of pulling her closer, he put his hands on her shoulders and made both of them take a step back.

"I'll never forgive myself if I get us both killed here tonight. Or if anyone walks in on us and sees you like this." His eyes were impossibly dark and intense. "Your passion, your sensuality—they're all mine, Kerry. *Mine.*"

She took a deep breath, and then another, knowing he was right and that they should behave more prudently. But after a lifetime of prudence, it was a lovely thing, frankly, to be risky every now and again.

Especially when it felt like he was *hers*, too.

"Besides," he added while she tried to get a grip on herself, "I wasn't kidding about my guys. I'd bet money on the fact that right now they're all talking about how gorgeous you are and what a lucky sonofabitch I am to get to spend even five minutes alone with you."

She would have blushed if her skin hadn't already been so flushed from his kisses. "They're just happy about the food."

"You really don't have the first clue, do you? No idea at all how beautiful or how sexy you are."

He brushed the pad of one thumb over her lips, and it was the most natural thing in the world for her to lick out against it, making him growl low in his throat as he barely managed to hold himself back. She did it again, partly because she wanted him so bad, but also because a secret part inside of her thrilled at knowing she could turn a man like Adam inside out with nothing more than the flick of her tongue against his skin.

"Just so you know, I'm using up every ounce of my self-control right now. You'd better prepare yourself, because things are going to get crazy once I finally get you naked."

She smiled so big her cheeks hurt. "I can't wait." And when he smiled back, just as big, she said, "I missed you this week." Her week would have been perfect if only he'd been a part of it.

"I wanted to cancel all of my meetings this week," he told her. "But I knew you didn't want me to be sitting in on all of yours."

She laughed, enjoying the picture of Adam crashing her client meetings, her weddings. He would be the very definition of a bull in a china shop. Despite that, she knew she would love every minute of having him there.

"Actually, it was really fun having you at the wedding on Sunday. Even if," she added, "my mother wasn't too pleased with me for kicking up my heels with one of the guests for a few minutes. I'm sorry if she made you feel at all uncomfortable. I'm sure she didn't mean to be quite so..." *Judgmental* was the right word, but she hated even saying it out loud to Adam now that she knew the real man behind the gorgeous face and charming grin. "So protective of me. She's always been like that with me and Colleen."

"Trust me," he said, "with a little sister and a zillion female cousins who are too pretty for their own good, if there's one thing I get, it's being overprotective. The only thing that would have upset me about my conversation with your mother would have been if she *wasn't* worried about you. Of course she wants the best for you."

"It's just…" Kerry had never told Adam about her father. She'd never really spoken to *anyone* about him, actually, not even close friends. Somehow, everyone had understood that the topic was off-limits. But when she was with Adam, all those usual limits just seemed to disappear. "My father walked out on us when I was a little girl. Just up and left. I don't know why. I don't even know if my mother knows exactly why. I guess he was just bored with having a family. And we never heard from him again. That's why my mom built her business—to save us. And that's also why she's always been so adamant about me and Colleen not getting involved with the wrong guy, because it's exactly what she did."

Adam gently stroked her cheek. "All parents should want their kids to have everything—especially the things they were never able to have themselves. Since love betrayed her, I can see why she wouldn't want it to do a number on you, too."

Relief washed over her that he understood so well. "It may also have been the first time she's ever seen me dancing with a man anywhere near as good-looking as you."

"Were those her exact words," he asked with a

grin, "or just your take on things?"

"Sometimes I forget that your head is already big enough." But she couldn't help laughing with him.

"Speaking of your mom," he said a moment later, "do the two of you co-own the business?"

"No. Why do you ask?"

"You said something at the wedding that made it sound as if you were still running it with her."

"My mother loved running the business, but being responsible for creating—and executing—one of the best days of people's lives isn't exactly the least stressful career in the world. Colleen was never interested, but since I clearly was, when I graduated from business school, my mother tried to give it to me."

"You and all those sexy-as-hell biz school brains. No wonder I love scrambling them up so much," he teased. "But you wouldn't just take the business from her, would you?"

"How could I? I wanted to make sure she'd be able to live comfortably in her retirement. And even though she'd always been a good saver, I knew that plenty of wedding planners would have jumped at the chance to buy the business from her just to get their hands on her contacts list. I'd had a couple of jobs that paid pretty well through college, so I was able to give her a down payment on what the company was worth along with a percentage of profits. Profits she'll always deserve for building something so wonderful."

Kerry had never told anyone so many of the details of how she'd come to acquire the business from her mother. Not even her sister. But it was always so easy to talk to Adam. She knew he wouldn't judge her. Not when he'd had plenty of reasons to so far, but never had.

He brushed a lock of hair away from her cheek, and just that faint touch of his fingertips sent thrill bumps rising across the surface of her skin. "You talk a good game," he said softly, "but we both know you didn't pay her for the business and cut her in on the future profits just to make sure she'd have a comfortable retirement. You keep her as a part of the business because you love her."

"The business was so much of her life—her whole life, really—for so many years that I didn't want her to feel like she had nothing once I took over. I want her to feel that if she ever wants to come back and work on a wedding, she doesn't have to ask, that everything is just as much hers as it's ever been. And I want to make sure that my standards of excellence are just as high as hers, so that she'll never be disappointed in the choice she made to turn her blood, sweat, and tears over to me."

"She'd love you just as much, even if the business went south. You know that, don't you?"

Kerry wanted to say, *Of course.* Wanted to believe that it was true. But though she nodded, Adam noticed her pause. Because he noticed everything.

"I'm not going to deny that I've met plenty of people who give out love tied to strings," he said, "but though I've only met your mother once, I'm positive hers doesn't come with any. How could it when you're the kind of daughter every parent dreams of having?"

The spot in her chest that had been tight and achy ever since her mother had shown up at the wedding suddenly loosened.

"How do you do it?" She struggled with the emotion rising within her—a mix of gratitude and breathlessness, leaving her feeling touched and overwhelmed. "How do you always know just what to say to make me feel better when I'm all twisted up in knots?"

"I'm usually the one saying all the wrong things, sometimes on purpose, sometimes by accident. But with you—" His dark eyes burned into her with deep emotion that seemed to equal hers. "With you, everything is easier. Better, too. So much better, Kerry, than with anyone else."

She'd never needed a kiss more, never wanted to lose herself in one the way she wanted to lose herself in his tonight. But when she heard male laughter coming from behind one wall—a wall that was only barely standing, according to Adam—she made herself draw back.

"I shouldn't keep you from your work any longer, especially not when I'm sure your guys will be wanting to head home as soon as they can. Text me when you think you might be free again, and we can—"

"Tonight. I can be free tonight in two hours. Three max."

Her heart leapt in her chest. "Are you sure? Because you—"

"Can't work these guys too much longer without all of us getting sloppy. And I don't want another night to go by without you."

"I'll be working, too, and I have plenty to keep me busy on my computer at the hotel, so promise me you won't rush and get hurt."

"I won't get hurt," he promised, but he made no promises about speed.

* * *

Four hours later, Adam finally walked into the hotel suite. He'd texted Kerry several times to let her know how things were coming along, but unfortunately, he hadn't been able to cut his guys loose until after nine p.m. By the time he'd finished closing up the site and dealing with paperwork that needed to be waiting on county desks first thing in the morning, another hour and a half had passed.

And every single second that he'd been working on the building, he wished he could have been here with Kerry, instead.

The lights were on throughout the suite, and his heart beat faster knowing he was only seconds from having her in his arms. Her name was already halfway from his lips when he saw her.

She was curled up asleep on a dining room chair. Her computer was open on the table in front of her, but the screen had gone dark...and she was so beautiful that his heart turned over in his chest. He swore it literally flipped head to tail, then back again.

A part of him didn't want to do anything to wake her. Not when she was clearly exhausted. But how could he let her stay in such an uncomfortable spot?

And more important, how could he possibly stop himself from touching her?

There wouldn't be any wild and crazy sex tonight, but that was okay. It was enough just to get to spend the night with her, even if she slept through the whole thing.

As gently as he could, he lifted her from the chair. She was soft and pliable and smelled amazing as her eyes fluttered halfway open.

"Adam." Her beautiful mouth curved up as her eyes closed again, and she snuggled into his chest.

"You're here."

"I'm sorry it took me so long."

"You're here now." He was laying her down on the bed when she opened her eyes again and said, "I'm so glad you're here with me." She reached out and put her hands on his face. "So handsome. Sometimes I wonder if you're even real."

He'd never seen her like this, halfway between awake and asleep, her words soft and a little bit rounded on the edges. "I wonder the same about you," he told her. "You're so beautiful that I lose sleep dreaming about you. So breathtaking that I lose brain cells every time I look at you."

"I dream about you, too," she said, her words barely above a whisper. "Every night." She threaded her hands into his hair. "Dream with me tonight, Adam."

He already knew he couldn't refuse her anything. Especially not on a night like tonight, when it really did feel as though some special spell wrapped all around both of them, making the divide between dark and light, asleep and awake, no longer clear.

Their kiss swamped his senses, dragging him deeper into her, then deeper still, until he couldn't remember a time before her, couldn't possibly imagine a life after her.

As he nibbled his way down to her exposed neck, she said, "I love the way you kiss me all over."

"I love the way you taste all over," he said as he covered her breasts with his hands and she arched into them with a sigh of pleasure. Moments later, when he opened up her shirt and unclasped her bra, her sigh turned to a breathless gasp as he stroked her bare skin.

"I love the way you touch me."

"I love touching you." He ran his hands down from her breasts over her taut stomach to unzip her pants. "I love how soft you are." He slid his hand beneath her panties, and she shivered with need. "I love how sensitive you are." As his fingers moved over then into her, she instinctively pushed up against his hand.

"I love the way you make me feel, Adam." Her breath caught in her throat again as he covered her breast with his mouth at the same time as he took her with his hand. "Only you can make me feel this good."

"I love knowing what I do to you." He stroked her nipple with one thumb, stroked across the arousal between her thighs with the other. "I love it when you let yourself go for me." Her gaze locked on his as her inner muscles tightened on him and her breath hitched. "Show me how much you love it, too."

"*Love.*" She whispered the word against his mouth as she arched into his touch, giving herself up to him without holding anything back.

All week long, he really had lost sleep fantasizing about her. And yet, even now, when he needed her so badly that his need was a constant ache throbbing in the center of his chest, the dream-state continued. Each new patch of skin he revealed tantalized. Every sexy sound she made as she opened one button after another on his shirt and ran her hands over his chest titillated.

But the best part of all was watching her smile and hearing her laugh as fabric tangled, as fingers fumbled, as kisses teased.

Finally, when there was practically nothing between them, Adam found himself wishing out loud, "I want to feel you. All of you." He knew it wasn't possible. Not tonight, anyway. But that didn't stop him from wanting to move inside of her, skin to skin.

"I do, too. All of you," she echoed.

God, it was tempting, so tempting to give in to that urge to be completely connected to her. *Soon*, he promised himself as he put on protection, soon they'd talk about being each other's one and only. Especially since she was already his, the only woman he ever thought about anymore. The only one who'd ever kept him up at night. The only lover to whom he had ever wanted to give all of himself.

"Love me, Adam."

Kerry was his dream woman come to life beneath him, her hands warm as she held on to his shoulders, her legs strong as she wound them around his hips and he began to move into her. And then they were rolling over so that she was every one of his fantasies come to life as she straddled and rocked, making the most beautiful sounds of pleasure while moonlight streamed over her.

She brought him right to the edge, then stilled just long enough for him to catch his breath before starting all over again.

Perfect.

Nothing, no one, had ever been so perfect as this incredible woman who'd just turned the tables on him. He'd always been in control in bed, always taken the lead, but tonight she led him every step of the way, straight toward heaven.

Again and again, she teased him with her curves, her heat, her kisses, until everything blurred in his head. Until his brain stopped functioning altogether, and he was operating on sensation alone.

The next thing he knew, she was on her knees, and he was, too. And, somehow, it was right where they both needed to be, with him right there behind her, taking and giving in equal measure. Her words all ran together in his head. *TakeNowPleaseNeedMore.* But he understood them all, because they were falling from his lips, too.

Sex had never been so wild.

Making love had never been so sweet.

And nothing had ever felt as right as flying out over the edge with Kerry, and then falling back onto the bed with her lithe curves still cradled against the front of his body.

But a few minutes later, as her breathing steadied and she fell asleep with him still spooned against her, he knew he was wrong.

This felt even more right.

CHAPTER SEVENTEEN

"Adam, I have the most amazing news!"

Kerry stood on the sidewalk with her phone to her ear on Wednesday morning, nearly a week after she'd last seen him at the construction site and their latest hotel suite. She'd been slammed with three back-to-back weddings the previous weekend—Friday, Saturday, and Sunday—and playing endless hours of catch-up in the office the first half of this week made for a really long break since she'd last seen him. Too long.

Especially considering how sweet he'd been about her sister last Friday night. When he'd learned that Kerry had a Friday night wedding, he'd offered to do any Friday night bar pickups if she needed them. Fortunately, Colleen had to fill in at work that night, so neither of them had needed to worry about her getting into trouble at a seedy bar.

Kerry and Adam didn't have plans to meet again until the following night, but she couldn't resist calling him with the good news. Could barely even wait to get

out of the realty office to dial his number from just
outside the building, standing on the sidewalk in
sunshine that felt just as warm and happy as she did
inside.

"The house is mine! I just finished signing all the
papers."

"That's great news. I'm so happy for you." But just
from the way he'd said her name, she would have
known he felt that way without him needing to say
anything more. "Let me steal you away for lunch
today."

"I have a meeting in a few minutes, and another
couple this afternoon, but I'm pretty sure I could meet
you for an hour at noon."

"Meet me at the house."

"The house? The one I just bought?"

He was laughing as he said, "That's the one. See
you at noon."

* * *

As Kerry got out of her car, she was surprised to find
Adam sitting with his back against the old oak tree on a
big blanket, a picnic basket beside him.

When he caught sight of her, he quickly stood and
pulled her into his arms. "Congratulations."

"Thank you." She kissed him then, and it was so
natural. So sweet, in fact, that she didn't stop kissing

him for a quite a while.

"If I'm going to get a kiss like that every time you buy a house," he said when they finally stopped kissing, "I'm going to ask my Realtor sister to show you a few more."

She laughed, but didn't move out of his arms. "I'm good with this one, thanks. Although the truth is that you're probably the only person on the planet who would congratulate me for buying this house." Not to mention the only one she wanted to celebrate with beneath the big oak tree.

He pulled a champagne bottle from the basket and popped the cork, which went flying off into the mess of the yard that, thankfully, was now all hers to deal with. It wasn't until he began to pour it that she realized it wasn't champagne. It was sparkling apple juice.

"I almost brought champagne," he told her when he caught her surprised expression, "but I thought it would be more fun for our picnic to be more like the ones you had when you were a kid."

"Oh, Adam." Her heart felt so full, almost overwhelmingly so. "Apple juice is perfect."

He held out his glass. "To your new home—and to the two of us bringing it back to its former glory together."

"I can't wait," she said as she clinked her glass against his.

They both sat on the blanket, and even though she hadn't been to a picnic since she was a little girl, it felt perfectly natural to sit beside Adam and look up into the beautiful branches of the tree that was even more majestic now than it had been twenty years ago.

She should have known that Adam wasn't done with his surprises as he began to pull out grilled cheese and PBJ and apple slices, all things she guessed he'd probably had on picnics as a kid. But they didn't look like something a deli would have put together.

"Did you make us these sandwiches?"

"I may not be a great cook, but I've always known my way around a sandwich."

She knew exactly how busy Adam's schedule was. He wasn't just one of the most highly sought-after architects in Seattle—his notoriety was international, with clients from every corner of the world beating down his door to get him to work with them.

And yet, he'd taken the time today to make sandwiches for their impromptu picnic.

Kerry immediately thought about her mother, wishing she could see how wonderful a friend Adam was. Although, surely her mother would read more into this picnic than was actually there, so it was probably for the best that she didn't know about it.

"The sandwiches look delicious," Kerry said, and when she took a bite of one, she realized he hadn't been exaggerating his sandwich-making prowess. "I didn't know peanut butter and jelly could be this good. What's your secret?"

He grinned at her. "Secrets have to be earned."

She grinned back, easily guessing the kind of payment he was looking for as she brought her mouth back to his again. She'd take any excuse to kiss him.

"Time to hand over your secret now."

But he just stared at her lips and said, "Secret?"

Loving being able to scramble his brain with her kisses, she laughed and reminded him, "Your PBJ-making secret."

He finally dragged his gaze—dark and full of desire—from her mouth. "I grind up the nuts myself. And more than just one kind of nut."

"Clearly, your genius isn't only in working with buildings."

He raised an eyebrow. "I thought you were worried about inflating my ego."

"That was before."

"Before what?"

The first thing that came into her head was *Before you made my world go topsy-turvy*. But she said, instead, "Before I realized just how modest you really are."

He shook his head, laughing. "I'm not modest."

This time she was the one raising her eyebrow.

"Any other architect of your stature would take every possible chance to remind the people around him of just how important he is and how ridiculously lucky they are to get to work with him. But instead of doing any of that, you're here having a picnic with me in front of a house that isn't grand enough to deserve even an hour of your attention, let alone several months."

"Grand is overrated."

Knowing that she was embarrassing him with her compliments, she turned her gaze to the house. "It's hard to believe it's mine now." She couldn't remember ever feeling this happy before.

"I wish I could have seen the Realtor's face when you said you wanted to buy it," he said with a grin. "Did you tell them you're planning to keep the house, rather than tear it down?"

"They practically said, *Are you sure you really want this place?* They didn't even try to negotiate. Clearly, they wanted to take my money and run before I changed my mind." She shook her head. "If only they knew that I had no intention of changing my mind, because this is where I'm meant to be."

"I agree," he said in a serious voice. "I mean, your current place is great, and I should know because I worked on renovating the building. But this house, this property, this neighborhood—it's all really you. Exactly where you're meant to be."

This rambling old house would never be the fancy, glossy, expensive place in the "right" part of town. But somehow this street with kids riding by on their bikes and moms pushing strollers and gray-haired women watering flowers in the front yard was really her in a way that nothing else had ever been.

She took in a deep breath of the air, sweet-smelling from the wallflowers in bloom along the side of the property, then took another bite of her delicious sandwich. She was washing it down with a sip of sparkling juice when he asked, "How were your weddings this weekend?"

"They were all good. All three couples are obviously very much in love, and I think things will last."

"But?"

She shouldn't be surprised anymore by the way he always heard the things she wasn't saying, but it was such a rare gift that she still never expected it. "Well, they were different from Jodi and Paul's wedding."

"How?"

Normally, Kerry wouldn't discuss her clients with anyone. But Adam wasn't just anyone. He was the one person who always seemed to understand her. "Jodi and Paul are best friends in a way that I'm not sure any of the three couples from this weekend are. I just feel like that makes such a difference."

"From what I can see with my siblings and cousins who are married, I think you're right on the money. Same goes for my parents. Mom and Dad always turn to each other first because they aren't just husband and wife, they're also best friends, which I think has made a difference for them over the years. In fact, this weekend, when I saw my cousin Ryan and his fiancée, Vicki, at the baseball game, they were more gushy over each other than ever—and they've been best friends since they were in high school."

"Did you have a good time at the game?"

"It was great. You would have had fun with us."

"At a baseball game?" She was surprised that he seemed to mean it. "Do you really think I'd like it?"

"Sure," he said easily. "Granted, the idea of you in tight jeans and a T-shirt with a beer in your hand is one of the sexiest visions I've had in a long time. But," he added while she blushed, "you're also competitive enough to really get behind your team. Which is usually the Mariners, by the way. Only when Ryan's in town do we root for the San Francisco Hawks."

She'd never had any interest in baseball, but she'd learned not to doubt Adam's instincts about things. If he thought she was going to love it, odds were good that she actually would.

"Next game," he told her, "you'll see for yourself when I drag you there with me. And hopefully the whole crew will be there the way they were this weekend. Although when everyone's there, it can get a little crazy."

"Why? Just because there are so many of you?"

"Partly. But mostly because everyone is so damned famous." He laughed. "Ford is a great guy, and he and my sister are perfect together, but it sure isn't always easy going places with a rock star. And then when you throw my billionaire brother and his movie-star wife into the mix…" Laughing again, he said, "It can take a while each time to get used to the bodyguards the stadium insists on sending over."

"Bodyguards?" It suddenly hit her. "Oh, no. I didn't even think of hiring bodyguards for Rafe and Brooke's wedding! How could I have overlooked that?"

He put his hand on hers. "You don't need them. Not for a lake wedding."

But she was still panicking. "Aren't some of your cousins famous, too? In addition to Ryan?"

"Doesn't matter how famous any of them are. No one is going to bother us at the lake. It's the perfect private spot for our whole family to get together. You have to trust me on this, Kerry. No bodyguards."

She made herself take a few deep breaths, but it was looking into his eyes that finally convinced her to stop panicking. "I do trust you." She let another big breath go before saying, "And what I meant to say before I started freaking out about bodyguards, was how great it is that you guys are all so close. It seems like you spend a lot of time together."

"We always have. They're a great group to hang out with. Do you have any cousins?"

"My mother was an only child, and my father's family didn't stick around any longer than he did."

"Regardless of whatever went wrong between your father and your mom, he never should have left his children." Adam looked disgusted. "Something similar happened with my cousins in New York. Their mom walked out one day on the four of them and my uncle."

"Oh, that's horrible." And she should know. "But you just have to move on and try not to let it affect you."

As she lifted her arm to swat away a fly, she caught a flash of her watch face and realized with no small amount of disappointment that it was later than she'd thought. "I wish I didn't have to leave for my meeting." She helped him put away the food and then brushed crumbs off her lap as she stood.

"I'm just glad you were able to squeeze me in," he said as he also stood. "We'll celebrate more tomorrow night, okay?" He lowered his voice and said, *"Naked* celebrating. And this time I'll be sure to have champagne to drink off your skin."

Tingles ran through her at both the good-bye kiss he gave her and the delicious thought of celebrating in bed with him. "I can't wait."

And she truly couldn't.

★ ★ ★

After Kerry left, Adam spent some time walking around the house and property and taking notes. All the while, he thought about the way Kerry had said she'd done her best to move on from her father's desertion without letting it affect her. But even though he knew how strong, how resilient, she was, he also knew from experience that all the things you tried not to let affect you, still usually did.

Take him, for instance. When he'd been a teenager and his father had lost his job, they'd nearly lost everything. Home—and doing whatever he could to help save it—had never been more important to Adam. To all of them. Adam had been too young back then to actually support the family financially, the way his oldest brother, Ian, had, but he'd still gone out of his way to mow as many lawns as he could. He'd hauled and stacked wood and cleaned swimming pools— anything someone in the neighborhood would hire him for. And going into all those people's houses had shown him, even more, just how important homes were for families.

Based on what had happened to his family, Adam knew it was no accident that he was fascinated with architecture, specifically reviving old buildings. Second chances were hugely important to him, too, which was why he very rarely built new.

And if he looked at what had happened to Kerry's family, it was no accident that she was in love with happy-ever-afters and was willing to do whatever she could to help people have the best possible start to their perfect forever.

Adam was so lost in his thoughts that he nearly tripped over a spindle from the railing lying in the middle of the porch. Bending down, he picked it up and was surprised once again by the level of craftsman- ship that the original owners had put into this house. They hadn't cut any corners, not in the design or in the crafting of the house. The only reason it was on the verge of falling down was because of the neglect of some distant grand-nieces and -nephews. Thank God someone like Kerry, someone who loved the house so much, had taken it over.

And, he thought with a grin that he knew bordered on egotistical, thank God she had him on her team. The two of them were damned effective solo—together they were going to be unstoppable.

As he took the spindle with him to his car, along with the picnic basket and blanket, he knew Kerry was right about the pull this place had. Something slightly magical. It wasn't hard for him to imagine living in this house, on this street, in this neighborhood. Not hard at all, actually, especially if Kerry was there with him.

And as he reluctantly started his car's engine to head back to work, his father's words from the day they'd looked over the property suddenly came to him: *"It's always hard to walk away from something beautiful, isn't it? Especially when you can sense that giving her your full attention will make both of you happy."*

And it was true that, since the moment he'd met Kerry, she'd completely stolen his attention. There had rarely been a day, rarely been an hour, that he wasn't thinking of her. That he wasn't wishing he could see her. Or that he wasn't longing to hold her in his arms.

And yet, he'd still tried to hold back. Still tried to stick to their arrangement. Still tried to keep from crossing over into what had always been a relationship no-fly zone, thinking that was the only way to be happy. Still believed he couldn't ever let one little four-letter word catch him in its grip without regretting it.

But what if his father was right?

What if giving Kerry—and their relationship—his full attention made both of them even happier than they had ever been without each other?

CHAPTER EIGHTEEN

When Adam was a kid, his father's wood shop was where he always could go when there was something he needed to talk about. Fortunately, things hadn't changed much after they'd grown up, and odds were pretty good on any given afternoon that Max Sullivan would be back there refinishing an old end table or sanding a length of crown molding. Which was why Adam had decided to take a detour to his parents' house instead of heading straight back to the office.

Of course, his mother would kill him if he didn't check in with her first. He found her at her writing table by a window in the living room.

"Adam, honey, what a nice surprise this is! I didn't think we were going to see you until dinner on Friday night."

He gave her a kiss on her cheek. "How's your writing coming along?"

She glanced down at the notebook in front of her and frowned. "Why didn't anyone tell me writing a book was so hard?"

"I'm sure it's great. Do you want me to read what you've come up with so far?"

She looked horrified. "No!" She laughed at herself. "Not yet, anyway, though it's a lovely offer." She noticed the spindle in his hand. "I'm assuming you want to see your father about whatever it is you're holding?"

Nodding, he asked, "Is he out back?"

"He is, and I know he'll be thrilled to see you. Especially since I'm pretty sure I heard cursing coming from that direction earlier."

Adam grinned as he headed into the backyard. His father had tackled some pretty difficult projects over the years, such as the armoire he'd built entirely from scratch. According to what his mother had just said, it sounded like a new project was in the works.

At the threshold of the wood shop, Adam poked his head in to make sure his father wasn't using power tools or anything that could cut off a finger, before he knocked on the door.

"Adam, it's good to see you." His mother was right—his father looked immensely relieved by the interruption as he moved away from his lathe. "I could use a beer. Do you want one?"

Opting not to point out that it was only early afternoon, Adam said, "Sure."

"What have you got there?" His father handed him the beer from the mini-fridge and took the spindle.

"It's from the big old house that you and I were looking at last week."

"I keep thinking about that place," his father said. "You don't see craftsmanship like this much anymore."

"How hard do you think it would be to find someone to do this kind of work that wouldn't break the bank? And is there even anyone out there who can handle doing it for an entire house?"

"I don't know for sure, but I can ask some guys who are much deeper into this kind of finish work than I am and get back to you." His father handed back the spindle. "Have you decided to buy the place, then?"

"Actually, a friend of mine bought the house."

"Is he thinking of keeping it?"

"She wouldn't dream of tearing it down."

Adam could see his father note with some surprise that the friend who'd bought the house was a woman. "Must be a woman who has a lot of vision, if she's not planning to tear it down the way most people would."

"She's got a ton of vision. More vision than anyone I've ever known." His father was now looking at him as if he'd grown a second head. His parents knew Adam had female friends, but they'd never heard him talk about one of them so passionately. "She's Rafe and Brooke's wedding planner. Kerry Dromoland."

Another flash of surprise flickered across his father's face. "I've heard great things about Ms. Dromoland."

"Everything you've heard is true. She's an exceptional wedding planner." Adam had promised Kerry that they'd keep their relationship a secret, but he trusted his father implicitly. "She's also the woman I mentioned to you the other day when we were looking at the house."

"If I recall correctly, you weren't sure the two of you were even friends yet."

"We are now." Adam struggled for a moment with how much to divulge, even to his father. "More than friends, actually. A hell of a lot more."

Adam hadn't been planning to come see his father today, hadn't been planning to tell him all about Kerry either. But now that he was here, he realized just how much he needed to discuss the situation with the man he respected most in the world.

"Rafe and Brooke asked me to meet with her a few weeks ago. They both had scheduling conflicts, but I'm pretty sure it was also a matchmaking attempt on their part, since they could have sent Mia or Mom instead of me. Anyway, during our first meeting, Kerry got to talking about a gazebo she wanted to have built on the beach for the wedding, and I offered to build it for her. Before I left the meeting, I asked her out, but she said no."

"She turned you down?" His father was grinning now, knowing how rarely a woman ever said no to Adam.

"Without a moment's hesitation. But I couldn't shake the sense that she was special, so I didn't give up. One thing led to another and—" No, he couldn't go any further with his explanations. Couldn't betray his intimate secrets with Kerry, not even to his father. "We're not officially dating, but we do see each other quite often."

His father nodded. "I see." And Adam could tell that he did, even though he didn't ask any clarifying questions about the whole not-dating-but-still-seeing-each-other thing.

"We both thought it would be easy to keep things clearly delineated. No complications, just two friends having a good time. After all, that's what we both wanted."

"Both of you?" His father looked more than a little doubtful. "We all love you, Adam, but you know we're not always crazy about the way you approach women and relationships."

"I know you're not, but there's never been anyone I wanted to have a real relationship with before. And Kerry, she's been waiting her whole life for the perfect guy, for someone she can count on no matter what. I know on paper that might not look like me, but—"

"But regardless of what your dating history looks like," his father finished for him, "if Ms. Dromoland doesn't know that she can count on you as a friend, then she doesn't know you very well."

"As a friend, I'm pretty sure she does know I'll always be there for her. But as more?" Adam walked to the doorway of his father's wood shop to look out at the oak tree in the backyard. It was big, but not quite as big as the one he and Kerry had just picnicked beneath. "When we first set up our...our arrangement...I told her she didn't have to worry about me falling for her. I promised her things wouldn't get messy. I said we would keep things simple, just two friends having fun." Adam appreciated his father holding his silence while he collected his thoughts. "But when we were over at the house today for lunch to celebrate her signing on the dotted line for it, I realized I wasn't just happy for her because she'd found her perfect house. The real reason I'm happy is because working on the house with her means we'll get to spend time together over the next year. A lot of time." His father joined Adam in the doorway as Adam laid it all on the line. "Before Kerry, I'd find any way I could to avoid entangling things with a woman. But now I'm going out of my way to find ways to tangle things up."

Now that Adam had started talking about Kerry, he

couldn't stop, couldn't find a way to stuff it all back in. "Seeing her is the best part of any day, the best thing that happens all week. I think about her all the time. I have to stop myself from showing up at her office and dragging her out to the park or for a sail or just to hang out doing nothing. Kerry shouldn't have been different. I wasn't expecting her to be different. Anyone but her, actually. But she is." By the time he finally finished talking, Adam realized Max was grinning at him.

"Look," his father said, "I'm not going to lie and say it's not terrifying. I'm not going to pretend it's not confusing as hell to feel something so strong that it rocks your world off its axis. Especially when it's something you might have thought you were never going to feel for anyone."

"We have an *arrangement*," Adam explained again. "One she's been really wed to." Just the way he'd been wed to it at first, too. It had seemed so perfect—getting to spend nights with a gorgeous woman who didn't want long term any more than he wanted it. "But then, somehow, somewhere along the line, things changed. And I don't want to stick to that arrangement any-more."

"Your whole life, when you've wanted to fix things," his father said in a serious voice, "you've fixed them. It's one of the reasons you're so good at what you do. Just as you've always known when something is so beautiful, so precious, that you can't possibly walk away without regretting it."

Max gave Adam a warm hug, one he was surprised to realize he'd really needed. Sometimes it didn't matter that you were a grown man with a hugely successful business—you needed to be reminded that the people who loved you most were there for you.

"I'm really looking forward to meeting her," his father said, "more than ever now. Friend or lover or girlfriend, however the two of you work things out, she'll always be welcome."

"You're going to love Kerry."

"I know we'll love her, because you do."

The truth of it hit Adam like a lightning bolt, and not from nearly as far out of the blue as he would have expected.

"You're right." He paused, reeling. "I'm in love with her." He let the word take hold in his head first...and then deep down in his heart. Right where Kerry had already gone. *"Love."* Amazingly, it didn't sound, or feel, as strange as he'd thought it would falling from his lips. "I love her."

His father was clearly beyond pleased, grinning ear to ear while he toasted Adam with his beer bottle. "So, now that you've got one big part of the equation figured out, what are you going to do about it?"

Maybe someone else would have given Adam

more time to get used to the idea of having done the impossible: actually falling in love. But the Sullivans weren't like other people, and when love struck, they didn't waste any time before they did whatever it took to make sure it lasted.

And hell, since he'd already gone and done what should have been impossible, how much bigger a leap was it to jump headfirst into crazy, too?

Adam grinned back, the answer as obvious now as his love for her. "I'm going to tell her."

He'd already been counting the hours until Thursday night, when he and Kerry were going to meet again. But now the anticipation was nearly going to kill him, because he couldn't wait to officially change the rules of their arrangement.

Adam Sullivan had finally fallen in love. And now that he had, there was not only no going back, there was also no one else he would ever love the way he loved Kerry.

She was his one. His only.

His *forever*.

CHAPTER NINETEEN

The following afternoon, Colleen was almost sparkling as she walked into the café where Kerry was meeting her for a cup of coffee. It had been so long since Colleen had looked happy—truly happy—that Kerry's heart filled with hope. Maybe her sister had finally turned the corner!

Kerry was really glad she'd moved her meetings around when Colleen had texted from out of the blue asking if they could have lunch. Two unplanned lunches in two days made Kerry's once perfectly rigid calendar look like a thing of the past, but it actually didn't bother her all that much. Not when she was feeling kind of sparkly herself lately.

"You look amazing," Kerry said when they hugged hello.

"I *feel* amazing." Colleen couldn't stop smiling as she sat down. The waiter came by and took their coffee orders, with Colleen adding a big piece of chocolate cake for them to share. "I swear this must be the best day of my life." She hugged herself. "Payton came back to me."

Kerry was so surprised that everything froze for a moment. Her brain. Her smile.

But especially her heart.

It was suddenly all too clear why Colleen was sparkling and filled with joy: The man she'd never gotten over had returned.

Kerry tried to find words, any words, to say to her sister. But she couldn't even seem to pry her lips apart at this point, not unless she wanted her sister to see her growling over Payton's return.

Fortunately, Colleen was too far over the moon to notice Kerry's reaction. "He was waiting on my front step last night with flowers. The most beautiful bouquet you've ever seen. He said he was sorry. So sorry that he ever hurt me. He said he's missed me every second we've been apart. He said he never stopped loving me, and then he begged me to forgive him." Colleen put her hand over her heart and sighed happily. "We weren't even inside the house and he said all of that. He couldn't wait another second to let me know that he's a changed man."

"Wow."

It was the best Kerry could do right then, but she knew she needed to do better. Adam had helped her with her sister enough times that now she found herself wishing he could be there with them again. Maybe he could have helped her figure out what to do and how she could possibly help her sister now. The strangers her sister met at bars had all been horrible, but Payton had never been much better. In fact, he was probably worse, because when he told Colleen he loved her, she believed him, and then she fell apart when he cheated on her repeatedly, stole from her, and then left her.

"What did you do?" Kerry finally managed. "What did you say?"

"You mean before or after we went inside and had the world's best make-up sex?" Colleen laughed, loudly enough that several other people in the coffee shop looked over and smiled at them. "I told him I'd never stopped loving him either." Colleen held out her hand, and Kerry finally saw the engagement ring. "We're going to Vegas tonight to get married."

"Tonight?"

Oh God, how could Kerry possibly talk her sister out of getting married when she had only a matter of hours?

"Sorry, sis," Colleen said with a shrug. "I know you probably want to throw us one of your fancy weddings, but that's never been my speed." And it was true that even as kids, her sister had never been the least bit interested in their mother's wedding business. "One of those Elvis-themed chapels is going to be *perfect*."

Kerry knew she had to be careful how she approached this situation, even more careful than she'd been before. "Are you sure you want to move so quickly? Maybe you could see how the next few weeks or months go, and then—"

"The way I feel about him isn't going to change." Colleen looked absolutely certain. "I've loved him from the first day. I'll love him until the last. So why should we wait?"

Because he doesn't seem to love you the same way!

It took all of Kerry's self-control not to blurt out the words that would, without a doubt, rip her sister away from her forever.

The chocolate cake came, and Colleen took a huge bite. "Got to get back some of those calories I burned last night. *All* night long, thank you very much. God, he's such an amazing lover. Better than ever before, actually, now that we're back together." She gestured to Kerry's fork. "You should eat some before I mow through the whole thing."

Kerry made herself pick up her fork, if for no other reason than to buy herself some time to figure out what to say. There had to be a way to get through to Colleen.

But before she could come up with any way to approach it that wouldn't have her sister throwing her fork at her and storming out of the café, Colleen said, "So, how's the hunk?"

Kerry froze again, this time with her fork halfway into the cake. "The hunk?"

Colleen rolled her eyes. "Oh, come on, don't play dumb with me and act like you don't know who I'm talking about."

If they were still as close as they'd once been when they were little girls, Kerry would have already told her sister all about Adam. About how happy he made her. About how he was teaching her how much fun it could be to actually *have* fun. And about how some-times...sometimes she found herself wanting more than just an *arrangement* of friends getting some sexy benefits with each other in a hotel once a week.

But ever since Colleen had first started dating Pay-ton, her sister had pulled away, and it had been a long time since they'd shared secrets.

Knowing it was by only the barest luck that her sister had been too self-involved to ask about *the hunk* before now, Kerry said, "Adam's fine."

"Fine?" Colleen took another huge bite of cake. "He looked a hell of a lot better than fine those two times I saw him. Just a few little details between sisters, that's all I'm asking for."

Knowing Colleen wouldn't stop pushing until she got something out of her, Kerry said, "We have fun together."

"Multiple-times-a-night fun, I hope. I mean, when a guy looks like he does."

Kerry knew the color taking over her cheeks was giving away just how true that was, even as she tried to shift directions by saying, "We're friends."

Her sister gave her a knowing look. "Friends who are clearly having slamming-hot sex." Colleen looked even more pleased when Kerry's blush confirmed it. "Good for you, finally letting go for once in your life. *And* with one of the hottest guys I've ever seen while you're at it!"

On the nights when Colleen had been drunk and said these kinds of things, Kerry had been able to blame it on the alcohol. But at noon on a Thursday in the middle of a crowded downtown café, she finally had to admit that Colleen truly thought she *was* uptight and boring.

"Now that you've hooked him in the sack," her sister continued, "we just have to figure out how to get him to declare his undying love for you and give you that ring I know you're longing for."

"I'm not longing for a ring!" Kerry shot back before she could moderate her tone. "I told you, we're just friends. The fact that we're having sex doesn't mean anything."

Colleen's eyebrows went up in surprise. "Wow,

look who finally got a backbone."

Kerry had to grit her teeth to keep from snarling.

"Look," Colleen said in a soothing tone, "I can see that you believe what you're saying, but the truth is— sex always means something. It's why I was so upset with Payton when he cheated on me. And it's also why I never slept with any of the guys at those bars."

Just as quickly as she'd fired up, Kerry felt herself deflate. She hadn't been surprised by all the talk about hot sex, but hearing this wisdom coming from her sister, who had been falling deeper and deeper down the rabbit hole these past few months? Honestly, it was almost as unexpected as Colleen's take on the importance of sex.

And then her sister surprised her yet again by putting her hand over Kerry's. "You're so in love with Adam. Anyone can see it in the dreamy expression on your face when you're talking about him. Anyone can hear it in the way you say his name, like it's the most beautiful word in the world." Colleen squeezed her hand. "Why won't you just admit it?"

Admit that she'd fallen in love with Adam?

Panic gripped Kerry like a vise, wrapping so tightly around her chest that she could barely breathe. "I'm not...I'm not in..."

She couldn't bring herself even to say the word *love*. Not when even that felt like too much of an admission.

"It's not a crime to fall in love, you know," Colleen said. "No matter what Mom always said. Just because her relationship with our father was bad doesn't mean that we should have to settle for boring sticks in the mud just to try to keep ourselves safe from heartache." Colleen looked into Kerry's eyes. "Forget what you've always been told. Forget what you've always thought you needed to do, the person you've always thought you needed to be. What do *you* want?"

"I just want to be happy."

"And does Adam make you happy?"

"He does." *So happy.* "But—"

"You're overthinking it all," Colleen said with a disappointed shake of her head. "Just can't get Mom's voice out of your head, can you?"

"It's not just Mom," Kerry said. How could she just leap and not worry about the fall? How could anyone? "I mean, you were so upset these past months, too."

"I know my relationship with Payton isn't perfect," Colleen admitted, "but I still love him, so of course I want to take him back and try again. And, honestly, I've never felt so happy in all my life. Don't you want to feel this good? Like you could fly? Like anything is possible? Like nothing could ever bring you down again?"

"Of course I do," Kerry told her sister. And the

truth was that she felt all of those things every time she was with Adam.

But the part of the equation that her sister was conveniently leaving off was—what if you were happy for a little while, and then later, it turned out to be only a fleeting happiness when the crash came and your heart was crushed into a million little pieces? Wouldn't that mean you'd been foolish to have placed all of your faith in that happiness?

Especially when Kerry not only knew enough about Adam's past to know what a huge risk it would be to give her heart to him, but she also knew precisely what he didn't want from his future. *"You're looking for forever with someone and I'm not,"* was what he'd flat-out said to her that day they'd agreed to meet at hotels for sexy fun. And then later, when she'd started to freak out about getting too close to him, he'd reminded her, *"We're both adults. It's not going to get messy."*

He was clearly a master at arrangements like theirs. Whereas she was the one in danger of making the mistake of letting her emotions tangle up with all the sex so that it started to look like love.

"He's here!"

Colleen's face lit up again, brighter than ever, as she leapt out of her seat. Kerry turned to see Payton walk through the door, smug as always in the knowledge that he had all the power.

He looked in no way regretful or apologetic. On the contrary, Kerry thought he looked more cocky than ever—now that he knew for sure he could screw around on her sister as much as he wanted and Colleen would wait for him whenever he decided to come back to her for a little while.

Kerry's fists curled beneath the tablecloth, and she had to work to shove down the fierce urge to punch him as he said, "Kerry, it's good to see you again."

Even though she knew how badly her sister wanted her to accept Payton back into their lives, Kerry simply couldn't lie and tell him anything about this situation was good. She wanted to drag him outside and tell him what a mess her sister's life had been for the past several months. She wanted to show him all the nasty bars Colleen had gotten drunk in. She wanted to introduce him to all of the creeps who could have hurt her sister. She wished she could show him just how deep the destruction he'd wrought had been.

Kerry was glad for her heels so that she was eye to eye with the jerk, and he wouldn't get to feel that he was towering over her. She had to forcefully unclench her teeth as she said, "Payton."

Thankfully, he was smart enough not to try to hug her, or even to shake her hand. But Colleen was so high up in the clouds that she didn't seem to notice any of the tension between her boyfriend—oh God, he was her fiancé now—and her sister.

"I was just telling Kerry how incredibly happy we are," Colleen told him. "So happy that we've decided to head to Vegas to make it official."

Payton smiled at Colleen. "You ready to go now, baby? I can't wait another second to make you mine."

"I'm more than ready." Colleen kissed him passionately in full view of everyone at the café.

"I'll pick us up a couple of coffees for the road while you say good-bye to your sister."

Kerry tried to smile back at her beaming sister. "I hope he's good to you, Colleen. I hope you'll be happy. That's all I want for you, too."

"I know." Her sister's smile suddenly fell away as her expression grew serious. In a soft voice that only Kerry could hear, Colleen said, "Thanks for all those nights you came to get me. Without you, I might have gotten into some really bad scrapes."

More than anything in the world, Kerry wanted to save her sister from another bad scrape. Quite possibly one of the worst of all—marrying someone who would never treat her right. Only, Kerry knew she couldn't save her sister this time. Just as Adam had said, Colleen would have to decide to save herself.

Which meant that there was nothing left for Kerry

to say, except for the one thing that would never change no matter how much friction there was between her and her sister. "I love you," she whispered.

"I love you, too, little sis."

And as they hugged, Kerry hoped her sister could hear everything she was forcing herself not to say aloud: *No matter what, no matter when, anytime you need me, all you have to do is call, and I'll be there.*

★ ★ ★

Kerry paid the bill for the coffee and cake, then went to the bathroom to splash some cold water on her face. It didn't help, unfortunately, and she still looked pale and shell-shocked by everything that had just happened. But she would have to find a way to put it all out of her head for a few hours, because she had some really important afternoon meetings.

A part of her wanted nothing more than to go to Adam's office and ask him to get in the car with her and speed to Las Vegas after her sister, to see if together they could figure out a way to stop the wedding.

But at the same time, the other part of her couldn't get Colleen's words out of her head. *"You're so in love with Adam. Anyone can see it in the dreamy expression on your face when you're talking about him. Anyone can hear it in the way you say his name, like it's the most beautiful word in the world. Why won't you just admit it?"*

Kerry's brain—and heart—were whirling around and around, faster and faster, as she stepped out of the café. Three and a half weeks ago, everything had seemed so clear. Until Adam Sullivan had come into her life and everything had started changing from one smile, one kiss, one night in his arms to the next.

Just then, her phone rang with her mother's ring tone. Kerry already had a splitting headache, probably from gritting her teeth so hard while trying not to punch out Payton. But that was no excuse not to pick up her mother's call. Especially when Kerry knew exactly why she was calling.

"Have you talked to your sister?" her mother said without preamble.

"Yes, we just spoke."

"I'm beside myself," her mother said. "Absolutely beside myself."

Kerry could already hear that her usually unflappable mother did indeed seem to be coming unglued. "Mom," she began, even though she wasn't sure what to say to make everything better, "I know how worried you are, but—"

"But nothing! After all he did to her, now she's going back to him? I tried to talk some sense into her, but she refused to listen to me. She's always listened to you, Kerry. You need to talk to her, tell her not to walk back into the arms of a man who has already proved that he can never be faithful."

Kerry knew better than to take sides, especially if Payton was going to be in Colleen's life for a while. She wouldn't lose her sister over him. But she couldn't upset her mother, either. For so many months she'd been teetering on a tightrope by covering for Colleen's dangerously wild Friday nights. Knowing the tightrope had just become even higher and thinner made her head throb so hard she felt sick.

"From the conversation we just had," Kerry said as gently as she could, "it sounds like she's made up her mind. But she knows we're here for her if she ever needs us."

"You're right. She's a lost cause. His hold over her is too big. Too strong. But, please, Kerry," her mother said in a desperate voice, "please promise me you'll never make the mistake your sister's making. I knew the first time I met Payton that he was trouble. He's had too many women. Had too much of a reputation. Just like your father." Her mother didn't say, *Just like Adam Sullivan*, but Kerry swore she could hear the words anyway. "Heartbreak is all men like that have to give. Promise me you'll keep being smart and sensible and wait for a nice man to come along. Promise me!"

Kerry's head was pounding so hard, and her chest was so tightly constricted that she was having trouble taking a full breath. Her mother's plea to *promise me you'll never make the mistake your sister's making* was getting all tangled up in her head with Colleen's admission that *I know my relationship with Payton isn't perfect, but I still love him, so I have to go back.*

In their family, so much pain had come from—and would likely continue to come—in the name of *love*. Before Adam, Kerry wouldn't have understood how her sister could go back to her ex the way she had. But now that Adam had shown her such joy and pleasure, she could see all too clearly just how easy it would be to fall into the trap Colleen was in.

The easiest thing in the world if it meant you could have a few extra precious days or weeks of pure happiness—even when you could see that a horrible fall was up ahead.

Kerry hadn't wanted to look too closely at any of her recent meet-ups with Adam. But she could no longer deny the awful truth that she'd been burying her head in the sand for far too long. She'd just wanted to let herself enjoy and appreciate it. Now, she finally forced herself to take out the microscope and face what had actually happened.

Things had probably started going off track on their very first night together, when he'd effortlessly made her feel so good. But it was the night they'd spent on her couch having pizza and watching a movie, rather than keeping to hot sex in hotels, that had truly started to knock away at the clear-cut boundaries they'd set up. At which point she'd doubled down on her mistakes by going to his house to be together—and then tripled down by staying the night curled up against him. Even when she'd tried to be smart and pull back, she'd simply been unable to resist dancing with him at the wedding, forgetting about everything but him for those few precious minutes in his arms.

So many times she'd had a chance to stop herself from going too deep and taking things too far, and each time she'd completely blown it. But none more so than the night she'd waited for him to come "home" from his late night on the job, as if they were a real couple. Just because their temporary home for the night had been a hotel didn't make it any different. Because when he'd finally come to their suite and found her asleep at the table, then carried her to the bed and made the sweetest love imaginable to her? Well, there were no words to describe their connection that night other than *making love.*

Kerry's stomach twisted as she finally accepted that, somewhere along the way, she'd let Adam become far more to her than just a friend with benefits.

So much more.

"Kerry, are you still there?" her mother asked.

Kerry opened her mouth, but no words came out at first. Only something that sounded more like a choked sob. "Yes, I'm still here."

"I know you can't control what Colleen does, and I can't either," her mother said. "But I just can't stand the thought of both of my daughters being hurt the way I was. I can't stand to see you go through what I went through, honey."

Kerry's tongue felt like crumbling cardboard in her mouth, and her vocal cords felt as though they were being strangled shut. But she knew she had to get out the words that her mother needed to hear.

"I promise." Kerry's voice didn't sound like her own. "I promise I won't make a mistake with a man like him."

And there was only one way to make sure she didn't. Tonight, when she and Adam met at another hotel, she was going to have to do the one thing she'd been trying to convince herself didn't need to happen: She was going to end their arrangement.

She'd be brave enough to do it face-to-face, and she would also make sure he knew that they'd absolutely continue to be friends and work on the wedding and the house, just as they'd previously discussed. But they wouldn't meet to have sex again.

And she wouldn't keep falling harder and harder for him with every kiss, every touch, every moment she spent lying in his arms, wishing she could stay right there with him forever.

CHAPTER TWENTY

Adam figured he should have been nervous about seeing Kerry tonight, considering he was about to declare his love for her. Instead, he couldn't stop grinning, nerves the furthest thing from his mind.

Everything that had happened between the two of them since the day they'd met—even the fact that Rafe and Brooke had picked her as their wedding planner out of all the wedding planners in Seattle—all of it now made sense.

He and Kerry had been meant to meet and fall in love. He had never even come close to falling for any of the other women he'd been with, because he'd been waiting for her.

And she'd been waiting for him, too. He was absolutely sure of it.

After all, when two people had as strong a connection as they'd had from the first moment they'd so much as looked at each other, there was no way in hell that they were supposed to be with anyone else.

Adam had always been fully supportive of his cousins and siblings who'd fallen in love, but he'd never truly understood how strong that love could be. It took you over, body, mind, and soul, but you weren't just totally okay with it, you were downright psyched to have found such powerful, real love.

Not to mention the fact that in-love sex was so freaking hot.

Who would have thought?

Adam was still grinning as he walked into the lobby of the hotel, mulling over the only remaining big decision for the night: Should he tell Kerry he was in love with her before or after they went upstairs and ripped off each other's clothes? Although, since telling her he loved her before, during, *and* after all sounded good, he figured there was really no point in trying to decide now, was there?

Turning to look out the big front windows to the sidewalk, his heartbeat immediately kicked up as he saw a flash of long dark hair and legs that went on forever beneath a soft pink dress. His grin widened as she stepped inside the building.

"Kerry." Damn, he loved her name. Loved saying it in public—and when they were making love and he couldn't get enough of her. Loved knowing that as long as he didn't screw everything up, one day there'd be *Sullivan* after it.

As soon as she heard her name and their eyes met, she stopped short. A couple behind her would have run her down if Adam hadn't pulled her out of their path and into his arms.

"Adam." She swallowed hard as she blinked up at him. Her eyes were huge in her face, and she looked pale.

"What's wrong?" But it wasn't hard for him to guess. "Is it Colleen?"

Her face crumpled. "Her ex came back, the one who cheated on her and drove her nearly crazy for the past few months. They're getting married in Las Vegas tonight. At some Elvis-themed chapel. She sprang it on me today at a café just down the street."

"Jesus." He stroked her hair as he brought her closer. He wished she'd called him instead of bottling it up until now, but he understood that sometimes you needed some time to process things before you called in the support team. It was the same reason he'd waited until yesterday to speak with his father about Kerry—because he'd needed to turn the situation around and around inside his own head until he figured out how to frame it with words. "You've had a hell of a day, haven't you?"

She took a step back so that she wasn't quite in the circle of his arms anymore. "I suppose it's better than the chances she was taking every Friday night at those awful bars. But he hurt her so badly when he left before that all I can do is worry about how hard she's going to be hit when he does it again."

Not *if* Colleen's ex screwed her around again. *When.*

Adam knew better than to try to stand up for the guy, especially considering he'd never met him. But he also hated knowing that Kerry was so torn up over her sister's decision. "You've always been there for her. If something does happen, you've got to trust that she knows you'll be there for her again." *And so will I,* he added silently.

Kerry's eyes rose to meet his, and for a moment he was glad to see her relax slightly. "That's what I told her."

Adam couldn't wait for everyone in his family to meet Kerry. They were going to love her just as much as he did, not least because she was as devoted to family as they all were.

A waiter walked by with a tray of cocktails, and Kerry said, "Do you mind if we get a drink first before going upstairs?"

He'd been planning to head straight to the suite with her the way they always had before, but she was still so tense. A few minutes sipping a drink was probably a good idea. A good prelude to the champagne he'd promised to drink from her skin, anyway.

"As long as you don't try to convince me to drink anything with the words *lemon* or *drop* in it," he teased.

The way her lips remained in a tight line instead of curving up before bantering with him the way she usually did told him just how much her sister's decision to get back together with her ex had thrown her. He put his hand on the small of her back and led them both over to the hotel's cocktail bar.

"Adam."

Adam was surprised to see his cousin Drake heading their way. "Kerry, it looks like one of my cousins from New York is here."

She turned, and when she followed his gaze, her eyes widened. "Are you talking about the guy who's even better looking than you are? He's your cousin?"

"If you're talking about the one who's *almost* as good-looking as I am," Adam said, "then yes, that's him."

His cousin gave him a hug, then immediately turned the charm Kerry's way as he held out his hand. "I'm Drake Sullivan, and it is a sincere pleasure to meet you."

"Kerry Dromoland."

"What are you doing in Seattle, Drake?" Adam asked. "And why didn't any of us know about your trip west?"

"My agent arranged a last-second meeting with the

museum for an installation they're working on. They've been having trouble getting the details exactly right."

His cousin was clearly irritated by this fact, and Adam forced himself not to razz him over it. Heck, he was just as much a perfectionist about the buildings he worked on as Drake was about his paintings.

Adam suddenly remembered, "This is the exhibition Will and Sebastian twisted your arm into doing, isn't it?"

When Drake nodded, with a side of snarl, this time Adam did laugh out loud. Will Franconi and Sebastian Montgomery were two of the five billionaires who ran The Maverick Group. They were not only frequent investors in various Sullivan businesses—including several of Smith Sullivan's movies—but they had also become good friends with Adam's family over the years.

Adam knew right when Kerry realized who she was talking to—the painter who had been called the "leader of a new generation" by *The New York Times*. "Oh. Wow. Your paintings are amazing. Truly, one of my goals is to be able to afford one someday. I should have connected the dots earlier, especially since I'm planning Rafe and Brooke's wedding and they gave me the rundown on everyone in your family. I know it's no excuse, but it's been a crazy day and my brain is a bit frazzled. I hope you'll forgive me."

"If you'll let me buy you a drink," Adam's way-too-charming cousin said with an answering smile, "all is forgiven."

Adam always liked spending time with his cousins, but not when they were hitting on *his* girl. "Shouldn't you be heading off for your important meeting at the museum?"

Drake shrugged as if that meeting barely mattered anymore. "I was planning to have a drink before I headed over anyway."

"Adam and I were about to have a drink, too," Kerry said. "And I'm sure you two want to catch up, so that sounds great."

Adam again put his hand on the small of Kerry's back before his cousin could swoop in, but as they headed into the bar, it wasn't jealousy that was hitting him hardest. It was the fact that it had started to feel as though Kerry was using both the drink and time with his cousin to avoid being alone with him for as long as possible tonight.

But that didn't make sense. Not when the last time he'd seen her, they'd been having a picnic beneath the big oak tree and things had never felt better. So good, in fact, that he'd finally realized he was in love with her.

"So," Drake said to Kerry after they'd found an

empty booth and ordered, "how did you two meet? Something to do with Rafe and Brooke's wedding? Or did you already know each other?"

The question was innocent enough, pretty much what anyone would have asked after seeing Kerry and Adam walking into the popular cocktail bar together. But by the way Kerry flushed, he knew she didn't see it that way. All because they had a suite waiting for them upstairs, one of many they'd made secret love in throughout the city.

"We didn't know each other beforehand," Kerry replied. "But Adam is helping to build a gazebo on the beach for the wedding, which I really appreciate."

"Am I getting in the way of you two getting down to business?"

Adam was about to say yes when Kerry said, "No. We've actually finished planning the gaz—" If she was trying to make it look like this was a business meeting, she stopped herself a little too late. She picked up the drink that had just been delivered and gulped half of it down.

Where was his calm and collected wedding planner? Had Colleen's news really thrown her off this much? Was being seen together by one of his relatives freaking her out?

Or was something else going on?

"Kerry and I hit it off when we started working on

the gazebo," Adam told his cousin. "So well, in fact, that I'm now also working with her to restore a house she just purchased."

"Right, the house!" Kerry put in gratefully. "We always need to meet to talk about the house." As if she realized that she was acting a little strangely, she quickly asked Drake, "Am I remembering right that you have three siblings?"

"A sister and two brothers," he confirmed.

"How's everyone doing?" Adam asked as he reached for Kerry's hand under the table.

"Same as always," Drake said. "Alec is busy building his planes, Suzanne is busy with her computers, and Harrison is busy with his academic research."

"I'm really looking forward to meeting all of them at the wedding," Kerry said. "Although I keep thinking my biggest job all weekend is going to be keeping everyone's names straight between your relatives in San Francisco, Seattle, New York, and Maine."

Drake laughed. "We Sullivans definitely know how to take over a country, that's for sure. I'll put in a vote for name tags," he joked, "and that way I won't forget any names, either." His phone rang then, and even though he clearly wanted to ignore it, he said, "I'm sorry, I need to take this."

As soon as his cousin stepped away from the table, Kerry pulled her hands from Adam's and said, "He thinks we're a couple."

"The way he was flirting with you makes me wonder if he does."

But she shook her head. "You've got to tell him we aren't. You've got to tell him we really were just meeting to talk about the plans for my house. Otherwise, he might say something to someone in your family, and then they'll—"

"Sorry about that."

Drake sat down, cutting Kerry off before Adam could find out what exactly she thought his family would do if they thought he was dating Rafe's wedding planner.

A beat later, Kerry slid from her seat. "Thank you for the drink. It really was lovely to meet you, Drake, but I'm sure you two would like to catch up without me before your meeting." She was talking too fast, her cheeks too flushed, her eyes looking everywhere but at Adam. "I've actually got to head out now to take care of some business I forgot about, so, Adam, I think it would be best if we rescheduled our meeting for another time."

"Kerry—" He was already halfway out of his seat when she put up her hand to stop him.

"No." She swallowed hard. "I really can't stay." Her skin flushed an even deeper rose as she shook her head. "Not tonight." And then she was spinning around on her sky-high heels and heading out of the bar in a flash of long legs and silky hair.

Drake looked from Kerry's retreating back to Adam. "What the hell is going on with you two? At first I thought you were an item, but now I'm getting some pretty mixed messages."

Hard-core frustration rode Adam as he said, "It's complicated right now."

But hopefully it wouldn't be for long. Because even if she'd just said she didn't want to talk to him tonight, he wasn't planning to wait. Still, he couldn't forget her request. Couldn't ignore how serious she'd looked as she made it.

"Look, Drake, I'd appreciate it if you could keep seeing Kerry and me together to yourself for now."

His cousin raised an eyebrow. "So you're not a couple?"

They were. She just didn't know it yet.

Instead of answering Drake's question, Adam threw some money down on the table. And when Drake said, "Good luck," it was clear that he thought Adam was going to need it.

CHAPTER TWENTY-ONE

What had she been thinking?

The question kept running through Kerry's head, over and over and over again, while she sat in the back of the cab that took her back to her house. Normally, she appreciated the peace and quiet of her home—but when she stepped inside tonight, she didn't feel at all relaxed.

How could she relax the slightest bit when she knew this wasn't even close to being the end of a day that had begun badly and gotten worse by the second? Though she'd left him sitting with his cousin in the hotel's cocktail bar, Adam Sullivan wasn't the kind of man who did what someone else told him to do when he didn't agree with it.

And it had been perfectly clear to her that he hadn't wanted her to leave.

It was bad enough that she had to break things off with him. But to run into his cousin in the hotel lobby and have Drake clearly think they were a couple right before she did it?

Had she really thought there would be no tears shed for Adam Sullivan? What a fool she'd been...

She closed her front door behind her and put her head in her hands. There was no point in locking it, she knew. Not when—

Adam's knock came at the same time as he said, "Kerry, let me in."

As she turned to open the door, she couldn't stop herself from bracing as if for battle. And from the look on Adam's face, he was clearly itching for one.

She decided not to pretend nothing was wrong. There was no point even trying to do that with Adam when he was one of the most direct people she'd ever known.

"I know you're angry with me." The second she'd asked him to explain to his cousin that they weren't really a couple, she'd seen the frustration move across his face. Frustration that seemed to have amped up several levels since then.

Now, she struggled to make herself say the words she needed to say. *It's over. We can't do this anymore. It's been fun, but I can't get in any deeper with you.*

But none of them would come, even though he was walking inside and closing her door behind him. The sound was loud enough with her already brittle nerves to make her jump.

He looked worried, then frustrated again as he ran a hand through his hair. "I'm not angry with you, Kerry. I'm angry with the whole damned situation. With continuing to play this game."

Finally, her tongue came unstuck. "It's not a game, it's an agreement. An agreement we made together."

"Call it whatever you want," he said as his brows came down low over his dark eyes, "we need to change it."

Surprise came first—surprise that he'd want to change what she'd assumed would be most guys' perfect arrangement with a willing woman.

And then, close on its heels, came longing. A desperate longing to have a real relationship with Adam.

But then, a beat later, panic swept in. Panic that gripped her just as tightly as longing did.

"No." She needed to take a step back from him, needed to have more space between them to be able to say, "We can't change it."

Even as his frown deepened at her refusal, she watched stubborn determination light in his beautiful eyes. Eyes that she'd felt were seeing all the way into her when they were making love and he was taking her to places she'd never even dreamed existed.

"Yes," he said in just as firm a tone as her *no* had been. "We sure as hell can change it. We don't need to sneak around anymore. We don't need to pretend to my family—or yours—that we're not an important part of each other's lives. We don't need to do things like ask my cousin not to tell anyone that he saw us together, or have you jump out of my arms when your mother finds us dancing."

"Why are you saying this? Why would you want this?"

"Kerry." He moved closer again, reaching out to stroke her cheek. "You know why. You know why I want to take a chance on you. Because you want to take a chance on me, too."

"No." Her voice sounded strangled as she repeated the two-letter word. "My mother took a chance on a guy like you and ended up all alone with two babies. My sister took a chance on a guy like you and drank herself into worse and worse situations every weekend until he finally deigned to come back home to her for a little while."

"Do you really think I'm like those guys?" He looked disgusted by the thought. "Don't you know me at all by now?"

"Of course I know you, Adam. You're a great person. You're a great friend. But you'll never be relationship material. *You* were the one who was totally clear with me from the first moment about not wanting a relationship. About not wanting a girlfriend, or God forbid, a wife."

"Well, maybe I've changed my mind!"

"Maybe?" His voice had boomed out across her foyer, where they were still standing, but so did hers as she shot the word back at him and whirled out of his arms. "That's exactly why I've tried to be so careful not to fall in love with you. Because I refuse to ever be any man's *maybe!*"

He reached for her again, even as she moved farther away. "I said the wrong word, Kerry."

"No, you said exactly what you think. What you feel. And I'm glad you did, because I've never wanted the two of us to lie to each other."

"Then we'd better not lie about this."

Before she could blink or breathe or move, he kissed her again. And then again and again, until her head was spinning from the taste and feel and wonder of him.

When he finally dragged his mouth from hers, his voice was raw as he said, "There's no *maybe* about the heat between us."

She stared into his eyes, dilated to an even darker brown now, and admitted, "I know." But focusing on the ridiculous amounts of heat they'd always generated together wouldn't help get them back on level ground. So she made herself push the heat back, and bring the prudence that she'd always lived her life by until meeting Adam back into the forefront again.

"Meeting your cousin at the hotel tonight really drove home the point that things can't be weird between us at the wedding next week. So I think it's for the best that we end things as friends. Friends who had great sex for a little while. But in the end, just friends. And since you'll be heading up to the lake this weekend to work on the gazebo, it's probably best if we just end that part of our relationship now."

He didn't say anything for a few long moments, and she thought that maybe he would let her go. And then she could shut the door behind him and let the tears she was holding back fall for everything she was making herself give up in the name of protecting her heart.

"I am your friend, Kerry. I'll always be your friend." He tightened his hold on her. "But I'm also in love with you."

Oh God, how could she have been more wrong? He hadn't been planning to let her go. Instead, he'd planned to pull out every card he could possibly play.

Even the last-resort love card.

"You don't—" Her heart wasn't beating right, and her breath couldn't quite make it in and out of her lungs. "You don't love me."

"Yes, I do. I love you, Kerry. I was planning to tell you tonight. Not like this, though. I was going to tell you when we were up in our suite, with champagne, when I thought everything was going to be perfect. And when I thought—" It was the first time she'd ever seen him look even the slightest bit vulnerable. "I thought you were going to say it back to me. I thought this was going to be our new beginning."

Again, she could barely find words, couldn't manage anything but shaking her head and saying, "I'm sorry."

"Don't be sorry, just love me back, damn it!" The force behind his words hit her so hard she was surprised she didn't fly back into the living room. "You do love for a living. How can you not know? Can you really not see? And are you really still that scared that I'll turn out to be like your father or like Colleen's boyfriend?"

She wanted to tell him she wasn't scared. But that wasn't true, so she told him what was. "I'm just being realistic."

"How the hell do you call refusing to believe that I love you realistic?"

"What you think you're feeling for me right now—it will fade. And when it does, you'll still be the man who told me flat-out that he's not looking for forever with anyone."

"I wasn't looking for forever. But then I met you and everything changed. You've got to believe me. You just said it—I've never lied to you."

So much of what he was saying *was* making sense. And yet, what if she let herself believe that the re-formed rake was real—and then it turned out that his declarations tonight were simply coming from a thwarted urge to claim her in front of his cousin? Or were the crazy-hot hormones from their kiss talking? Or was it simply the fact that she was the only woman who had ever challenged or said no to him?

When she didn't say anything—all her thoughts were way too jumbled to be able to straighten them out into words—he said, "I know you've never lied to me, so I'm just going to ask you one more question tonight. Do you love me, Kerry?"

She swallowed hard. It had all seemed so simple at first. They were just going to have sex. It was going to be fun and exciting. And mean *nothing*.

But *nothing* had turned into *everything* from their very first kiss. From the first time he'd held her in his arms. From the first time she'd looked into his dark, intense eyes and been helpless to look away.

She couldn't stop her tears from falling. "Maybe." More tears fell, fast and hot down her cheeks. "Maybe," she said again, the only word she could get out.

He'd never touched her more gently than when he wiped away her tears, smiled down at her, and said softly, "You're not a *maybe* kind of woman. Just the way you once told me I'm not a maybe kind of man."

Her brain was in tangles, and her heart was in tatters. Still, she tried to hold on to the one thing she'd promised herself, and Adam, that they wouldn't ruin.

"Are we—" It was hard to talk past the tears clogging her throat. "Are we still friends?"

"Yes." He didn't pause, didn't need to think about it for even a split second. "Always."

Relief flooded her. Relief that she hadn't ruined everything after all.

"I'll always be your friend, too," she told him. "Always."

And as they stood facing each other in her foyer, it finally hit her that they'd had their last time together already…and she hadn't even known it. Hadn't had a chance to savor every last moment in his arms.

Regret swamped her. Regret so strong it was like a physical pain slamming straight into the center of her chest.

Just weeks ago, she'd found herself standing in front of him and saying, *One night.* Now—too soon— she found herself saying, "One last time."

She was too lost in her own emotions to be able to read his clearly. But he didn't keep her guessing for long, not when his arms were around her by the time she took her next breath—which he promptly stole from her with a kiss that made her knees buckle. And just as he'd always been before, he was right there to catch her. He swept her up into his arms, his mouth never leaving hers, not for a single second, as he carried her into her bedroom and stripped away their clothes.

Their kisses never stopped as he sent her reeling first with his hands, and then came over her and drove her up so high she would have been gasping for oxygen if she hadn't been able to take it straight from his lungs.

Never again would she know this pleasure.

Never again would she know the sweet sensation of his mouth on hers.

Never again would she feel his hands molding her curves as if he were sculpting them.

Never again would she look up to see him above her in bed, his eyes going darker and darker as he took them both higher and higher.

Never again would he tangle his fingers in her hair as he kissed her while fireworks exploded between them.

Never again would she fall asleep in his arms, warm and safe and impossibly happy.

Never, ever again...

★ ★ ★

Adam had heard every word Kerry had said before she told him she wanted *one last time* with him. But he couldn't believe any of them. Wouldn't let himself believe she meant them.

They couldn't be ending everything right when they'd just begun. Even if she was utterly certain it had to be so. Even if she had a reason, an argument for everything. Not even if her reasons and arguments made sense.

Some things didn't make sense, but that didn't mean they weren't right. It didn't mean they weren't meant to be.

And it didn't mean they shouldn't last forever and ever. Past that, even.

Adam had refused to let himself memorize her with his hands as they made love. He hadn't let himself drink in her scent as if it were the very last time he'd ever be this close to her again. He'd fought the desperation to take her again and again so that she'd be left with the imprint of his body on hers, in hers.

Because this wasn't *the end*, damn it.

Tonight he'd hoped—assumed—that he could convince her to change their arrangement. He'd thought that tonight would be the night when she'd officially become his girlfriend and he'd be her boyfriend. He'd thought that when he said the words *I love you* that he'd immediately hear her saying them back to him.

But he'd never been so off base, never miscalculated so badly before. And now he needed to regroup, needed to figure out what the hell to do next, so that she would come back to him. Come back and see just how much she meant to him.

See that she was absolutely *everything* that mattered.

In the aftermath of their wild yet sweet lovemaking, Kerry was warm and soft as he held her. It was tempting to use this moment when her defenses were down to try to convince her to change her mind again. But one of the things he loved so much about her was how well she knew her own mind. She was stubborn, just like him. It wasn't easy to be rational right now, but he knew that if their positions had been reversed, the one sure way to make him run would be to push him.

So he wouldn't push, at least not tonight. He'd force himself out of her arms. He'd make himself put his clothes back on. He'd order his legs and feet to walk out of her door as if their arrangement had actually ended tonight the way she'd told him she wanted it to.

But, damn it, he wasn't giving up. Because he couldn't give up on the biggest love he'd ever found in his life.

The biggest love he'd *ever* find.

CHAPTER TWENTY-TWO

Friday

Adam was the only one not paired off at his parents' dinner table. His father—and his mother, who he could see had been filled in on the situation with Kerry—had clearly been disappointed that she wasn't with him.

They hadn't had to ask him how things had gone with declaring his love to her, not when he knew his haggard expression gave him away. He hadn't slept a single second of the night after he'd left her bed. How could he, when he'd practically had to chain himself up to keep from heading right back to her?

As he watched Ian with Tatiana, Mia with Ford, Dylan with Grace and Mason, and his mother with his father, Adam saw even more clearly what he'd found in Kerry. Not just a beautiful woman. Not just an intelligent friend who always kept him on his toes. Not just a lover who rocked his world. But his other half. The person who made him whole.

None of the other women he'd dated had even a

tenth of Kerry's substance. Her strength. Or her capacity to love. No wonder he'd never believed he'd have forever. None of the women he'd dated had been forever women.

Not until Kerry.

During dinner, his family had been talking about Rafe and Brooke's upcoming wedding and how good it would be to see everyone. Finally, he remembered to tell them, "I ran into Drake last night."

"He's already in Seattle?" Mia asked, clearly surprised.

"Not for the wedding. For a museum show. Sounds like they weren't hanging or lighting his paintings to his satisfaction."

"Artists," Ian said with a grin. "They're so picky about having everything just the way they want it."

Tatiana grinned back at him. "And aren't you lucky we never give up until we get exactly what we want?"

"So lucky," he agreed, kissing her to back up his words.

Normally, this was where Adam would groan and roll his eyes and tell them to get a room. When he didn't, even Mia looked worried.

Mason started fussing right then, and Adam decided he owed the kid one. "I'll take him outside," he said as he reached for Grace and Dylan's son. "Want to count the stars with me, kid?" Mason stopped fussing and held out his little arms.

Adam and Mason had just made it out to the grass and had turned to look up at the sky when his father stepped up beside them and said, "Any chance you need another star counter?"

Little Mason loved his grandfather and gave Max Sullivan a happy smooch. For a long while, the three of them stood in silence beneath the bright lights dotting the dark blue above.

"If Kerry's the one," his father finally said to Adam, "fight for her."

"I'm planning on fighting with everything I have."

His father's arm came strong and warm across his shoulders. With a squeeze, he took Mason from Adam's arms and left him standing alone in the middle of the backyard that he'd grown up in. Alone with thoughts that grew clearer, more focused, and more determined by the second.

Just as he'd been totally focused on getting Kerry to see him again after the first time they'd met, now he had an even bigger purpose: He wasn't just going to convince her to start dating him again—he was going to convince her to marry him, damn it, no matter what it took. And given that they were both going to be at the lake for his brother's romantic wedding, the universe was clearly handing him the chance of a lifetime.

★ ★ ★

Saturday

Everything at the wedding Kerry was putting on at the top of the Sky View Observatory was going like clockwork, thankfully. The newly married couple was very rich and very exacting, and she'd been working her tail off for months to make sure nothing fell through the cracks.

She'd barely been able to sleep since Thursday night, when Adam had loved her *one last time* and then left her with a good-bye kiss so sweet that she could have sworn it was still lingering on her lips. But even though she should have been exhausted, she felt totally wired and had been glad for such a big and detail-heavy wedding to force her brain to hold focus on something other than Adam.

At least, she shouldn't have been thinking about him, shouldn't have been missing his voice, his smile, his touch the entire time. From the vows and the first kiss, from the cutting of the wedding cake to the moment the band played the first bars of the first dance.

In a heartbeat, as the music began to play, Kerry was immediately swept back to another wedding. To another first dance. And all she could do was wish that Adam would magically walk through the doors, pull her into his arms, and sweep her onto the dance floor.

She didn't realize she'd stood frozen for the entire song until someone jostled her on their way to the dance floor. Hoping no one realized that she'd checked out for the past five minutes, she got back to work.

But no matter how much she tried to push it down, the soul-deep longing for Adam never went away.

★ ★ ★

Sunday

"Thank you for meeting with me today, Ms. Dromoland."

Kerry's mother inclined her head slightly and smiled as she chose a bench beneath a leafy tree and sat, looking out at the blue water sparkling in front of them. "This park has always been one of my favorite places to be on a warm afternoon such as this."

Adam smiled as he sat beside her. "It's one of my favorite places, too."

But Aileen Dromoland didn't smile back as she turned her gaze from the water to him. "I'm assuming you've asked me here to discuss Kerry."

He looked her straight in the eyes and didn't waste one second before telling her, "I love your daughter."

"Any man with half a brain would love my daughter," she said, her expression not having shifted at all despite his profession of love. "But few would *deserve* to love her."

"I agree," he said without any hesitation. Kerry's mother raised an eyebrow, but let him continue. "I know I have a long way to go to deserve Kerry's love, but I'm not just going to *try* to be good enough for her. I'm going to *be* good enough."

In just a few weeks, he'd learned so much, so quickly, about love. It wasn't enough just to try, to hope, to wish. Love meant laying every single thing out on the line and trusting that the other person would lay everything out, too. Without fear. And without regret.

"How exactly are you planning to do that?"

"By always putting Kerry first. By always respecting her. By always appreciating her. By always sharing everything with her. And never, ever hurting her."

Emotion flickered in Aileen's eyes, emotion that looked to Adam like a combination of past pain resurfacing—and, possibly, if he was lucky, the first beginnings of new hope for the future.

"If you are expecting me to talk to Kerry and present your case to her—"

"That's not why I'm here." He'd present his own case to Kerry, damn it. And he'd shower her with so much love that she'd never again be able to doubt how he felt about her. "I'm here because any mother who cares about her daughter as much as you love Kerry deserves to know how much she's loved."

Aileen looked out at the water for a few moments, and Adam followed her gaze. A small tugboat was dragging in an enormous barge. It should have been impossible for something so small to be so strong, but Adam now knew that the smallest things—like a simple word with only four letters, for example—could be the strongest force in the entire world.

"If you love her so much, then why did she break up with you?"

Yet again, he didn't hesitate to tell the truth. "Because I was an idiot."

Aileen looked at him with surprise. "Did you just admit you made a mistake?"

"More than one," he said, nodding.

"And Kerry? Did she make any mistakes with you?"

"Almost as many as I have."

This time she didn't look shocked. Instead, her lips seemed to be twitching at the corners. "Are you really sitting here telling me that both of you acted like idiots?"

He grinned, knowing his instincts about Kerry's mother had been spot-on. Her elegance and self-control might make her seem slightly cold and forbidding at first glance, but beneath that veneer she was clearly as warm as her daughter. "Pretty much."

A flash of a smile moved across Aileen's face, but just as quickly, it fell away. "Last week, my other daughter made a personal decision that I found extremely difficult to accept. So difficult that I asked— begged, actually—Kerry to make me a promise to be careful so that she would never put herself in the same terrible position as Colleen. But now—" For the first time, Kerry's mother looked her age. "Now I'm wondering if I might have gotten things wrong."

"I suspect there are very few things you've ever gotten wrong."

She studied him for a few moments, and he could see where Kerry came by not only her beauty, but her intelligence, her strength, and her compassion, as well. "I'd like to think there aren't too many," she finally said, "but you've certainly surprised me. And I'm not surprised very often anymore. Particularly when it comes to love and relationships."

"Your husband," Adam had to tell her, "was a fool to have left the three of you."

"Yes," Kerry's mother agreed with a little catch in her voice, "he was. A terrible fool. And I was an even bigger one for not seeing it until it was too late. But then—" She quickly pulled herself back together. "I wouldn't have traded him for anything if it meant not having my girls. They mean absolutely everything to me."

"I would do anything for my family, too."

Again, Kerry's mother studied him, so closely that he wondered if she was actually trying to read his mind. "I can see why you grew on Kerry. Despite your devil-may-care reputation, family is clearly important to you. It doesn't hurt, of course, that you aren't hard on the eyes. But I've never known Kerry to be swayed by a pretty face. If anything, I'm going to guess that she was harder on you for it."

He laughed out loud at that extremely accurate statement and held out his hands. "I'm pretty sure she only let me off the hook because I had nothing to do with the way my face is put together. That's entirely down to my parents."

"I met your mother and father many years ago. I believe they were going through one of life's rough patches at the time, but when they spoke about you and your siblings, it was as if everything was perfect. That's how I knew they'd come through all right. Because you had each other to lean on. I'm glad to know that I was right and that each of you has had extraordinary success in your careers. All of your brothers and your sister are either engaged or married now, aren't they?"

"They are," he confirmed, even though it was clear that Aileen had done her research on him and his family. Which wasn't hard to do when most of them were either famous or spectacularly wealthy.

"Why are you the only one left? Were you even looking for love when you met my daughter?"

"No." Just as he would never be anything but honest with Kerry, he would never lie to her mother, either. "Love was the very last thing I was looking for." He paused and smiled. "And the very best thing I've ever found, accidentally or otherwise."

"I've always believed that nothing in this world is more beautiful than true love." She held Adam's gaze. "The two of you were beautiful when you were dancing together at the wedding. I've never seen Kerry look so happy."

"I want her to be happy," he said. His throat grew as tight as his chest had been ever since he'd made himself walk out of Kerry's apartment three days ago. "Kerry's happiness is all I want. Her happiness is *everything* I want."

"This morning, before coming here to meet you, I was worried that you are a man who quite obviously always gets precisely what he wants. But now?" Aileen Dromoland smiled at him, a smile that told him more about her change of heart than any words ever could. "Now I'm glad."

* * *

Monday

Kerry and her mother both arrived at the waterfront restaurant at the same time. They'd always been on track like that, and it was nice to know that some things never changed.

"You look wonderful, Mom," she said as they were shown to their seats beneath a colorful awning.

"I'm so glad you could squeeze me in for lunch today, honey."

"And I appreciate you saving me from lunch at my desk behind my computer," Kerry said with a smile. One that nearly faltered as she watched a couple embrace. They couldn't take their eyes—or hands—off each other. For a little while, that had been Kerry. With Adam.

"Have you heard from Colleen since she came back from Las Vegas?"

Her mother's question knocked Kerry back to her seat on the deck over the water. "Yes, she emailed me the pictures of their ceremony." Carefully, so that she wouldn't set her mother off, Kerry added, "She looked happy."

"She did." Kerry was still reeling at her mother's shocking agreement when her mother added, "Hopefully, a miracle of miracles will happen and it will last this time. But I actually didn't come to lunch to talk about Colleen."

Assuming her mother wanted to be caught up on the business, Kerry said, "Things have been so busy lately that I haven't checked in with you nearly enough. But I can give you a quick rundown of our most recent weddings if you'd like."

"There's no need for that," her mother said with a shake of her head. "You've always done far better than I ever did with the business. I don't need to know how work is. I need to know how *you* are."

Kerry tried not to let her mouth fall open at the way today's lunch was going. Her mother had always been there for her, of course, but never in such an in-her-face way. "I'm..."

"You look like you're not sleeping well." Her mother's hand came over hers, warm and comforting. "And even worse than that, you look sad."

Kerry knew she should be coming up with excuses to allay her mother's concerns. She could blame it on work, or maybe allergies, couldn't she? But the truth was that all the sleep she hadn't been getting since the night Adam had loved her *one last time* was making her brain slow, like mush.

"The last time I saw you, when you were dancing with Adam Sullivan, you looked so different. So happy. At least, until I showed up," her mother said with a rueful smile. "I didn't mean to ruin your beautiful moment."

Kerry wanted to tell her mother that she hadn't ruined anything. But that was a lie she couldn't get past her lips. Instead, she told her what she was absolutely positive she wanted to hear. "Adam and I, we aren't"— she could barely keep her voice from breaking before she got to the final word—"together."

This was where her mother was supposed to sigh with relief. Instead, she frowned and said, "I've always gone by first impressions. A skill that I passed on to you. However, what's taken me sixty-odd years to recognize is that sometimes those first impressions aren't right. Sometimes you need to take a step back to take stock of what the *actual* situation is. Take your father, for example. He swept me off my feet. But the man he turned out to be after those first impressions had faded... Well, you know precisely how that turned out. I don't always get it right, Kerry. Particularly, I'm afraid, when it comes to the man you were dating."

"But Adam and I were never dating."

Only, was that really true? Because even though they'd had an *arrangement*, hadn't they repeatedly broken the rules they'd set for themselves?

"Well, maybe we..." Kerry was so tired from fighting her feelings that she nearly laid her head down on the table. "I don't know what we were." Her chest was clenched tight as she admitted, "I don't know what we *are*."

"Oh, honey." Her mother's arms came around her, holding her tight. "Maybe you should give yourself some room to find out."

Kerry was officially beyond speechless now. "Wait." She was sure she had this wrong. "Are you actually telling me to date Adam Sullivan, one of Seattle's most notorious playboys?"

Her mother brushed the hair back from her face, just as she had when she was a little girl and it had come out of her ponytail. "I love both you and your sister, but the two of you have never been the same. You've always had a good head on your shoulders. Whether it's business or love, I trust you, honey. And I'm proud of you. So for once, instead of promising me to be safe, I'm hoping you'll make me a different promise. A promise to trust your instincts. And if you fall in love, to let yourself love with your whole heart."

* * *

Tuesday

Adam left for the lake right after meeting with Kerry's mother on Sunday. And since the moment he'd arrived, all he wanted to do was call Kerry, hear her voice, and tell her she should be standing on the beach with him, in his arms.

He wanted her back now. Yesterday. Tomorrow. *Always.*

But he knew she needed time, needed space. The time and space to miss him. And to long for him the way he was longing for her, every second of every day.

Soon, he reminded himself for the zillionth time, she'd be here for three days of wedding romance, not to mention a dozen Sullivan happy-ever-afters all around them. But Adam had never waited for anything in his life, and it was killing him not to speed back to Seattle, charge into her office, throw her over his shoulder, and lock the two of them in one of their fancy hotel suites until she accepted what he already knew for sure—that they belonged together.

For the first time in days, he smiled, thinking of what her reaction to *that* would be. First cool as she would try to freeze him out, then hot as she would blast him for being so presumptuous. But he'd do anything to get her to consider taking him back.

He was glad that he'd had so much work to do building the gazebo for the past two days, though every nail he pounded, every board he cut, every swipe of the paintbrush made him think of how excited Kerry had been about this addition to the wedding plans. Adam had always been good at carpentry, but he'd never done work this good. He'd never wanted to please anyone more than he wanted to please Kerry, in any and every way that he could.

Normally, when he was at the lake he liked to spend as much time with his family as possible. But since he wasn't good company right now, he'd tried to steer clear of the happy couple.

There'd been no getting out of the bonfire the three of them were sitting in front of tonight, though. Just as there was no getting away from the concern in Brooke's eyes as she watched him from across the fire and asked, "Is everything okay, Adam?"

Rafe handed him a beer. "Is one of your projects at work giving you trouble? You mentioned that building last week that was practically falling down when you took it over."

"Work's fine."

Adam took a long pull from the bottle, feeling a tug of guilt about not confiding in his brother and Brooke about Kerry. But he'd promised her that it would stay only between them—with his father as the only exception. Adam couldn't betray Kerry's trust by telling everyone in his family about them. One day soon, he hoped she'd be here with him, and they'd tell everyone together.

But for now, all he could say was, "I'm trying to work out something in my head and hoping it will come out right."

In the firelight, he could easily read the shock on

their faces. "When have you ever not been sure about something?" Brooke sounded as surprised as she looked.

"Guess there's a first time for everything, isn't there?" Even the one Sullivan who'd never planned to fall in love losing his mind over it. Knowing there was no point in continuing to spread his dark cloud over the two lovebirds, he stood up. "I'm going to head in. Enjoy the fire."

Thankfully, they didn't ask him to stay.

★ ★ ★

"Rafe, I think your brother..." Brooke was still staring after Adam, though he'd already gone into the house next door to theirs, which Max and Claudia Sullivan owned. "I can't believe I'm going to say this, but I think Adam's in love."

"Since I can't think of anything else that could possibly mess with him like this, I'm going to guess you're right on the money."

"Adam Sullivan in love. I can hardly believe it." Brooke shook her head in wonder. "But who could possibly have stolen your brother's locked-up heart?" Rafe gave her a huge grin, one that tuned right into her almost-married-couple ESP. "Oh, my God." She grabbed her fiancé's hands. "Kerry!"

He nodded. "Of all the people in the world to end

up falling for a wedding planner, Adam's got to be the best."

Suddenly, Brooke's smile fell away. "Wait, he was talking about hoping things would work out. Do you think that means she doesn't love him back?"

Rafe also frowned. "My brother definitely has his faults, but he's also one of the best men I've ever known."

"Surely she's got to see that," Brooke agreed.

But as they held on to each other in front of the fire on the beach, both of them were silently hoping for the same thing: that Adam would end up getting his happily ever after. One as wonderful as the love that Rafe and Brooke were about to seal with vows and wedding rings in only a few short days.

★ ★ ★

Wednesday

Kerry was getting desperate. She'd try anything to get to sleep at this point. Warm milk. Chamomile tea. Even a hot rum toddy. Today, she prayed a long walk up and down the downtown Seattle streets between meetings would wear her out by evening.

She'd walked past plenty of construction sites over the years, but none of them made her heart race until she'd met Adam. Suddenly, she found herself looking at all the crews a little more closely, searching for that familiar swagger, for that cocky smile that made it impossible not to smile back.

And then—she swore she saw him. Tall, dark, broad shoulders, moving through the job site like he owned the world. Kerry's heart raced, her palms got sweaty, and she had already turned in from the sidewalk to head his way when the guy turned around.

It wasn't Adam.

Her heart fell so hard, so long, so painfully, that she had to put a hand on a metal rail to steady herself. Of course Adam wasn't here in Seattle. He'd been planning to head up to the lake that weekend to build the gazebo.

He hadn't texted, hadn't emailed, hadn't called since Thursday night, and neither had she. It was going to take them a little while to reset their boundaries to just friends, she knew that. But even if she was never going to kiss him again or make love with him again, she *missed* him. Missed her friend, the best one she'd ever had. She missed his teasing, missed his laughter, missed being able to talk with him about anything at all.

Kerry was nearly back at her office when she stopped and turned around. She hadn't planned to head up to the lake to set up for Rafe and Brooke's wedding until tomorrow morning. But she couldn't stand it anymore.

Even if it was too soon, even if she and Adam were both still too close to the end of one phase of their relationship, missing him was a deep ache that came from way down inside. And as far as she could tell, there was nothing that she could do here in Seattle to make the ache go away—not wine or food or TV or burying herself in work.

Only Adam could make her happier.

* * *

Adam put the final touches on the lattice on the gazebo and stepped back to look it over. It was as perfect as anything he'd ever built. Rafe and Brooke had come out earlier before leaving for their overnight trip into Seattle and exclaimed over how great it was. The hug Brooke had given him had been big enough, and gone on for long enough, that he'd shot his brother a questioning look over her shoulder. But his brother had just shrugged, so Adam figured it was probably wedding nerves.

Either that, or the two of them were worried about him big-time, given the way he'd brooded over the bonfire for the full five minutes he'd joined them last night.

Hell, he thought as he stripped off his shirt and shoes so that he could toss himself off the end of the dock in his shorts, he was almost starting to worry about himself, too. All night, and every minute that had ticked by today, he'd had to practically nail his fingers to the gazebo to keep from getting in his car to go get Kerry.

How was he going to make it until she showed up tomorrow? At this rate, one more day was going to kill him when each hour, each second, had never gone so slowly.

Damn it, he was going to her. *Now.*

Adam was halfway up the beach, planning to grab his car keys and drive into Seattle, when he heard a car pull up behind Rafe and Brooke's house.

And saw the most beautiful woman in the world step out of it.

CHAPTER TWENTY-THREE

Kerry hadn't been surprised to find Rafe and Brooke's driveway empty when she'd pulled in behind their lake house. They'd told her they weren't going to be back until late that night, but since everything was unlocked, she should let herself in and use anything she needed. They'd also told her that if she needed help with anything, Adam would be there working on the gazebo and staying next door at their parents' lake house. Everyone else in the family would be arriving the following evening, while guests who weren't related would come a day later for the actual wedding.

Adam's car was parked next door, and just seeing the vehicle that they'd once nearly made love in made her heart beat so hard that she could hardly breathe.

If she could barely keep it together just looking at his car, how the heck was she going to deal with actually seeing *him* again? But she knew she had to figure out a way to do just that, and quickly, because she had an amazing wedding to put on.

Friends, she reminded herself. She and Adam were just going to be friends now. Friends who might not actually have talked to one another for nearly a week, but still—she hoped and prayed—friends.

The sun was setting as Kerry stepped out of her car. Since she would be staying at an inn a short distance away from Rafe and Brooke's cottage, she left her things in the trunk. Taking a deep breath of the wonderfully clean lake air, she headed toward the beach where both the wedding and the reception would be set.

The first thing she saw was the most incredible gazebo ever made, one so beautiful that her jaw actually dropped. Adam Sullivan wasn't only a brilliant architect, he was also an artisan of the first order. She'd seen his plans, of course, but seeing the structure brought to life simply took her breath away.

Her eyes grew wet as she thought about Rafe and Brooke standing in the center of the gazebo saying their vows to each other. *Perfect*. It was absolutely perfect, and her emotions tore more deeply into her.

So deeply that when the sun momentarily shifted behind a cloud and she realized Adam was standing on the beach looking straight at her, she didn't have even the barest chance of giving herself another of her many reminder lectures about why keeping the boundaries clean and clear between them was the smart thing to do.

Kerry couldn't think straight anymore. Couldn't figure out how to do anything but *want* as she kicked off her heels and ran toward him.

And, of course, his arms were open for her when she threw herself into them—just as open as they'd always been.

"Adam."

She couldn't press her lips against his soon enough. Couldn't wrap herself around him nearly close enough. Again and again, she kissed him, and he kissed her back with just as much need. Just as much desperation.

"Too long." She kissed him again, running her hands over his bare back. "It's been so long, too long. I missed you so much."

"I missed you, too." His kisses were hard and deep, and still she wanted more. So much more. "Never again."

"Never," she echoed.

But then, instead of taking more, he drew back from her. "I promised myself I wouldn't do this. That I wouldn't let sex make us forget everything else. We need to talk, Kerry. Need to figure things out."

"We will. I promise we will." And even though she knew he was right, she couldn't keep her hands or her mouth off him. "Later. We'll talk later. About everything."

He took her mouth again, rough and sweet and wonderful, before pulling back once more. "Promise me, Kerry. Promise me that you won't run, won't shut us down. Promise me you'll talk to me. Really talk, even if it's hard."

"I promise. Just please, *please*, make love to me. In the water, on the sand, in a bed. I don't care where, just as long as I'm with you."

Thank God, her pleas and promise finally convinced him to give up the last vestiges of his control as he said, "Hold on to me." He lifted her up so that she could wrap her arms and legs around him. "I need you everywhere, sweetheart. Every last one of those places. Tonight."

"*Yes.*" His kiss warmed her everywhere that the lake cooled her as he took them into the water. "Everywhere. *Anywhere.*"

Adam was wearing only shorts, but her lightweight dress immediately stuck to her skin, becoming transparent as it soaked up the water. When she heard ripping as he tore the dress off her, no sound had ever been sweeter. He covered her breasts with his mouth, first one, then the other, making both of them moan from the shocking pleasure of being together again.

Nothing else existed for them as they rediscovered each other with lips and hands, with gasps and sighs, with water sloshing between and all around them.

Adam's shorts were thrown on top of her clothes in a nearby rowboat, and with the water buoying her weight, it was so easy to cling to him and nearly take him inside the way they'd both wanted to so badly before. No protection, nothing between them at all.

"There's no one else for me, Kerry. I swear I'm clean and safe."

"I am, too," she told him even though she knew he could already have guessed it, since she hadn't been at all promiscuous before they'd met. "Take me like this. Just like this."

"Will you—"

"No. I'm on the Pill."

The sun had nearly set all the way by then, but there was just enough light for her to see the ecstasy in his expression as he moved into her at the same moment that she brought her weight all the way down onto him.

"You feel so good." He kissed and licked and bit at her mouth, at her chin, at the curve of her shoulder as he pushed up into her. "So damned good."

But she couldn't speak at all anymore, couldn't do anything but try to take him even deeper, even closer, with the water cradling them and the sun setting behind them. He held her hips in his big hands, rocking her down over him again and again until her breath was coming out in panting sobs and the water was rippling in a perfect circle all around them.

She felt utterly raw and exposed, but when he was loving her like this, it didn't feel wrong to let her walls all fall away. Not when she knew he'd already dropped all of his.

"I love you."

He'd said the words to her last week, but her heart had been locked up tight that night. Now, with the locks stripped away by longing, she finally heard him. Finally understood that he wasn't just saying what he thought she wanted to hear.

"I love you."

Every time he said it, the three little words went deeper into her, straight into the center of the heart she'd so carefully guarded her whole life.

"I love you."

His mouth was barely a breath from hers, and where he would usually have been kissing her as she came apart in his arms, tonight he whispered the words over and over again—*IloveyouIloveyouIloveyouIloveyouIloveyou*—in a kiss made entirely of love.

Kerry went tumbling into a release so powerful, so astonishingly wonderful, that she could have sworn fireworks were shooting out over the lake. But tonight, every beautiful explosion, every dazzling detonation was inside of her as Adam's lips finally crashed into hers again, and he kissed her through his own release.

The surface of the water around them calmed long before her own heart rate steadied. As she laid her head on his shoulder, the truth was that Kerry never wanted to let go. Never wanted to have to think past the beauty of their physical connection. Never wanted to have to dissect anything more than the fact that Adam made her feel safe and warm.

And loved. So loved that she reeled from it. She couldn't quite believe that anyone could feel so deeply for her, deeply enough that he would say the words to her again and again and again the way Adam had.

He stroked her back. "I should take you inside and dry you off before you get cold."

"I'm not cold," she protested, but she knew her body temperature would soon drop. It was just that as soon as they got out of the water and got dressed and weren't making love anymore, she'd have to make good on her promise. Her promise not to run, but to talk. Really talk to him about the two of them.

The moon illuminated his face as he put a hand on her cheek so that she would have to look him in the eye. "I know you promised to talk to me, but it doesn't have to be tonight. Just getting to be close to you again is enough for me right now."

It was so tempting to take him up on his offer to push off their talk. But there was too much between them, too many things left unsaid, too many needs and desires pushing at their boundaries, for them to simply get dressed and get to work on the wedding.

"No, we should talk now."

His eyebrows went up. "Right now? Because I'm not sure I can get enough synapses to fire when we're like this."

It was so perfectly right, so wonderfully natural to be wrapped up in his arms, that it took her a few seconds to realize they were still totally connected in every way they could be under the water. Nervous laughter escaped her.

"You're right, we can get dressed first."

"God, I love to hear that sound. Your laughter." He closed his eyes, as though the emotions he was feeling were too strong for him to deal with. "It's one of the most beautiful sounds in the world."

Her entire chest warmed even as shivers started to take over the rest of her.

"Come on, beautiful, let's get you into a warm shower."

Kerry had never been an exhibitionist, had never thought she'd do anything as crazy as having sex in a lake, but as he handed her his T-shirt from the dock to put on and she walked out of the water nearly naked and holding Adam's hand, she felt strangely calm about the incredible breach in the propriety she'd been raised with.

And, of course, when they finally made it to the shower, there wasn't any chance at all that they wouldn't come together again. Just as fast as they had in the lake, just as desperately, with her back against the tiled wall and his hands tangled in her hair while he kissed her the entire time that he loved her back over the edge of exquisite pleasure.

He didn't say *I love you* this time, but she heard it in every stroke of his body into hers, in the pounding beat of his heart against hers, in the dance of his tongue over hers.

She hadn't slept well for the past week, and as soon as he draped a big plush towel around her body and began to gently dry her skin, her eyelids started to droop.

"You're exhausted."

"No," she protested. "I'm okay. We can still—"

"Talk after you rest."

He lifted her into his arms before she could make any more protests and brought her into a rumpled bed that smelled wonderfully like him. She should have told him she was staying at the inn and that she needed to take her nap there. Instead, she said, "You never make your bed, do you?"

"Never could figure out why I should bother when I'm just going to get back into it again."

"Because," she said before yawning big and long,

"it looks prettier when it's made."

Her entire body felt lax and loose again after making love with Adam twice in a row. But it was more than just sex that had her finally feeling like she could relax.

It was knowing that he'd still be there when she woke up.

"If you ask me," he said as he looked down at her, "the bed has never looked prettier than it does right now."

She was so very tired, but the desire in his words had her blood heating again. "You promised to make love to me in all three places I listed. You've given me two, if we switch the shower for the sand." She reached for him. "Now I want the bed."

And, of course, he gave her everything she wanted.

Just the way he always had before.

CHAPTER TWENTY-FOUR

Kerry was surprised to find sunlight streaming over her when she woke the next morning. Woke in a strange bed, no less. One that she didn't recognize. Not until it all came rushing back to her as she came fully awake.

Adam.

Feeling like the sun had finally come out again when she'd seen him after too many days apart. Running into his arms. Making love with him in the lake. And then the shower. And then again in this bed.

She wanted to stay wrapped up in the sheets, under the beautiful quilted comforter, and just let herself stay steeped in his scent and her memories of how good it had been to be back in his arms. But she was here to put on a wedding, so when she saw by the small clock on the bedside table that it was already ten in the morning, she jumped out of bed.

She hadn't been sleeping well all week without him and knew she must have crashed after that last time he'd made love to her, slow and sweet. That third time, he hadn't been in a rush, had seemed determined to give her more pleasure than she'd ever guessed was possible for any one person to feel. Again and again, he'd taken her to the edge, then over, until she'd lost track of where one orgasm ended and the next began. And then, when he'd finally taken her...

She lost her breath all over again just remembering how it had felt as though Adam was giving her everything, his heart and soul, in those beautiful moments. But even as more pleasure took her over, even that pleasure took a backseat to the emotion pumping from him to her.

So much emotion that she could still hardly believe it. Could all of that really be for her? And if it really was, could it possibly last?

Looking around the small sun-filled bedroom, she saw her bag standing against the door and realized Adam must have brought it in from her car. How long had he been up? And where had he slept last night?

Knowing she couldn't risk running into any of the other Sullivans looking like she'd just fallen out of bed, she went into the connected bathroom and took a quick shower. After putting on her clothes and making sure her makeup hid the remaining vestiges of her sleepless week without Adam, she went out in search of him. On her way down the hall, she saw that the sheets in the guest bedroom were rumpled and his clothes from yesterday were on top of it.

God, she was so confused. More confused and con-flicted by what she wanted, and what she thought she shouldn't want, than she'd ever been in her entire life.

Turning the corner into the kitchen, she saw Adam standing by the corner windows. He was looking out at the lake, but she couldn't stop looking at him.

There was a smile on his lips when he turned around and said good morning, but she could see all the questions in his eyes, and knew that he was waiting for her to make her decision—to be with him for real this time. Or not.

"You should have woken me up," she said, her words seeming far too loud, too hard, for this beautiful morning on the lake. But she was nervous. And Adam Sullivan had always thrown her off her game. "We never talked last night, and I promised you that we would."

"You needed the sleep." He put his coffee cup down and began to move across the room to her, making her heart pound even faster than it already was. "You didn't even wake up when I made myself go and sleep in the other bedroom."

"You didn't have to go."

"I didn't want to. Leaving you in the bed alone was the last thing I wanted to do, but since we hadn't talked yet—"

A knock sounded at the door, startling both of them. Frustration rode Adam's features as he went to open it. Rafe and Brooke—whose wedding happened to be the reason she was here at the lake in the first place—were standing on the front porch.

* * *

"Yay, I'm so glad you're here!" Brooke rushed inside to give Kerry a hug. "Rafe and I saw your car and wanted to make sure to welcome you properly."

It was clear to Adam that Kerry was glad for a few moments to try to gather her composure while she hugged Brooke and Rafe hello. From the moment he'd turned to see her standing on the threshold of the kitchen, he'd been able to see the wheels of her mind spinning like crazy.

"I got in late last night," Kerry explained after the greetings were done. "I'm actually supposed to be staying at the Inn on Main Street."

Guessing that she felt that she needed to justify why she'd clearly spent the night here with him at his parents' lake house rather than at her planned lodging, Adam added, "I could see that she was tired from the drive from Seattle, so I convinced her to crash here last night."

Kerry shot him a grateful glance, and he went to pour her a cup of coffee. Every second of the night after leaving her alone in the bed, he'd wanted to go back to her bedroom. But though he hadn't gotten any sleep, he was glad to see that she looked far more rested than she had last night. It had worried him to see her that tired—and to know that he had to be the reason for it.

He'd meant it when he told her mother all he wanted was to make her happy. The thought of making her sad destroyed him.

But though she'd initially been flustered, both by seeing him in the light of day after their long night of lovemaking and then by Rafe and Brooke showing up at the door, he was impressed by the way she shifted back into professional mode. This was his brother's big wedding weekend, and no matter how much Adam wanted time alone with Kerry to give everything he had to convincing her to be with him, he would never forgive himself if he did anything to ruin his brother's wedding. At this point, he was just grateful to be near the woman he loved for the next three days.

Patience, which had never been his strong suit anyway, was nearly killing him this week.

"How are you both doing?" Kerry asked Brooke and Rafe, her slightly flushed cheeks the only sign that she was at all ruffled by Adam being in the room with her. "I can't wait to go over everything with you today."

"We're good," Rafe said as he drew Brooke close and kissed his bride, then kissed her again before letting her go. "Real good."

Kerry beamed at them. "I'm so glad to hear that." Tires crunched on the gravel outside just then, and she looked at her watch. "That must be the delivery trucks with the rental furniture. Let me just direct them where to put everything, and then the three of us can sit down to run through the plan for the weekend." She turned to include Adam. "We should also figure out exactly where to put the gazebo. It's absolutely amazing, Adam, and I want to make sure we have it in just the right spot."

Kerry hadn't quite made it to the still-open front door when his parents, rather than the delivery people she'd been expecting, stepped onto the porch.

"Rafe! Brooke! Adam!"

His mother and father looked thrilled to see them, just like always. It didn't matter if only twenty-four hours had passed since the last time they'd been together. Adam never had to question his parents' love for him.

But Kerry had done exactly that for more than twenty years with her father. And, now that he knew her so well, it wasn't hard to guess that losing her father's love had made her feel as though she should question everyone else's love for her, too. Not only

that of her mother and her sister, whom she was
continually afraid of disappointing—but Adam knew
his love was the biggest question of all for Kerry.

Max and Claudia Sullivan both turned to Kerry at
the same moment, and Adam made the introductions
before anyone else could. "Mom, Dad, this is Kerry
Dromoland."

His mother held out her arms, and Adam was glad
to see how readily Kerry walked into them. "It's so nice
to meet you, Kerry. I've heard such wonderful things
about you."

His father stepped in next, holding out his hand to
shake hers. "It really is a pleasure to meet you. Truly."

Quickly pulling herself together yet again, Kerry
smiled at them both. "I'm sorry we haven't met before
this. I've really been looking forward to meeting both
of you, too. I know you must have heard this a thousand times before, but you have extraordinary
children."

"Thank you."

Adam's mother looked *very* pleased with Kerry, and
Adam knew she was already trying to figure out what
her grandchildren would look like from a combination
of Kerry's and Adam's features.

Normally, that would have bothered him. But
now? Hell, he was wondering the exact same thing.
More than wondering, actually—more like ready to get

going with making those kids with Kerry and starting the family that he'd never wanted before, but now couldn't see a future without.

"We don't want to get in your way, Kerry," his father said, "but anything you need help with, I want you to promise that you'll let us know. Anything you need, no matter how big or how small—don't hesitate. As far as we're all concerned, you're one of the family this weekend, and we couldn't be more pleased about it."

Kerry continued to smile at his parents, but Adam was so attuned to her that he felt the emotion well up in her as if it were his own. "Thank you so much. That means the world to me." When the actual delivery truck came just then, she rushed out.

Rafe and Brooke followed her, leaving Adam with his parents.

"She's beautiful, Adam." His mother was still watching Kerry from the living room window. "Even from meeting her for a few minutes, I can see that her beauty isn't just on the outside."

"I agree," his father said, but the questions in his eyes for Adam were crystal clear.

"No one knows about us," Adam told them both. "No one but you two." He ran a hand roughly through his hair. "And right now, honestly, there isn't anything to know. I'm crazy in love with her, but—" He bit back a frustrated curse.

His mother came to put her arms around him. "The way you look at her—and the way she looks at you when she doesn't think anyone else can see. Honey, I don't have one single doubt that you two belong together. She'll see it soon, too. I know she will. Some things just take time to work themselves out. Just try to have a little patience. And faith that what your heart knows is true really is."

"Patience." Adam growled the word as though it were the worst thing in the world, and his parents both laughed.

"Come on," his father said. "Getting that heavy furniture set up according to the plan your beautiful wedding planner came up with is sure to help keep your mind off things for a little while."

But even though Adam knew his parents were right about having patience and faith, they were totally wrong about one thing.

Nothing could pull his thoughts away from Kerry.

CHAPTER TWENTY-FIVE

Kerry felt like she'd blinked, and suddenly the big family dinner was about to begin.

It had been one of the busiest days she'd ever spent getting ready for a wedding. Not only because of the work she'd had to do to get things in place for the huge family dinner on the beach tonight and for tomorrow's wedding, but also because she'd met so many famous—and best of all—truly nice Sullivans that her head was spinning.

Sullivans had come from all over the country for Rafe and Brooke's wedding. Adam's four siblings from Seattle and his parents, Max and Claudia, were there, of course. Adam's siblings alone were impressive enough with Rafe, the private investigator, and Brooke, a chocolate-maker extraordinaire; Mia, the Realtor, who was married to Ford, one of the biggest rock stars in the world; Ian, the billionaire businessman, and his movie star fiancée, Tatiana; and Dylan, who was renowned for his hand-built yachts, his writer wife,

Grace, and their toddler son, Mason.

But then there was the San Francisco crew—Chase, the famous photographer, his quilter wife, Chloe, their young daughter Emma, and new baby, Julia; Marcus, the winemaker, and his pop star wife, Nicola; firefighter Gabe, his numbers-whiz wife, Megan, and their daughter, Summer, and baby, Logan; Irish pub owner Jake, his librarian wife, Sophie, and their toddler twins, Smith and Jackie, who had been making everyone laugh all day long with their antics; race-car driver and auto mogul Zach and his dog-trainer fiancée, Heather; pro baseball player Ryan and his talented sculptor fiancée, Vicki; movie star Smith and his fiancée, Valentina, who co-wrote and produced movies with him; and choreographer and dancer Lori, with her rugged cowboy husband, Grayson. What's more, their mother, Mary Sullivan, was one of the warmest people Kerry had ever met.

Kerry had already met Adam's painter cousin, Drake, but today she'd also had a chance to meet the rest of the cousins from New York, all of whom had come without dates. Suzanne was a computer genius, Alec built luxury planes, and Harrison was a professor. Kerry had also enjoyed meeting Adam's Uncle William and watching Max and William together, brothers who were still obviously close even though they lived on opposite coasts.

Adam's cousins and his Uncle Edward from Maine had only just arrived before the rehearsal, so she hadn't had a chance to chat with them yet. Which was probably just as well, because she was already on name overload. Tomorrow morning she'd be fresher and would be able to get to know all of them, too.

Again and again throughout the day, she'd been struck by how close, how solid, the Sullivan family was. None of them seemed to care that they were an extremely famous and successful bunch. The only thing that had mattered to any of them during the day had been who could make the biggest cannonball splash off the docks and who had more hot-dog-roasting skill.

Kerry honestly never thought she'd live to see movie star Smith Sullivan go head-to-head in a paddle-boarding contest with rock star Ford Vincent. A contest that ended with both of them trying to dunk the other and everyone else laughing their heads off from rowboats and kayaks before getting in on the fun.

Now, for the family-only dinner, Kerry had strung fairy lights across the beach and placed the tables beneath them. With the moon and stars shining down and the water lapping on the shore, it was one of the most romantic locations she'd ever seen.

Kerry wouldn't normally have been at the rehearsal dinner, but Brooke and Rafe had insisted on it. Knowing she wouldn't be working for the next couple of hours meant that she could finally take a few moments to sit back and sip a glass of wine while enjoying the beautiful location.

She had been to the lake once before, right after Rafe and Brooke had hired her, so that she could see what she'd have to work with for the wedding and reception, and had been amazed by its beauty. But now that she'd spent twenty-four hours here in and out of both Rafe and Brooke's cottage and their parents' house next door, now that she'd sunk her toes into the warm sand, now that she'd been in the crisp, clear lake—she'd fallen just as much in love with Lake Wenatchee as the rest of Adam's family. No wonder Rafe and Brooke had decided to settle here full time. And Adam had been right about the private location. They definitely didn't need any bodyguards here.

Or maybe it just seemed so romantic to her because the previous evening had been pure romance from start to finish as Adam had showered her with love any way he could—with words, with his body, with love radiating from his eyes, with every touch of his hands on her skin, with every single kiss.

Adam didn't have a plus-one, so it had made sense for Rafe and Brooke to suggest that she sit next to him at dinner. He hadn't come to the table yet, but she'd seen flashes of him in constant motion all day long.

Usually alongside his father, who had clearly meant it when he'd said, *"Anything you need."*

Just like Adam. Because he'd always been there for her, hadn't he? No matter what, right from the start, without question or hesitation. He'd helped her with the gazebo, her sister, the house.

And then last night, she'd desperately needed him, and he'd been there to catch her in his arms and make everything that had felt so wrong when they were apart right again.

But all day long, not being able to actually sit down and talk through everything with him had made it all feel wrong again. Not their lovemaking last night, but the distance that still lay between them. Distance that she'd deliberately put in place a week ago when she'd been so sure that they couldn't be together.

Only, what if she was wrong? What if her mother was right about first impressions being wrong sometimes? And what if sometimes the most right thing in the world was the most unexpected? Not to mention exhilarating and frustrating and addictive?

With the dinner starting in less than five minutes, Kerry was heading across the beach to take her seat when she heard delighted giggling. She turned to find Adam standing in the middle of the gazebo, holding little Emma and Jackie in his arms, one on each side.

He had showered off the hard, sweaty work of the

day and was now wearing a dark suit that made him almost too handsome. Too handsome for Kerry's heart to figure out how to return to beating normally, anyway.

The girls were singing songs that she was fairly certain were from the movie *Frozen* in high-pitched, often out-of-tune voices, and Adam was dancing with them. The girls were obviously head over heels in love with him—and he looked just as thrilled with them. From one cheek to the next, he peppered them with kisses that had them giggling even harder.

It was, hands down, the most beautiful thing Kerry had ever seen in her life. Watching Adam shower his family with love was so beautiful, in fact, that she suddenly couldn't remember a single reason why she'd pushed him away.

Because Adam Sullivan, she now knew with perfect certainty, was an amazing man. A loving son, brother, cousin, and uncle. He never hesitated to give all of himself to his family.

Unlike her father.

Kerry's father had never given her anything. Not his love. Not his support. Not one dance that she could remember. No kisses on cheeks. No nights helping with homework. No advice about dealing with boys.

She'd thought she'd dealt with it, that she was over it. She'd even told Adam—*you just have to move on and try not to let it affect you.* But now, for the first time, Kerry realized that the big empty hole in her life where her father should have been had never fully closed, no matter how many years had passed.

Worse still, she could now see that she'd lived with that fear her whole life. Not only that men would leave her behind without a second thought, but that everyone she loved would leave her.

Hadn't she always worried about disappointing her mother? And hadn't she walked on eggshells with her sister because she hadn't wanted Colleen to turn away from her, either?

The enormous epiphanies were still hitting her one after another just as Adam turned and saw her standing there, watching him dance with the little girls. A few moments later, they wiggled down and ran off, hand in hand, leaving her face-to-face with the man who had reached deeper and deeper into her heart from the first day they'd met.

She loved him.

Kerry Dromoland loved Adam Sullivan with every breath, every heartbeat. And she would love him from now until eternity, if they were lucky enough to have that much time together.

All week, everything she'd been feeling, everything she'd been wanting, the things her mother had said to her—they'd all been swirling around and around inside of her. And then yesterday…

Yesterday there hadn't been anything in the world that mattered but Adam.

Only Adam.

Always Adam.

"Kerry."

His voice was warm and full of so much love it floored her, but she was already heading for him. She was nearly in his arms again when the tinkle of silverware on glass chimed out over the beach.

Max Sullivan's amplified voice sounded. "Claudia and I couldn't be happier that all of you were able to come from near and far to celebrate Rafe and Brooke's wedding."

Adam stepped down from the gazebo and took Kerry's hand in his. "Let's go enjoy dinner. And then after, we'll talk."

"Promise?"

This time she was the one needing to know for sure that she wouldn't miss her chance with him. Her chance to tell him everything that was now burning a hole inside of her. She wanted to tell him she loved him, had the words right there on the tip of her tongue, when he reached out to stroke her cheek.

"Everything, Kerry. That's what I'm promising you."

With no time to say anything more, he simply put

his hand on the small of her back and walked with her to their seats.

★ ★ ★

Ninety minutes later, Kerry was dying. Literally about to burst.

The dinner was wonderful, and the toasts were all beautiful and funny and heart-wrenching. But the truth was that she hardly noticed any of it, because all she wanted was for it to be *over already* so that she could get Adam alone and they could talk.

Fortunately, though, she wasn't so twisted up that she missed when Rafe and Brooke turned to focus their attention on her. "We want to take a moment to thank Kerry Dromoland for doing such an amazing job of putting our wedding together. We're just so glad she could be here with us tonight, especially because there are an awful lot of us and we're a lot to take in."

Everyone laughed at that, and Kerry managed a smile as she mouthed, *Thank you.*

Rafe continued to speak into the microphone, saying, "I know it must feel like we've already been toasting each other all night long, but does anyone else want to chime in before we let you loose on the bonfire?"

"I do."

An entire beach full of Sullivans looked at Kerry in

surprise. Only Adam didn't look surprised. Probably because he'd always been able to read what she was feeling on her face, seeing all the things she'd always been able to hide from everyone else.

What she was about to do was the most unprofessional thing in the entire world. But she didn't care if she got a reputation for being the worst wedding planner on the planet after this. She couldn't hold in what she was feeling anymore.

Kerry stood up beneath the fairy lights and the moon and took the microphone from a grinning Brooke. "I've been putting on weddings practically my whole life." She hadn't planned a word of this, but that didn't matter. Not when every word she spoke into the mic was coming straight from her heart. "I thought I knew what love was, because I watched it every day. But it turned out that I didn't really know anything. I didn't know what love really was until I met…"

She stopped, put the mic down, and turned to Adam.

"Until I met you."

Tears were falling down her cheeks, and Adam was right there, brushing the streaks of emotion away.

"I never knew, either," he said, "not until you."

"I want everyone to know how much I love you, Adam." Her throat was clogged with tears and emotion. He hadn't wanted to keep their relationship secret from anyone anymore, and she'd been wrong to try to keep his family—and him—in the dark. "I know I probably ruined everything every step of the way—"

His kiss stole the rest of the words from her lips…and gave her everything she'd ever wanted.

Love.

Adam was all there was for Kerry as they stood on the beach, surrounded by his family, the water lapping against the shore and the stars shining down over them. His arms around her, his mouth on hers, the way he just kept telling her he loved her with a kiss that swept all the way through her soul.

When they finally came up for air, she was shocked to realize that all of the Sullivans were applauding like crazy. Absolutely losing their minds over her declaration of love for a man they all adored.

But she knew that no one would ever adore Adam more than she did.

CHAPTER TWENTY-SIX

"I've been wanting to dance with you again for weeks."

Adam drew Kerry close, loving the feel of her heart beating against his as they danced to the music filtering down to their private spot on the beach.

"So have I," she told him, "but I have so many things I need to tell you, too. Things I've never told anyone else. Things I never wanted to own up to about myself, not until I almost lost you."

"You never even came close to losing me." And it was true. "You're the partner I never knew I needed, Kerry. The other half that actually makes me complete. You and I, we're good alone. But together? Together we're unstoppable. That's why I would have worked forever to win your heart. And I would have waited forever for you, too."

She stopped dancing, but didn't let go of him. "That's what I couldn't understand." Her eyes were so big, so full of emotion as she said, "Even now, I'm sure it's going to take me a while to really, truly believe that you love me as much as you do."

"So much, sweetheart."

She smiled then, such a bright and beautiful smile that she nearly turned night into day with it. "I love you that much, too."

"I know you do. Your love runs deep, so deep and strong that I've always been astonished by it."

"I could never understand how my father…" She took a shaky breath, but pushed ahead. "How he could have left the way he did, how he could have left at all if he loved me. I know I told you I had dealt with it, that I wasn't letting it ruin my life, but now I can see that wasn't entirely true. Because a part of me couldn't believe that I would ever be enough to make the people I loved stay. After he left, I think I spent pretty much my whole life trying to be prepared for everything, to make sure I could avoid every possible crisis. But avoiding all those potential falls meant I could never let myself appreciate the amazing things all around me. Most of all, you."

"Did you just call me amazing?" he teased, wanting to see her smile again even as she got everything off her chest.

Her laughter made him happy. So happy that he wondered how he'd managed to live thirty-four years without hearing it. "Beyond amazing, Adam, enormous ego and all."

Now he was the one turning serious. "My ego and I made a lot of assumptions about you and me, thinking that just because I was one hundred percent ready to be in love, you must be one hundred percent ready to love me back. I'm sorry for barging into your heart like a bull in a china shop."

"You once told me that two people don't have to be completely the same or look at everything the same way, for a relationship to work. These past weeks with you have been exciting and frustrating and happy and crazy-making. And the truth is that I can't wait for seven more decades just like these with you. Everything might not always be calm and easy, we may get messy and raw sometimes, but I know that as long as I'm with you, they'll always be wonderful, too. So, if you ask me, barging like a bull into my china shop sounds just perfect. I don't want to change one single thing about you, Adam, and I couldn't stand it if you tried to be someone you aren't."

A violin was playing a romantic melody, one that floated across the still lake water to them, as she said, "Marry me, Adam. Be mine forever."

He kissed her soft then hard, teasingly then deeply, over and over again.

"Is that a yes?" she asked.

"Not just a yes," he told her, grinning like a fool. "It's a *hell yes* to marrying you and having picnics with our kids under the oak tree of our rambling old house during the day and making love beneath the stained-glass windows upstairs every night." He kissed her again. "And that's me saying yes to holding hands as we rock together on the front porch." Another kiss, one filled with pure love. "But you should know that I'll never stop making you blush by kissing you in front of the whole world and asking you to dance at the most inappropriate times."

"Promise?"

"You want to know how long I'm promising you, Kerry?" He brought his lips to hers and whispered, *"Forever."*

* * *

Back at the inn, they stripped each other so fast that the door was barely shut and locked behind them when Adam came over her on the big bed, deliciously hard and heavy as he kissed her. And kissed her. And kissed her some more, until her head was spinning even faster than it already had been back on the beach.

Every part of her wanted every part of him as he began to run those drugging kisses down over her cheek, her jaw, her neck, her shoulders.

"What are you going to plan for our wedding?" he asked her between kisses.

"Wedding?" It was hard to think straight with his

tongue swirling lazily over the tip of her breast.

His laughter vibrated against her sensitive skin as he moved to tease her other breast. "You just asked me to marry you, remember?"

"Yes." He slid his hand down over her stomach, then between her thighs. *"Yes."*

His laughter turned to a growl of satisfaction. "Maybe you're thinking of the honeymoon, then?" he said as he began to run nipping little kisses down over her rib cage. "Somewhere hot and sunny where I can keep you naked for a week."

She was barely able to think, let alone speak, as he dipped his tongue into her belly button. But somehow she managed, "Two weeks."

He rewarded her excellent suggestion with another breathtakingly hot kiss, one that had her arching her hips to get closer to his mouth. Spending one night a week with Adam had been incredible. But knowing he would be hers forever? Knowing she'd be laughing, and teasing, and loving him every single night—not to mention anytime they could get away from work during the day?

Her body exploded in a kaleidoscope of pleasure, one that she was desperate to share with him. And thank God, he could read her mind just as he always did, because even as ecstasy took her over, he did, too, in one gorgeous thrust.

She couldn't hold him tightly enough, couldn't wrap herself around him closely enough. And this time, when he whispered that he loved her against her mouth between kisses, she whispered it right back, over and over and over again, until she knew he'd never, ever forget just how much she loved him.

Or that all she ever needed was *him*.

EPILOGUE

Drake Sullivan enjoyed Rafe and Brooke's wedding. Not only because he got to spend time with his family, but also because the laughter all around him was a much-needed infusion. He'd tried to paint last night and had ended up with something that could have been done far better by a child. Which he'd just confirmed when Chase and Chloe's little daughter, Emma, gave him a drawing she'd been working on at her seat during the reception. He could see the budding artist in her, from the way she watched everyone and everything around her so carefully—and from her extremely long attention span as she'd worked on her drawing with her tongue between her teeth.

She'd drawn the lake with the dock jutting out into it and the mountains rising up behind it. Her drawing was confident and, honestly, pretty damned brilliant. "This is great, Emma. Can I keep it?"

She beamed up at him. "I made it for you, Mr. Drake. You have to keep it." She gave his legs a quick hug before running off to play with her cousins, who were calling her name from down the beach.

"Looks like you have a little admirer." Drake's sister, Suzanne, was smiling as she walked up to him. He showed her the drawing, and her eyebrows went up. "Wow, that's really good."

"Better by a mile than anything I've done recently, that's for sure."

His sister put her hand on his arm. "Your muse still messing with you?"

Drake had never believed in a muse before. Painting had always been there for him, a natural extension of himself. At least, it had been there until the past six months or so. "I'm thinking of heading out of the city for a while when I get back."

"Montauk?" she guessed.

Drake nodded. He had a little cabin on the water there that he didn't use nearly enough. But maybe if he got away from the noise, the activity of New York City for a little while, and surrounded himself with water and sand like this, he'd get back what he was starting to feel he'd lost.

"Maybe I'll come visit," she said, but he knew better. His brilliant sister could rarely pull herself away from her computers long enough to get out to the far tip of the Hamptons.

Still, he wanted her to know she was welcome, so

he said, "Come anytime, Suz."

Their brothers, Alec and Harrison, walked up to them just then. Despite their physical similarity—both of them tall and muscular, with dark eyes and hair—the luxury airline mogul and the university academic couldn't be more different.

"Everyone, including Dad, is placing bets on who's next," Alec said.

Not following, Drake asked, "Next?"

Harrison clarified, "They're betting on which one of us is going to go down in the flames of love like Adam just did."

With his painting going badly enough that he was going to have to cancel an important exhibition soon if he didn't snap out of it, Drake couldn't help but feel as though he had more than enough trouble on his hands without bringing a woman into it. But his siblings? Sure, he could see one of them falling crazy in love out of the blue.

"Who's in the lead?" he asked.

The last thing Drake expected was for Alec to grin and say, "You."

★ ★ ★ ★ ★

For news on upcoming books, sign up for Bella Andre's New Release Newsletter:

www.BellaAndreFans.com/Newsletter

ABOUT THE AUTHOR

Having sold more than 5 million books, Bella Andre's novels have been #1 bestsellers around the world and have appeared on the New York Times and USA Today bestseller lists 28 times. She has been the #1 Ranked Author on a top 10 list that included Nora Roberts, JK Rowling, James Patterson and Steven King, and Publishers Weekly named Oak Press (the publishing company she created to publish her own books) the Fastest-Growing Independent Publisher in the US. After signing a groundbreaking 7-figure print-only deal with Harlequin MIRA, Bella's "The Sullivans" series has been released in paperback in the US, Canada, and Australia.

Known for "sensual, empowered stories enveloped in heady romance" (Publishers Weekly), her books have been Cosmopolitan Magazine "Red Hot Reads" twice and have been translated into ten languages. Winner of the Award of Excellence, The Washington Post called her "One of the top writers in America" and she has been featured by Entertainment Weekly, NPR, USA Today, Forbes, The Wall Street Journal, and TIME Magazine. A graduate of Stanford University, she has given keynote speeches at publishing conferences from Copenhagen to

Berlin to San Francisco, including a standing-room-only keynote at Book Expo America in New York City.

Bella also writes the New York Times bestselling Four Weddings and a Fiasco series as Lucy Kevin. Her "sweet" contemporary romances also include the USA Today bestselling Walker Island series written as Lucy Kevin.

If not behind her computer, you can find her reading her favorite authors, hiking, swimming or laughing. Married with two children, Bella splits her time between the Northern California wine country and a 100 year old log cabin in the Adirondacks.

For a complete listing of books, as well as excerpts and contests, and to connect with Bella:

Sign up for Bella's newsletter:

www.BellaAndreFans.com/Newsletter

Visit Bella's website at:

www.BellaAndre.com

Follow Bella on twitter at:

twitter.com/bellaandre

Join Bella on Facebook at:

facebook.com/bellaandrefans

Made in the USA
Middletown, DE
20 July 2016